# WHAT WAS MOTHER DOING ALONE ON THAT EVIL NIGHT?

Her nightdress was stained and soaking as she returned the spade to its place on the barn wall. The early light filled the sky as she walked back toward the house, not noticing the second-story windows where her eldest daughter looked down in horror, and where the son named after her husband watched as he had from the beginning, with a smile as strange as her own.

# Buried Blossoms

## STEPHEN LEWIS

A JOVE BOOK

BURIED BLOSSOMS

First Jove edition published March 1982

First printing

Printed in the United States of America

---

Jove books are published by Jove Publications, Inc.,
200 Madison Avenue, New York, N.Y. 10016

## Stephen Lewis, 1947–1981

Beautiful dreamer, waken to me
Starlight and dewdrops are waiting for thee;
Sounds of the rude world heard in the day,
Lulled by the moonlight have all passed away.

—Stephen Foster, "Beautiful Dreamer"

prologue
1942

THE MAN IN the bed, bandages covering his eyes, guzzled and choked, spitting out some of the juice he'd taken through the straw in the glass.

"I'm sorry—" he apologized.

"There's no harm done," a woman's voice answered, taking the glass away, dabbing his chin with a facecloth. Blindly, he reached out and grasped at her hand, studying it with his fingers.

"Soft. Cool, too—if you'll excuse me for being so personal, Sister."

"I'm not one of the nuns," she told him, returning the pressure of his touch.

"No? You're not a nurse. I *know* that."

"How do you know?" she asked him.

"Because the nurses are always in a hurry. They're always rushing."

"I'm afraid that's because there aren't enough of them," she explained. "And so many patients coming in all the time."

"Are there—lots of them like me?" he asked, his voice quivering.

"Oh, most of them aren't quite as handsome," she replied lightly.

Almost all the soldiers who were sent to the ward of Divine Providence Hospital asked the same thing in one way or another. Were there many others like themselves? Had the war taken the eyesight of lots of men like them?

When she'd started her work as a volunteer, they had told her that patience was the main thing. It took a man time to come to terms with the realization that he'd never see again, time to learn to use his other senses to the fullest.

"If you're not one of the nuns and you're not a nurse," the man asked her, "why are you here?"

"Just to help."

"But isn't it depressing? I mean, wouldn't you rather work at a USO canteen or someplace like that?"

For an instant, an image of lights and dancing, of a stage and an orchestra, came to her, then it was gone.

"I'm happy here," she told him. And though she didn't say it, she knew what it was like to be in a hospital, to be another patient and not a real person.

For a moment anger filled her, anger at the shock treatments, and the drugs, and the indignities she'd suffered. But then that, too, was gone. It was another memory, only a memory, and she was different now. Better. Well, they'd told her when they'd released her from the hospital in Worcester where they'd transferred her from Northhampton.

It had been a nicer hospital, only a few miles from this one. But there'd been bars on the windows, and though she'd never been mistreated or given cause—"Never a moment's trouble, that one . . . if only they were all like her," a nurse's voice sighed in her memory—the attendants had been cruel at times to some of the other patients.

She'd seen it and been silent, as if she were like the man whose bed she stood over, blind. Blind, and silent, too, for seven long years. And for those seven years, she'd fooled them into thinking that she was deaf as well, unable to hear the doctors discuss her case and its "classic symptoms."

They'd tried to talk to her. They'd given her electric shocks. There'd been pills of all sizes and shapes, but she'd stayed the same. Only the shots—". . . An experiment. A new approach to treatment for people like you," another voice explained in her memory—had changed it. She hadn't wanted the injections, not even the first one. Pills could be spit out into uneaten food. Even when she swallowed them, it didn't make a difference. But injections, needles into her bloodstream, had frightened her.

Not the needles themselves, but the idea that they might render her defenseless, might make her talk and tell too much.

But when she had spoken, she'd been pleased to find that she said only what she chose: the secret, the part of her life that had brought her to the hospital and all that had led up to it were a dim and distant dream.

The secret was safe, burned away by the jolts of electricity, and the pills, and time itself.

"I wish I could see you," the man in the bed told her, still holding her hand. "I know you must be beautiful."

Another image flashed through her mind. Herself, younger, years before. She had been beautiful then, and she felt an ache for what was gone. With her free hand, she touched the red scar the burn had left on the side of her face. She avoided mirrors—they hadn't let her see herself at first, and when she did, she hadn't wanted to look again— but she knew it was there, hideously disfiguring. That was why she had wanted to work with the blind soldiers, she'd explained when she'd volunteered. She didn't want to frighten the seeing men with her looks. With the blind, she could be useful, and her face wouldn't matter.

"Is there anybody else you'd like to write to?" she asked the man in the bed. "I'd be glad to take another letter for you if you want to dictate it—"

He shook his head. "No, you were sure nice to write down that letter to my folks. I don't want those soft hands of yours to get tired."

"Would you like me to read to you, then?" she offered. "There are magazines, newspapers—"

"The paper," he interrupted. Then he sighed. "I sure will miss reading the paper."

"There's Braille," she told him. "And the radio has the news, too. You won't miss a thing."

"I guess not," he agreed tentatively, releasing her hand. "Hey—you won't mind if I drift off on you, will you? The medicine makes me do that sometimes."

"Of course not," she answered, settling into the chair beside his bed and unfolding the newspaper. Every soldier in the hospital got a copy each day, even though it struck her as senseless that they were passed out on this ward.

"Let's see . . ." she began. There was a speech that President Roosevelt had made, and she read that first. Then a story about an English girl, only seven years old, who'd saved her baby brother during an air attack. There was a report on the trial of a black marketeer, which she decided to skip, and an encouraging interview with General Eisenhower that she read aloud in its entirety.

It was a few moments before she realized that somewhere during the General's comments, the soldier in the bed beside her had fallen asleep.

Quietly, so as not to disturb him, she refolded the paper. A page slipped out and fell to the floor, and a headline containing the word Eastfield caught her eye.

She didn't want to read the article, but she couldn't stop

herself. And as she read on, her eyes widened with each word, her heart pounded.

*It was over, finally over! And she was finally, fully safe!*

She crumpled the page into a ball, and tossed it into the wastebasket, silently leaving the room.

"A shame about that one, isn't it?" a nurse asked her in the hallway, nodding toward the room of the patient she'd just left. "You know, they really thought that operation might save his vision."

"There are some things it's just as well not to see."

"Huh?" the nurse asked. "Hey—are you all right? You look like you've just seen a ghost!"

The words made the volunteer laugh, for she had seen a ghost on the page of the newspaper. Not just one ghost, but many, ghosts of people and years. But now the ghosts were gone, like the years and the life they'd stolen from her.

Still, one thing was certain: she could never again be haunted.

"Frannie," the nurse said, "I just can't figure you out."

part one
**1896**

## - 1 -

"MRS. HAZELTINE!" the shopkeeper said, leaving the bolt of fabric in his customer's hands and hurrying around the counter to greet her. "How do you do, ma'am?"

"Very well, thank you, Mr. Emery," she answered, her light smile including the other patrons who made no effort to appear as if they were doing anything but staring at her. She caught a glimpse of herself in the mirror where women held pieces of cloth up against themselves, considering the color and imagining the cut of the garment they'd sew, and she raised her finely arched eyebrows in either amusement or pleasure.

"My," she said to herself. Her long, tapering fingers touched the starched scalloped lace of her collar, her nails, shining and rounded, glided over the delicate pleats of her skirt. Her parasol, like her dress, was white...always white, as if she were more bride than wife. She flicked a speck of dust from the parasol handle and turned to Mr. Emery, ready to do business.

"How may I help you—" he began, his left hand rolled into a fist and his right covering it. His arms were tight at his sides, his body hunched and pitched forward in a slight bow when he noticed his own sleeves. "My coat. Begging you pardon, ma'am, but it was so warm. I'll get it—"

Olivia Hazeltine waved the offer away. "That's a handsome vest," she told him, her eyes sparkling. "Did Mrs. Emery make it?"

The man nodded self-consciously. "It's a new gabardine, very light. Summer gabardine, they're calling it. I think there's enough left if you'd like some for Mr. Hazeltine—"

She laughed gently. "He prefers to order his suits from London."

"Of course," the shopkeeper said, apologizing. "Of course he does, ma'am."

"But I would like some thread."

"Certainly," he answered, retreating behind the counter, pencil and paper in his hand.

"A spool of red, another of blue, and two of white," she told him. A moment later there were more than a dozen spools on the counter, blues from dark royal to pale robin's egg, reds from deep pink to cardinal. "Oh dear," she said, considering them.

"Begging your pardon," Mr. Emery said. "But is it for the Celebration?"

She looked at him, puzzled, then she noticed the placard mounted near the register.

Town of
EASTFIELD
Bicentennial
Celebration
July 4, 1896

"Ah, the Celebration," she said.

"I thought perhaps you might be sewing a costume or decoration," he explained, looking to his other customers for support. "Like so many of the ladies."

Olivia Hazeltine looked at the women in surprise, then at Mr. Emery. "Really? Why it never occurred to me."

He was nervous, afraid of having been too forward, appreciative of her patronage but unsure of how to deal with her. "I know that Mr. Hazeltine's speech will be a highlight of the ceremonies," he offered in amends. "Yes, I'm looking forward to it. Mrs. Emery and I, that is."

She smiled and began picking up the spools of thread one after the other.

"If I can help you make your selection—" he began.

"I think I'll take them all," she said sighing.

"All of them?"

"It is best to be prepared," she observed. "Oh, please don't forget the white."

"Yes, Mrs. Hazeltine," he said, busily wrapping the package. "Two of the white." When it was tied with string, she reached for it. Again he hurried around the counter. "Allow me," he insisted, standing back to let her pass.

The afternoon sun blazed beyond the open doorway. Before she crossed the threshold, Olivia opened her parasol.

"It's bad luck," one of the women said darkly, speaking for the first time. Realizing she'd said the words aloud rather than thought them, she brought her hand to her mouth as Olivia's light laughter filled the small store.

"We make our own luck," Olivia announced, lifting the parasol and stepping outside under its protective cover.

The women hurried to the window, watching Mr. Emery escort her down the street. Like her dress, the pair of horses that pulled her carriage were white. They kicked the ground and shook their manes as she approached, pausing to stroke them. The shopkeeper assisted her as she climbed up, then handed her the parcel.

"It *is* bad luck," the woman who'd spoken first reiterated.

"With all their book reading, you'd think she'd know that much."

"He's the one what reads the books," her companion corrected. *"She* takes magazines."

"And how do you know that?"

"Doesn't my own brother-in-law work in the post office?"

"So he does."

"Well, he's the one what told me. She takes the *Journal,* and the *Companion,* and a good dozen more—"

"Do tell!"

"That's not taking into account the newspapers," she informed the other two, savoring the gossip. "There's the *Times* from New York, and the *Beacon* out of Boston. Not to mention the *Springfield Republican."*

The woman who'd been looking at the fabric clucked her tongue. "I suppose the *Eastfield Crier* isn't good enough for our Hazeltines."

"Oh, they take that, too, Mrs. Putney. Yes, they do take the *Crier*. Of course I suppose it's only right that they have to know what's going on in the world, with his being a man of affairs—"

"All I know," her friend said, "is that it's bad luck to open an umbrella indoors. A body doesn't have to read any papers or books or magazines to know that. It's common sense."

"Umbrellas," the first woman considered. "Do you think it holds for parasols too?"

"Lucy, don't be a ninny! Of course it does."

Mrs. Putney clucked her tongue again. "Well, I don't suppose it makes much difference in *their* case. Not when you consider what he's already got coming. Mark my words, the fancy Hazeltines are going to get theirs, all right. The Lord doesn't forget."

"Mrs. Putney!" Lucy Tremont said.

"It's the truth, isn't it? What have I said but what everybody knows?"

"But talking about it in public—"

"And who hasn't talked about it, I'd like to know? Oh, the subject is out of fashion these days. Ever since he come back and took the Works over from old Mr. Palmer, it's changed. He's *quality* all of a sudden, with that fancy house and a place on the speaker's platform at the Celebration, if you please!"

Lucy and her friend Mary Dayton looked at each other, considering it.

"He has done a lot for the town—" Mary began.

"A lot *to* the town, if you ask me!" Mrs. Putney corrected her. "All kinds of strangers moving in, and now that trolley car going right down Water Street, with all that clatter!"

"They say that Paul Hazeltine is the man who put Eastfield on the map," Lucy offered. "Why, before you know it we'll be as big as Springfield—"

"Springfield is Springfield and Eastfield is Eastfield. The town's been on the map long enough with no help from the likes of him, and it will still be there when he and his get their comeuppance. And well they will, mark my words! The lot of them."

Olivia's carriage drove by. The women hurried from the counter to the window.

"Not the whole family, do you think?" Lucy asked. "My but that hair of hers is lovely, isn't it? The red in it catches the sun. That's why she always carries the parasol, I'm sure. Because redheads have such fair, delicate skin."

"My mother was a Garrison," Mary informed them. "The Garrisons all have red hair and fair skin. And sun or no sun, they worked that farm up to Northampton, my own mother with them. Without a parasol, thank you."

"Still, she does make a striking appearance," Lucy insisted, watching wistfully as the carriage moved out of sight.

"Who wouldn't when you're to the manor born, as they say, and marry more money to boot?"

"But she *does* add a certain something to the town—"

"For all we see of her! They're too good to mix."

"Now then, ladies," Mr. Emery said, back behind the counter. "Where were we—"

Mrs. Putney eyed him coldly. *"We* have been right here in your shop, Mr. Emery, waiting—and without complaint—while you took her ladyship out of turn and saw her to her buggy. I'm glad for you that business is so good you can up and leave your shop and your customers. Since we've had to wait, we've commenced to talking, and now you'll kindly return the favor."

Lucy giggled as Mr. Emery, flustered, retreated to the stockroom under Mrs. Putney's stare.

Once she'd finished with him, she turned back to the two other women, still at the window.

"All I know is, put everyone's troubles in a bag and you won't want to be picking hers," she told them. "Not even with the money and the house and the way she looks. The Lord does *not* forget—He'll deal with them in His good time."

"But her?" Lucy asked. "And the family?"

Mrs. Putney was annoyed. "We may go to different churches, but we do have the same Bible. What does the Bible say about the sins of the fathers? They'll be visited on the children is what. And the wife."

Lucy thought about it. "It doesn't *say* the wife as well—"

Mary Dayton had taken Mrs. Putney's side. "It doesn't *have* to say it. Anybody with a brain in their head can figure it out. Unless they don't have the sense to wait until they're out of doors before they open an umbrella."

"Poor Olivia," Lucy said, closing the subject.

Poor Olivia, then. For even if she was the wealthiest and most beautiful woman in Eastfield, her house, clearly, was marked.

# - *2* -

THE CELEBRATION WAS a matter of civic pride and a reflection of prosperity. Springfield had marked its bicentennial in May with a parade that was ten divisions long and with several days of speeches and ceremonies. Representatives and delegations from all over Hampden County and from as far away as Boston had been on hand. But Springfield, after all, was a city: Eastfield was a town, and though it had had the formal designation for two hundred years, it was only recently, as recently as Paul Hazeltine's return, that the last vestiges of a villagelike atmosphere had begun to disappear.

Still, the local selectmen agreed, there was no point in letting Springfield have all the thunder. Combining the Celebration with Independence Day meant making the most of a holiday weekend, and assured a good crowd. There'd be the parade of course—not nearly as big as Springfield's, but big enough—and speeches on the Common. There would be games and amusements for the young people, and an amateur show in the Town Hall, proceeds (after much debate) going toward the erection of a statue in honor of Mathew Wyndham, acknowledged as the town's founding father, on the Common.

The local historical societies had pored over their papers in the hope of finding some previously neglected mention of Wyndham. Unable to discover one, they set about re-telling his tale in a manner that made him seem like something other than the unpleasant, mean-spirited man he'd obviously been.

Arriving in the New World in 1648, he'd brought his skill as a carpenter to Springfield, the settlement founded by William Pynchon and named after the town the founder had come from in England. From the start, Mathew Wynd-ham had made trouble or been a party to it. In 1651, he supported a fellow artisan, a bricklayer, in accusing Hugh and Mary Parsons of witchcraft.

During the investigation, Wyndham swore to Pynchon, among whose titles and positions was that of magistrate, that he'd seen the Parsonses dancing "in a field, by the light of the moon." Hugh Parsons, he claimed, had tried to be-witch him, and when he resisted, casting Parsons from his house, a nearby pail of fresh milk had at once turned dark and sour.

The case was sent on to Boston, but not before Mary Parsons had turned against her husband. Pushed beyond the brink by the proceedings, she had murdered their infant son. And, too, not before the respected Mr. Pynchon delivered a stern and accusing speech in the hearing room, during which he reminded those giving testimony—and Mathew Wyndham in particular—that false witness for the sake of "personal gain and alliance" was as grievous a sin as witch-craft and indeed a sight worse. Wyndham, the records re-veal, thereupon had a violent outburst worthy of one pos-sessed, during which he vowed to even the score with the magistrate.

His chance came sooner than he might have expected. Pynchon, who was a Biblical scholar and somewhat liberal

Puritan, wrote a book entitled *The Meritorious Price of Our Redemption*. He theorized that the Crucifixion was not, as the Calvinists held, an expression of God's anger and vengeance against mankind, but the work of the Dark One, using the Romans and Jews to his nefarious purpose.

Publication was marked by outrage in Boston. The book was decried from the pulpit, along with Pynchon, who was branded a heretic. The furor culminated in the banning of the book in Boston, and a book burning on the Common. William Pynchon was stunned and saddened, and powerless against the union of critical clergy and personal enemies.

Mathew Wyndham led the latter contingent in Springfield, where the author had hoped to wait out the crisis. The carpenter saw to it that the cries and fires stirred across the colony were echoed and fanned closer to home. Adopting a posture of moral outrage, he was at the forefront of those who held that Pynchon's retraction of his work was not enough: only a trial could rectify the heinous crime he'd committed against society.

Broken and sick at heart, William Pynchon regretfully left the settlement to which he'd devoted himself and his life and returned to England.

The vanquishing of his sworn enemy did little to make Mathew Wyndham more agreeable. In 1655, he was fined three pounds for working on the Sabbath, with witness brought by one Elias Colt. The same year, the carpenter tried his proven tactic again, accusing Mr. Colt of "the practice of Witchcraft and cavorting with Old Nick." This time, however, he was less successful: for his efforts, he received a fine for slander, as well as a public whipping.

For the next eight years, Wyndham was a regular visitor to the court. He was charged fourteen times with offenses including "rowdy manner in the Publick House," "drunkenness on the Common," and "profane speaking." The fines and his affinity for strong drink did not temper his surly spirit or ruin his business. Instead, the carpenter turned into something of a dandy. Gold and silver trim, like silk, were strictly forbidden under Puritan law to those who had estates of less than two hundred pounds. The selling of spirits to the Indians, "Agawam and other," was likewise prohibited. For some time, there had been accusations that one or more men of the town had built a still somewhere in the woods, and were running a profitable business in bootlegging to the natives. The name of Mathew Wyndham figured repeatedly in these stories, along with that of the bricklayer whom he had supported in the witchcraft inquest of the Parsonses.

For lack of evidence, no formal charges had been brought, but Wyndham was put on trial for sporting a silken jacket "in the Regimental style, with Goldeney Buttons." He insisted that it was his right, and when asked how a carpenter with a known prediliction for heavy imbibing could amass what amounted to a fortune by sanctioned means, he defiantly told the court that it was his business and his alone. Before a fine could be levied, or the charges of manufacturing and selling liquor to the Indians brought, Mathew Wyndham headed east, out of the Springfield Settlement and into the woods.

The town, obviously relieved and well rid of the troublemaker, made no effort to return him.

Twelve miles downriver, he established his own domain, fishing and hunting, building himself a cabin, and making cider and a cherry liquor that was particularly favored by the Agawam tribe. The Indians in return gave him supplies and at least one young woman.

Unlike William Pynchon, who'd come to the Colonies with a fervent desire to build a settlement, Mathew Wyndham was dedicated solely to his own comfort. He was left to his own devices until 1675, when Phillip, the Indian

King, took to the warpath. Like neighboring Brookfield and Deerfield, Springfield was attacked and burned.

No records exist of the conversation that took place when a delegation of men from the Settlement, headed by John Pynchon, the son of his enemy, visited Wyndham, beseeching him to return and use his professional skills to help rebuild the razed community. Later histories suggest, however, that the former carpenter laughed or spat in the face of his callers, telling them that he didn't care a damn what happened to Springfield. He was east of it and rid of it forever, and cared only about his "Eastfield" where hostile Indians posed no problem whatsoever.

Families from the settlements began to spread out on both sides of the Connecticut River. Wyndham found himself with neighbors who, unlike himself, had gone through the formality of obtaining Land Grants. But the memory of raids and attacks was still fresh in the minds of those who had recently moved, and his presence, in view of his excellent rapport with the local tribes (and, possibly, the power of his product) was thought to be protective.

Undisturbed, except by paying or trading customers, Mathew Wyndham lived until 1684, when he died in his sleep in November. His Indian wife went back to her people, and his neighbors, following the examples of Westfield in 1669, Suffield in 1674, and Enfield in 1683, petitioned to form the Town of Eastfield in 1686.

The Celebration stirred a good deal of public discussion and private debate concerning the suitability of the glorification of Mathew Wyndham. The purists argued that history was history after all, and there was no denying that the carpenter, however bad his character, had founded Eastfield.

Several of the ladies active in their church auxiliaries and the local chapter of the Christian Temperance League argued

that history regardless, the founding father was a most un-
suitable candidate for any sort of memorial, and an unde-
sirable influence for the young people of the community.

The question was argued heatedly at a series of town
meetings. Finally it was suggested that Miss Violet Herrick,
who directed the Eastfield Public Library, be assigned the
task of writing a brief official (and inoffensive) biography
of Wyndham. She was also to submit several possible in-
scriptions for the proposed statue, which could then be put
to a vote.

Miss Herrick struggled with her plight, confessing to
friends and fellow members of the Eastfield Literary League
that she was torn between her obligations as a custodian of
fact and truth and her duty to the community. Eventually
she offered a document which omitted more facts than it
contained.

Mathew Wyndham was described as a "brave settler who
left the safety of his native England's pleasant shore" for
the New World. "His hand helped to build homes for others"
before "the pioneer spirit" led him to be the first settler "in
the place we know as our beloved Eastfield," where he
"made peace with the Redman."

The biography was voted acceptable only after the ref-
erence to the Indians was deleted; then came the discussion
of how the subject should be depicted in bronze. Since
Wyndham was not the type of man to have had his portrait
done, none existed. A committee was formed to pursue the
question, and eventually it was decided that he be depicted
as a bearded workman, strong of jaw and broad of shoulder,
and decidedly more handsome and tall than Springfield's
Mr. Pynchon.

One of the town selectmen, feeling that the whole business had gone on long enough, suggested that Wyndham
be depicted holding a string of wampum in one hand and

a bottle in the other. This brought a good deal of laughter, but would cost him reelection. In the end, it was decided that the bronze would show a man holding a musket in one hand to represent the pioneer spirit, and a hammer in the other, symbolizing both his trade and progress.

In this way, Mathew Wyndham's unrepented sins became Eastfield's collective sins of omission, hardly sins at all under the circumstances, it was felt, and certainly more comfortable to live with than the truth.

The controversy was entertained at such length largely because there were so many who enjoyed it. The older it is, the glossier its patina, the more easily history lends itself to revision: those who have not heard a former version are unlikely to question the accuracy of the version they hear. Wyndham was an ideal subject for debate and argument which could really offend no one too deeply. Such a topic was convenient, since the matter of Paul Hazeltine's place in the Celebration could not be spoken of in public.

There was no question of ignoring him in the ceremonies. In the nine years since his return, the effect of his presence had been dramatic. In the way that one man, given the right conditions of timing, can influence an entire community, Paul Hazeltine was the embodiment of the new prosperity Eastfield was enjoying, a living symbol of progress. As such, his position in the community was assured. He had not sought it, and in fact kept the town at a distance, but there was no question that as the wealthiest man in town he was the most prominent, and therefore the only candidate for the position of principal speaker.

As soon as he'd come back to Eastfield, he had negotiated with old Mr. Palmer for the purchase of the Palmer Buggy Works. Palmer had run the business as his father had before him. The men of Eastfield whom he employed, grateful for the work and having no expertise other than specific trades, had no reason to criticize or suggest improvements in their employer's methods. What Paul Hazeltine knew about carriages had only briefly remained to be seen.

For the first weeks of his management, the new owner had contented himself with silent observation of the Works, only occasionally asking a brief, specific question. Were the wood fittings turned on the premises, he wanted to know, or at the mill? What became of the scraps of leather?

A month later, he began to institute policies and practices of modernization. Every phase of the business was changed in some way, from the keeping of ledgers and records to the purchase of materials. Paul Hazeltine saw no reason for the association with a cousin of Mr. Palmer, who was in lumber in Amherst, to continue—so he purchased the Eastfield Lumber Company, offering the former owner a management contract.

He drew up charts that broke the process of carriage making into steps, and introduced a method of something he called "rotation," which meant that there would always be carriages in each of the steps of production. The foremen and manager, long accustomed to the old Palmer routine, listened to Paul Hazeltine with feigned expressions of respect, politely nodding when he announced the averages he'd taken of the time needed to mount wheels and finish seats.

They had no choice but to implement his plan, to pass on to their rough-handed men the new employer's concern with "efficiency" and his desire to increase production. The respect was earned when the ideas proved workable. The Hazeltine Buggy Works, as they became known, expanded and grew, with the introduction of two new models of carriages and many new jobs. Orders and production increased, and, within two years, a new facility was erected to accommodate them.

The town was now mentioned in newspapers and magazines, with the Hazeltine Buggy Works cited as a model factory. Success brought new workers, who in turn brought new businesses to Eastfield.

There were many, as a result, who had no reason to speculate as to Paul Hazeltine's past. But there were more who knew that he had not begun his life in the fancy house on River Road.

The construction of the house, in fact, had been as much of an event as the purchase of the factory. With the same methodical interest he'd shown in taking command of the Buggy Works, Paul Hazeltine had devoted himself to the building of the house on ten acres of land at the edge of town, running back from the shore of the Connecticut River. A prominent Boston architect had arrived to supervise construction from his plans, consulting with his client on every detail, as if the house were a monument to last for all eternity. Often the workmen would wait, finding the idleness surprisingly awkward, while the architect went to the Buggy Works to discuss with Mr. Hazeltine the shade of a new shipment of stone, or while Paul, visiting the site, suspended their work to examine the progress in a manner that was as leisurely as it was silent, as if time and money were of no matter.

Those with time to spare divided it between the edge of the Hazeltine property where they observed construction with an interest befitting the erection of a new town hall, and the railroad depot, where almost daily furnishings—the like of which Eastfield had never before seen—arrived.

Some were crated, leaving the curious to speculate on the contents.

Naked to the eye, though, there was a succession of treasures. Tufted leather sofas and heavy carved chairs upholstered in fine brocade; Oriental screens on which birds of embroidered gold and silver thread cavorted against silk skies of shaded blues and pinks; tables of strange, rich inlaid woods; cabinets and cases of all manner; paintings of distant, fantastic landscapes unrivaled even by those in picture books . . .

The depot took on the atmosphere of a fair. The barn at the Hazeltine Buggy Works, where the furnishings were being stored until the completion of the house, was like a museum through which the workers carefully and uncomfortably walked when the lunch bell rang. They examined (but did not touch) the sinks with their faucets in the shape of golden fish, and the furnishings; the boxes labeled BOOKS and SCIENTIFIC EQUIPMENT, viewing them all with a mixture of wonder and apprehension.

On weekends, when it was Hazeltine's custom to travel to Boston by train, the riverbank became the fairground. Mothers would half-heartedly tell their children not to play on Mr. Hazeltine's land, taking care not to make their admonishments too severe so that they might have legitimate cause, after a while, to search out their young and thus witness the progress of the great house for themselves, though of course from a suitable distance.

It occurred to a number of mothers that their daughters might be suitable candidates for a match with Eastfield's leading bachelor. They saw themselves visiting the house on River Road, strolling through the gardens, relaxing among the treasures their husbands brought news of from the Buggy Works. They chose to ignore as idle gossip the rumor that Mr. Hazeltine was keeping company with a wealthy Boston girl (whom, it was said, he visited each weekend). Introductions, still, were all but impossible to arrange.

Paul Hazeltine had no friends in town. He never attended church or social functions. As a result, the amenities were dispensed with and proprieties foregone, replaced with forced and awkward moments in which the acquaintance of embarrassed or overly eager young ladies was thrust upon him in the middle of the sidewalk, or at the railroad station.

He tolerated these undisguised attempts with civility and mild amusement, in the same way that he took for granted the awe of his possessions and respect for his accomplishments, including the wage increase that had gone into effect at the Buggy Works upon the occasion of its second expansion. Deference was met with distance. His steel-blue eyes remained cool; the lips unsmiling beneath his carefully groomed mustache. Aware of the eyes of the townspeople that were always upon him, Paul did not come closer to them, nor did he look away. Checking the arrival of items at the railroad siding against a master inventory, he sometimes turned to the hungrily curious crowd with a glance that told them in no uncertain terms that he was of them but apart from them; that they had best look while they had the chance, for they might never be close enough to see these things again.

This demeanor might have been more easily accepted from one with a background of wealth and position, but Paul Hazeltine was newly rich. His family had been born poor, and they'd died the same way, buried at the far end of the Trinity Church yard. The headstones, small and untended, were simple witnesses of arrival and departure, and tragedy of no small kind. The little girl's first:

ELISABETH HAZELTINE
1866—1870
*Gone the Flower Before It Fully Bloomed*

The year, from the start, had been cruel, with the cold lasting late into the spring and the ground remaining frozen when it should have given itself to tending. Crops, when they grew at all, were sparse and scrawny. Before there was time to feel the blow, cows took sick. With summer came influenza, raging through the area like a killing wind, entering every household. The first frost, which came too early, was said by the doctor and the clergy—in rare agreement—to be a "blessing," though nobody was quite sure why. The only hope was that what was to come would be better than that which had gone before.

The Hazeltines, having buried their daughter, were far too concerned with their own survival to do more than work until they were exhausted. They kept their own counsel, with little notice from or of the town.

In February their small farm burned, and Agnes and Peter Hazeltine with it.

There were some in Eastfield who remembered the night, but all of them had heard the story so many times—and told it, too—that it was as if the whole town had been on hand to see the boy of thirteen, all Paul had been then, run from the blaze. Standing in the field, his thin face impassive, he'd watched the beams and planks flare, huge matchsticks lighting the sky. And he'd seen the two smaller sticks among them, live and bending, twisting in a short and frantic dance of death as their cries, for an instant only, pierced the crackling that filled the night.

There was no kin to take the boy in: a family named Abernathy, who'd moved to Ludlow shortly after, had taken Paul home that night. The next day Reverend Willis called to inform them of the arrangements: the Church Relief would bury the Hazeltines, and after the service the boy's future would be decided.

What occurred next was as well known as the time of day, but the story was told often, and always with a pause at this point.

"For who among us can question the wisdom of His ways," Reverend Willis asked the few dutiful mourners gathered beside the simple pine boxes, "or can know of what is life?"

Oblivious to the sanctity of hallowed ground, or the presence of the small assemblage, or any sense of decorum, Paul Hazeltine had at that moment turned away, but not before damning God, and His ways, and the small group at the graves. With the curse on his lips came a fire—fierce as the flames the night before that had made his boy's face a man's, its brooding expression set forever—in his eyes.

"Where are you going?" the reverend asked, all dignity lost as the boy strode through the cemetery.

"Away," Paul called over his shoulder, not slackening his pace.

"But where? When will you be back?"

"Ask God," he spat, with a hatred the observers found as chilling as the winter day itself.

The service was resumed for the sake of the dead, and when it was over, Paul Hazeltine was nowhere to be found. The story, however, survived, repeated around Eastfield as shocking gossip at first, then as a lesson to ungrateful or willful children who, it was hoped, would be brought around by the tale of a lost young man who had turned on the town and its charity and God, with consequences so dire that they could scarcely be imagined. Let the children think, as the story implied in the version they heard, that while the faithful prayed at the graveside, the hand of the Almighty had reached down, returning Paul's curse and transporting him from Eastfield directly to Hell. The citizens, for a while, wondered what fate had befallen him, though in time their attention turned to other matters and the wondering stopped.

The graves were simply marked, the ladies of the Church Relief Committee agreeing that the less said the better.

AGNES HAZELTINE
1839—1871

PETER HAZELTINE
1836—1871

Paul Hazeltine became a shade, a shadow, lost to God and them and probably himself as well, and what difference did it make? With time, the story of his disappearance faded into the fabric of Eastfield's history.

Paul's return, unheralded and unexpected and all the more dramatic after sixteen years, was observed with an amazement that approached awe. The lone, kinless boy, who had vanished with only the clothes on his back, had become a man of resources, apparently limitless, that began to unfold like the pages of a book.

He had been to sea, it was said, rising from a deckhand to a merchant in import and export. He was said to have done extremely well in business in any number of places— New York, Boston, San Francisco. Clearly, he had amassed a fortune which he made no effort to hide from the town of Eastfield.

More disturbing was the fact that his fortune was growing.

Puritanism was gone, but its tradition was a factor that shaped the character of the place and the people. For his hubris and his shameful deed (his age at the time of his parents' death and that tragedy itself not withstanding), he had not been harmed or humbled, but apparently rewarded. It was, at the very least, a poor example.

But the Lord, the women of the town reminded one another, worked in mysterious ways and in His own good time. Who could say that He had not raised Paul Hazeltine, and was raising him still, to heights that would make his fall all the more punishment? If his position as principle employer and prominent businessman earned Paul Hazeltine a measure of respect, it was not given wholeheartedly in every case. Besides those who felt that his success was a deceptive calm before a certain storm of retribution, there were those who resented him simply because he was the embodiment of all that they envied and longed for.

Between these two groups, an attitude toward Paul Hazeltine was sparked, then forged into the fiber of Eastfield. If he wanted to keep to himself, it was just as well, people thought.

Amenities, of course, had to be observed. The deference of a shopkeeper for his customer, and the respect of a worker for his employer were as much common as common courtesy. As was polite applause for a man speaking on a public occasion, even if he had been a wicked boy whose punishment had not, as yet, been visited upon him, though it surely would be, in time.

## - 3 -

"LOVELY," OLIVIA HAZELTINE OBSERVED, peering into the center of the rose she'd just cut. She turned it slowly between the fingers of her gloved hand before gently placing it with the others in the white lacquered wicker basket hanging from her arm. Lovingly, she stroked the blossoms as if they were small, sleeping animals. "Perfection," she whispered.

Brigid, the hired girl, shifted in the morning sun, careful not to sway the parasol that protected her employer. "Yes, missus—"

"Of course it was the bananas that made all the difference."

"Ma'am?" Brigid asked.

Pleasure was replaced by concern. The color, the little of it that there was, faded from Olivia's porcelain cheeks. "You *did* bury the banana skins around the rose bushes as I asked you. You didn't forget?"

"Oh, no, ma'am. The banana peels. I did that."

Olivia patted the girl's cheek as if it were one of the roses. "Fine, dear. It makes *all* difference. Of course with camellias, it's a different story entirely. Camellias want tea leaves, you see."

"Tea leaves," Brigid repeated, remembering the wash that had to be done and the dining table to be set. All that, and the cooking to boot, and here she was listening to talk about banana skins and tea leaves.

"That should do for the table," Olivia announced, clipping a last rose, handing the basket to Brigid. "Do try to remember to *place* them in the vase, won't you. Don't stick them all in at once, but place them carefully, one at a time. Just as they grow. Mr. Hazeltine does enjoy an attractive arrangement."

Brigid nibbled at her lip before deciding to speak. "I always heard it was best to leave 'em outdoors, missus. They draw the benefits of the air, they do—"

Olivia tossed her head back and laughed. "Indeed? Why, wherever did you hear such a thing? It's nonsense, dear. Sheer nonsense!"

"Yes, ma'am."

"Mother!" the shriek came from the side lawn, and the two women turned to it. Seconds later, a small girl in a starched pinafore ran toward them, the blue ribbon that banded her hat flying in her face. A boy, younger but big as the girl, followed, laughing as she cried, breathless, clutching at her mother's skirt.

"He took my doll! He won't give it back, Mother—"

"Did not! We were playing. It was my turn to hide it—"

"Children!" Olivia said, her tone quieting them. "If this is the way you're going to behave, I don't think your father will let you go to the Celebration."

The threat quieted the girl's tears, but the boy glared at her.

"Tattletale!" he spat.

"Apologize to your sister, Paul."

He muttered an apology, and Olivia's good humor returned. "That's better. Francine, go along with Brigid and let her fix your bonnet. Wash your face, while you're at it. Run along now."

Brigid led the children up the path, stopping at the steps before the door. "About the table, missus," she began.

"Yes?"

"Will the children be eating with me? In the kitchen?"

Olivia looked at her in amazement. "Why ever would they do that?"

The hired girl's color rose with her embarrassment. "Well I thought that with your company, you and Mr. Hazeltine might want them out of the way."

"Out of the way?" Again Olivia laughed. "Certainly not, Brigid. Mr. Hazeltine feels that the company of our guests will be instructive to them."

When Brigid and the children had gone inside, Olivia strolled toward the sundial on the right side of the walk, admiring the marigolds that grew around it. The lawn, soft and green, stretched from the house to the manicured hedge like a blanket or carpet, while the thick hedge itself provided a barrier between the grounds of the house and the wild growth beyond it.

The Way, as they called the drive that led to the house, ran at a gentle angle from River Road, which in turn followed the course of the Connecticut River. Through the trees, Olivia could hear the sounds of horses and carts, more than usual since it was the day of the Celebration. The rhythm of hoofs and wheels slowed at the places where the house could be glimpsed through the thick summer growth of birch and alder and weeping willow.

They were aching for a good look, Olivia knew. There'd been a time, at the very beginning, when she'd thought of satisfying their curiosity, of opening the house and grounds to them. A lawn party, she'd thought, with lemonade and little cakes...

She'd been newly arrived in Eastfield, as new as the house Paul had built and presented her with, and like the house, she'd been something of a novelty. The townspeople were courteous, certainly, nodding, offering the polite smiles that were her due as the new Mrs. Hazeltine. A part of her had imagined going beyond the surface of the greetings, making friends among the local people with whom she and Paul might have dinner; women friends she might call on, and who might call on her for tea or little luncheons.

The thought of a party, an "at home," budded and grew, and one day she broached the subject to Paul.

"Certainly not!" he'd replied with a severity that took her aback. He'd touched her cheek to let her know that he wasn't angry. "Well intended I'm sure, my dear, but quite impossible. Whatever possessed you to consider such a notion?"

He was so much more intelligent than she was, brilliant in fact, she knew. Quite suddenly the imagined joy was gone, and she felt embarrassment in its place. "I—I only thought it might be pleasant, husband. And they do seem so interested in the house..."

"Let them satisfy their interest from the public road, then. I'll not have them here."

It was not her nature to voice her disagreement with him under any circumstances; she rarely even pursued a topic of conversation he did not wish to discuss. But the looks she'd seen in the appraising eyes of the women of Eastfield, and her own fear of having him think her foolish, had made her continue.

"It was only that they are our neighbors—"

"Hardly!" Paul Hazeltine corrected her. "If they happen to live in the same region as we do, it's an accident of geography and nothing more. A useful one, I admit, when it comes to my business—but it goes no further than that,

Olivia. It cannot. We have nothing whatsoever in common with any of them, nor they with us. Is that clear?"

"Yes, husband," she'd answered meekly, thinking how much he reminded her at that moment of her Uncle Allister, with whom she'd lived in Boston after her parents were drowned in a boating accident. She'd been a child, only five, and in time she'd come to forget them, thinking of the stern and demanding uncle and Aunt Katherine, his meek and often ailing wife, as a normal family. Still, there had been times when she watched from the parlor window of the house on Charles Street as children played in groups, longing for a friend to share the hours in the darkened house where one could never make noise, because Aunt Katherine was resting or Uncle Allister studying his paper.

Over the years, the longing had subsided. Olivia had found it easier to avoid the window and to turn instead to the books provided by Miss Hathaway, her governess. Excursions were rare: her aunt feared all manner of germs and diseases which might be returned across the threshold. But in books, and in her mind, Olivia could travel as far as she wanted at her whim.

The idea of a party had been a lark, an indulgence. All the more silly, Olivia realized, when she considered that it was the very type of life she'd lived in Boston, her "unworldliness," as he'd put it, that had caused Paul to court her. Of course their courtship had begun quite by accident when he came to call on her uncle in regard to a business matter. It had continued, even more surprisingly, in the face of both her uncle's and her aunt's stern objections.

Paul Hazeltine, Uncle Allister said, was a scoundrel—and a Protestant scoundrel at that. But conditioned as she'd been over the years to accepting the commands of a strong man, Olivia not only found herself flattered and in love, but under the influence of a man whose sense of purpose and determination made even Uncle Allister's pale. When they refused him permission to call on her, Paul Hazeltine took matters into his own hands.

The notes and messages he'd sent her made her head spin: she had felt like a character in a novel, the sort of novel her uncle would never have knowingly allowed her to read. The instructions Paul gave her made her tremble, but she'd followed them, inventing errands to mask their meetings. He'd not only been quick to state his intentions, but had devised the means of realizing them, pointing out that she was a grown woman of independent means, able to marry whomever she pleased.

If her uncle saw the wisdom of coming around, Paul had said, that would be so much the better. But if he persisted in opposing the match, there were steps to be taken. Olivia had been unable to sort it all out as he discussed the inquiries he'd made at her bank, which was also his own, and recounted to her the extent of the fortune her parents had left her in her uncle's guardianship. Money, in any case, made no difference and posed no problem: Paul told her that he had amassed more than enough of his own, all they might ever need.

"Trust me," he'd told her, and, transfixed by the firm line of his jaw, the steel blue of his eyes, the touch of his hand on her own, Olivia had been powerless to resist. She'd never considered a future for herself, fully expecting to end her days as she'd all but begun them, catering to her uncle, caring for her aunt through an endless succession of illnesses and recoveries, real and imagined. That she might find love, that a man might find her, was more than she'd dared to dream.

Their clandestine meetings had gone on for nearly a year. Then, without warning, their secret had been revealed by an associate of her uncle's who had seen them sitting to-

gether on the banks of the Charles. The news reached home
before she did. Uncle Allister had met her at the door, red
with rage. She'd closed her eyes, summoning Paul, wanting
and needing him. Instead, she'd fled to her room in tears,
cursing her lot, convinced that a lifetime of excruciating
memory was to be the penance for the taste of pleasure
she'd so briefly known.

That Sunday, as usual, she had accompanied her uncle
to church. Aunt Katherine, who normally attended with
them, was in her bed, suffering with a spell. The ride, like
all their time together since his discovery of what he termed
her "betrayal," was silent. She'd spoken only in response
to the Mass, and at the church door, where Father Brennan
had wished them both a good day. Then, from the sidewalk,
she'd heard the familiar voice of Paul Hazeltine calling her
name.

"Come away at once!" Uncle Allister insisted, unable to
control his rage. He seized her arm and began pulling her
toward their carriage.

"Wait!" Paul commanded, planting himself in their path,
moving when they moved so that the confrontation could
not be avoided.

"You are not a gentleman, sir!" her uncle had said, the
veins in his neck and forehead throbbing, his face red with
anger. "I forbid you to see my niece."

And there, on the very steps of Saint Joseph's Cathedral,
Paul Hazeltine had defied him. The calmness of his demeanor contradicted her uncle as much as his words.

"I'm afraid, sir," he said coolly, "that you have no choice
in the matter. I have asked Olivia to marry me and she has
agreed, and that is the end of it—"

Her Uncle Allister released his grip of her only long
enough to slap Paul Hazeltine's face. But her suitor returned
the blow with a force that sent Allister Langley sprawling

to the ground as the startled pastor and parishioners looked
on.

"I forbid it! I forbid it, do you hear! I'll disown you,
Olivia. I'll lock you out of my house—"

"She has no further need of your house or anything in
it," Paul Hazeltine said, extending his hand. The power of
his eyes made her feel as if she were losing her own
balance. "Come, Olivia."

As if she were in a trance, she started to reach for him.
Then, when their fingers were almost touching, she stopped.
"But where? Where, Paul?"

"With me," he said, and before she knew that she'd
decided, her hand was in his and he was leading her to his
carriage.

Only when they had pulled away, when the stunned spec-
tators could no longer follow them, did the magnitude of
what she'd done dawn on Olivia, and with it a mild hysteria.

"I shall have to beseech him!" she sobbed. "We must go
back, Paul, so that I can beg his pardon—"

"Nonsense," he said, matter-of-factly.

"But it's my home! Uncle Allister and Aunt Katherine
. . . my things . . ."

"Your home is with me, or it soon will be," he told her
with a rather amazing calm. "We have no need of his blessing, or his pardon, or your things for that matter. Even if
I were unable to provide for you, Olivia—and I am, make
no mistake—you have no need for anything you've left
behind. My things are yours now. We'll have a house of
our own to hold them, Olivia. As for pardon, it is your
uncle who should ask yours. He has mismanaged your
funds, my dear. He's no better than a common thief—"

"Perhaps he needed it—" she insisted.

Paul took her hands, staring into her eyes as if he could
see her soul. "I am to be your husband and you, my wife.

Forget him. Forget it all. Let your life begin now, with me.
*Our* life, Olivia."

"Yes, Paul," she heard herself say, feeling like a sleep-
walker. The boundary between dreaming and the reality of
wakefulness, such as it was, was confused. Was she imagining it all, Olivia Langley wondered. She had been with
him, been *his,* only a few short minutes, yet the past—that
which had been her life for so long—had in that time become remote. When she tried to remember the details of
it, it appeared to have taken place so fast and so long before.
That life, she thought, even the most vivid moments of it,
had been a kind of sleep, a waiting for this man with eyes—
a blue as deep and cold as an old jay in late November—
that held her. How he had come to her, and from where,
and why he had chosen her did not matter. He was someone,
something that had happened to her, transforming her existence.

For a time, though she had not dared to express the
feeling for fear of somehow disturbing the perfect landscape
of his vision of her, she had suffered moments of anxiousness. Never having been in the position of having to make
choices, she'd dreaded the mistake unmade, the decision
made unwisely. But if her aunt and uncle had directed the
course of her life with a rigid precision, Paul Hazeltine, it
quickly became apparent, was willing—eager, even—to
exert the same influence, merely redirecting the flow.

Where would she live, Olivia had wondered that day as
she sat in the carriage beside him. There were hotels, to be
sure, though she had never been inside them, not that a
single young woman could in any case consider taking a
hotel room. Propriety aside, there was the mechanical as-
pect, the details of how, exactly, to go about it. How would
she explain to the people she knew what had happened, so
suddenly, when she barely understood it herself?

By that evening, Paul had installed her in the Beacon Street home of a couple named Boland who accepted her not as a stranger thrust upon them, but as a guest whom they might have been expecting.

The Bolands, Paul told her, were his friends: they would be hers, too. To her delight, Olivia found herself at home in the sunny bedroom suite with its soft white curtains and the ivory vanity set laid out as if it had been waiting for her to claim it. Dorothea Boland was somewhat older than Olivia herself—how old, Olivia did not ask, for to do so would certainly have been rude—but it was as if there had been a space in the woman's life that had been made for Olivia to fill. If Dorothea found it odd that her guest had arrived for what was certain to be a lengthy if indeterminate stay, she gave no sign.

That first Monday, when Paul—who had of course spent the night in his own rooms, "nearby the Bolands," he told her, without being more specific—left to return to his business in Eastfield with a promise to return the following weekend, the two women shopped. For the first time in her life, Olivia wasn't told to make sensible purchases under the watchful eye of her aunt, but was instead encouraged to indulge herself. Samples of fine fabrics, the softest silks, the finest cottons, were presented by dressmakers. "Yes, of course," Dorothea told her, confirming the pleasure she took in the the feel of the materials, the subtlety of the shades, the endless sketches. The color and the cut would become her. There were shoes to be bought, lingerie to be run up. There were items of sheer whimsy, such as a pin box that played "Plaisir d'Amour" when its lid of delicate china roses was lifted. A parade of seamstresses came to the house to measure and fit. Dorothea's own maid washed and rearranged Olivia's hair, using an imported shampoo, so much more luxurious than the castile she was used to, that polished the highlights in her hair until it shone like burnished gold. Instead of being caught back in a bun, an illustration from one of Mrs. Boland's many French magazines served as example. Her new coiffure was pulled up from the nape of her neck, her hair waved and pinned to the crown of her head with tendrils falling about her cheeks.

"You'll grow accustomed to it, my dear," Dorothea assured her. "It suits you so."

To her delight, Olivia did, and with an ease that amazed her. The reflection that gazed back at her from the mirror of the dressing table she'd come so quickly to think of as her own struck her as finally hers. She learned the names of the rich and delicate sauces served at the Bolands' table as if she'd known them rather than the plain and bland cuisine necessitated by her aunt's delicate constitution all her life. Within a week, she'd been transformed, and when she greeted Paul, who arrived in time for dinner on Friday, in a dress of soft chiffon with delicate flounced sleeves (it had been delivered and finally fitted only that morning, Dorothea having told her that with money, all things were possible), the approval, the appreciation in his eyes nearly moved her to tears.

"You must always wear white, my dear," he said, kissing her hand.

He gave her a velvet box, which she opened to find a string of coral beads.

From the first, she'd been awed by the way Dorothea presided over her table. Conversation was bright and lively, so different from the silence of the meals she'd taken with her uncle, who believed that conversation impeded the digestion. That first weekend, she'd had to struggle to retain her composure, afraid of saying the wrong thing and thus betraying her ignorance. But Paul spoke of Eastfield, and his factory, and the house he was already planning to build.

A smile, a glance, an attentive tilt of her head, Olivia observed, satisfied and charmed him. After dinner, while the men finished their brandy and cigars before joining them in the drawing room, Dorothea had toyed with one of Olivia's tendrils as if she were a child who had pleased a parent.

"You needn't worry," the older woman assured her. "You're quite what Paul wants, Olivia. He adores you. It's very plain to see."

Later, then again and again in the following months, she learned to recognize the pleasure in his eyes when he looked at her; to luxuriate in the sensation of being a woman adored. During the week, when business took him back to Eastfield, guests frequently appeared at the Bolands' table. Olivia found that her natural simplicity and lack of worldliness was perceived by others as an innocence with a charm of its own. The shopping excursions continued, and there were outings to the symphony or the theater. Dorothea took her to museums. Olivia was enchanted by the whole waiting world that she was seeing for the first time. When she was with Paul, she was careful not to ramble on about her new discoveries and cautious, for the most part, to temper her enthusiasm with what she believed to be a ladylike reserve. When she spoke, in any case, he appeared to notice her face, the movement of her lips and the darting of her eyes, far more than her words.

With no resistance, then, for there was no part of her being that was not intent on pleasing him, Olivia Langley let herself be fashioned into the woman Paul Hazeltine wanted. In Eastfield, he was building the house they would share: in Boston, she was being molded into the wife of his design. An observer (though those friends of the Bolands' and Paul's whom she met seemed delighted and accepting at once, as though she had not only been expected, but had been there all the while, and in any case kept their observations to themselves) might have likened her to clay. This would have been an unfortunate image, not nearly so trite as inaccurate.

For instead of being inert and emotionless, Olivia was passionately dedicated to her own reshaping, to becoming the thing the man who loved her and had let her love—*at last!*—wanted. She rejoiced in discerning those things which most pleased Paul, in making herself all the more desirable.

Seven years had passed, years in which the house and Olivia had been finished. Her life with him, and her children, and their future, were things that Olivia Langley would have found impossible to imagine. Yet Olivia Langley Hazeltine had come to cherish them with a devotion that now made it impossible for her to think that her life might be or have been any other way.

If her husband chose to rarely mix socially with his neighbors and the people of the town that was *theirs,* it was fine. If, however, he would deliver the keynote address at the biggest celebration in the history of Eastfield, it was natural and fitting. She would welcome those guests he might occasionally invite, and fill herself so fully with him that there would be no place to miss the friends, the guests, she might have wanted.

For his was a world of his own, and he had built it—its confines as rigid as the high hedges and thick trees bordering the yard where she strolled—to both include and contain her. And that, Olivia thought, smiling, holding her parasol delicately over her shoulder, was how it was and surely would always be.

## - 4 -

JUNE'S RELENTLESS HEAT had parched the Common. The members of the Celebration Committee had hoped for a late rain, picturing the newly whitewashed bandbox and the reviewing stand, with its tricolor bunting, as they might have looked against the green grass.

The festivities, noted in a special souvenir program, were not scheduled to begin until noon, but by early morning the Common had been crowded with families, their blankets spread and their picnic baskets open. Random groups of children played improvised games of ball, or rolled hoops, or annoyed the peddlers and vendors who offered lemonade, ices, and flags. Babies cried as the heat rose; men removed their jackets, rolling up their shirt sleeves in spite of their wives' protests and wiping the sweat from their faces and necks with handkerchiefs.

By half past eleven, the temperature had reached a stifling ninety-eight degrees, and the Common was a sea of bodies, too tired and too tightly packed to move. Latecomers, finding no room left on the arid yellow grass, had to settle for the shadeless sidewalk of Front Street, facing the green, some of them spilling over to State and Market Streets as well.

The banner—TOWN OF EASTFIELD BICENTENNIAL CELE-
BRATION/JULY 4, 1896—hung limp in the heavy air. The
bunting wilted, and the marching bands and paraders, clustered together in their costumes, tugged at their collars for
respite. In addition to the groups from Eastfield—the fire
brigade, the Grange, the church groups, and the rest—there
were representatives from Springfield and Holyoke, Amherst and Ludlow.

The matter of choosing a Grand Marshal for the parade
had been a subject of considerable debate among the Celebration Committee. A number of the local clergy had been
suggested, then rejected, since each committee member
wanted to nominate the spiritual leader of his or her church,
and because the whole idea, on further consideration,
seemed undignified. The leading citizen of Eastfield, Paul
Hazeltine, to whom the honor might otherwise have gone,
was an unpopular choice: there was about him a stern coldness, and aloofness, that made it virtually impossible to
imagine him leading a parade, and it was enough that he
would be delivering the keynote address. The governor had
been invited, but had sent his sincere regrets. The honor,
by default, fell to Mayor Kallen.

By noon, the crowd was as restless as it was festive. The
reviewing stand, filled except for the first-row seats reserved
for the Hazeltines, was the scene of frequent consultations.
The statue of Mathew Wyndham at the far end of the Common, draped in muslin for the ceremonial unveiling later
in the day, had attracted children, who were peeking beneath
the cloth: "You *must* do something," Violet Herrick told
Mayor Kallen. "Can't one or two of the policemen guard
it—"

"Now, now . . . calm down, Miss Herrick," the mayor
said, noting that the reporter from the *Springfield Republican* and the other men of the press were witnessing the

scene and smirking at one another. "Our peace officers are marching in the parade." He lowered his voice. "Besides, Violet, what does it matter? Everyone's seen the statue already. You only decided to cover it a week ago."

"It's the principle of the thing!" she insisted, near tears.

"All right. Once the parade starts, the children will be much too busy to bother the statue."

"Really! If that's your attitude—" The noon bell rang from Trinity Church, interrupting her. Miss Herrick changed her tactic. "Why hasn't the parade started, may I ask? You're *late*, Mayor Kallen."

He cleared his throat. "I thought we might wait for Mr. Hazeltine."

"Indeed!"

He cleared his throat. "Yes . . . well, perhaps it would be best to begin." One of his aides was dispatched to tell the calliope man to stop playing, and the mayor himself, smiling and nodding as he moved through the crowd, hurried to State Street, where the marching groups were assembled. A stir of excitement moved through the crowd on the Common as mothers scanned the outskirts of the area, looking for their children but too tired and too crowded in place to do more than call to them.

Then, as the sounds of instruments being lifted and tuned came through the air, the crowd settled, expectantly.

A bass drum sounded, then sounded again.

All eyes turned to State Street.

With a sudden start, to cheers of approval and excitement, a Sousa march began. Mayor Kallen, in the morning coat and top hat the committee had insisted on, rounded the corner to Front Street, followed by the newly established Eastfield Bicentennial Marching Band. The band and its uniforms, like everything else about the Celebration, had been matters of discussion and dissension. It was readily agreed that Leonard Fontaine was the only man capable of organizing the group: he played the organ and led the choir at Trinity Church (the only congregation in Eastfield with such an instrument), and was considered by all to be the resident expert on the subject of music. His abilities, expertise aside, had been tempered by the shortage of qualified musicians he had to work with.

It was not that Eastfield did not have its share of instruments and those who liked to play them, but rather a matter of suitability. Lettie Yardgrove, who'd recently ordered and received a new parlor grand piano from Sears, Roebuck and Co., voiced the opinion that the band should include pianos and organs, to be taken from parlors of those closest to the parade route (a somewhat selfish qualification, considering that she herself lived at the corner of Front and High streets). The instruments, she suggested, might be placed on wooden platforms with attached wheels, which could then be pulled by horses. After heated debate, the motion was defeated.

The real issue of supplementing the relatively few trombones and cornets posed a problem. Other, bigger nearby communities would be sending their bands to the Celebration: how would it look if Eastfield were shabbily represented? Students from the First Eastfield School, selected by the principal, Lucas Garvey, were pressed into service, hastily acquainted with drums and bells and triangles. Relatives of Eastfield residents, after one of the several town meetings on the subject, were asked to bring their musical instruments when they came to the Celebration.

The resulting assemblage, if it might have sounded somewhat cacophonous to the unsuspecting outsider, was cheered heartily by the crowd on the Common. In their white trousers and jackets (or shirts in some cases, for after a great deal of debate on the matter, it was agreed that shirts would suffice for those who could not or would not afford white jackets), the strains of the opening Sousa march were nearly overwhelmed by the sounds of the people of Eastfield hailing their sons and husbands and brothers.

The Hampden Fire Brigade followed, white horses pulling a gleaming new fire truck with its coiled white hose and extension ladders. The drill team from the YMCA school in Springfield came next. Church groups, civic delegations, a band of youngsters from the County Orphans Home . . . one followed another along the parade route, down State Street, across Front, around the Common, and back along Front to Market.

Children, the children of Eastfield who had never seen such sights or such a crowd except in picture books, watched in wide-eyed wonder. Husbands and wives put aside the bickering of the morning and other mornings and nights to smile at each other in the sheer pleasure of it.

Mayor Kallen, heading the parade, smiled and beamed, tipping his high silk hat, appearing not to mind the heavy morning coat in the least, as if he had some special, singular dispensation from the heat. The crowd on the Common stood, those in front at first out of excitement and then those behind them, if only to get a better view, as a carriage rolled by, a hand-lettered sign proclaiming OUR OLDEST AND NEWEST CITIZENS. Nettie Green, ninety-two years old, had no idea of what was going on, of course—she was stone deaf, and prone to dozing, but she smiled, pleased with the ride and the attention. Little Roger Berlinger, likewise unaware of his place, his moment in history, howled in the arms of his mother, who held him too tightly as she sat beside Nettie, smiling in nervous embarrassment.

The parade was concluded by the Celebration Committee's proudest accomplishment—the Pageant of History.

At first, it had been suggested that great moments in Eastfield's history be acted out, with townspeople recreating the various scenes. Even Miss Herrick, however, was hard pressed to come up with several great moments in history that had actually taken place in Eastfield, or close enough to be incorporated for the purpose. Instead, then, a costume parade had been decided on.

Those who had lived in or around the town long enough searched attics and cellars, barns and trunks and boxes for suitable attire. Where no garments existed, Miss Herrick provided sketches from books, and Mr. Emery was induced, in view of the high patriotic and civic nature of the cause, to donate what material he could be talked out of and to sell the rest at his wholesale cost. At night, when they might normally have done the supper dishes and perhaps sat and enjoyed an hour of relaxation once the children were in bed, the women of Eastfield had cut and sewn and fitted, washed and pressed, and polished brass buttons. And now, after all those hours of work and all the discussion of who would portray what period, the Pageant of History began.

EASTFIELD'S FIRST CITIZENS, a sign announced. Mathew Wyndham, all agreed, was getting more than his due: there was no need to single him out again, nor to portray the Indians to whom the land had belonged before it was settled. Lucy and Hank Tremont, dressed as pilgrims, walked in the center of the parade route, their two children between them. On either side rode the Parker brothers, Nate and Calvin, whose horses were the finest looking as well as the fastest in town, excepting the Hazeltine horses, of course. The brothers were dressed as English soldiers, and carried muskets that had been borrowed from the Gavin family, who could trace its history back to the town's beginnings.

COLONIAL DAYS, the next sign said, followed by a group of men and women dressed in heavy clothes that might have been worn at harvest time. They carried rakes with missing teeth, heavy old shovels culled from the cobwebbed corners of barns and sheds.

Next came a black-bordered sign, EASTFIELD'S GLORIOUS PATRIOTS. Five men in uniforms of the Continental Army walked in step, followed by five women in black, representing the grieving families of those who died in the American Revolution.

TIME MARCHES ON—EASTFIELD GROWS, a sign announced. The greatest number, twenty six in all, walked behind it, wearing all manner of their ancestors' work clothes and finery. There was chuckling on the green, fingers pointed at the old, wide bonnets and cloaks, at the awkward-looking suits. Florence Emery wore a burgundy ballgown with fancy beading.

THE WAR BETWEEN THE STATES—EASTFIELD MEETS THE CHALLENGE. The Tenth Regiment, commanded by Henry Briggs, was represented, as were the Twenty-Seventh Massachusetts Volunteers. Luke Kelsey, Henry Bryant, Damon Carr, Solomon Frazier, and William Lowndes rode in full uniform to the applause of the crowd. Behind them, women dressed in the style of the time followed, carrying knitting needles and yarn, knitting as they went, to commemorate the contribution the women of Eastfield had made to the war effort, not only tending their homes and fields when needed but making such a concerted effort to the Union Bandage Drive that there had been a letter of gratitude from the governor himself.

PEACE AND PROSPERITY, the final sign read. An effort had been made by the Committee to assign specific places in line in this last category, as in the others, but by now the excitement had grown to the point of contagion. With none of the decorum Miss Herrick and the other organizers had repeatedly insisted on, the remaining paraders strode and skipped along, a hodge-podge of costumes from after the war to the present. Children, attracted from their viewing positions, followed merrily. Dogs, every dog in town that wasn't tied up, ran in circles behind them, barking to the merriment of the crowd. When the last of them had passed, a cheer went up from the Common.

The Trinity Church bell rang for a full five minutes.

Already marchers were making their way into the crowd, their costumes exchanged for more comfortable clothes. Picnic baskets were opened; sandwiches offered, salads and cakes set out to be admired first by, then shared with, neighbors and friends.

On the reviewing stand, Mayor Kallen, who had grown quite accustomed to his hat and had no obvious intention of parting with it, shook hands and accepted congratulations: the day had begun triumphantly.

"My friends!" he called, raising his hands to settle the crowd. "Friends and guests!" Slowly, people resettled themselves on the Common. The talk and the laughter subsided.

"Dear friends and guests," Mayor Kallen called. "Welcome to this historic day. And let us start by commending that which has gone before—the glorious parade organized by our Celebration Committee!"

The crowd responded with cheers, and Miss Herrick, in spite of herself, smiled, red-faced.

"Yes, friends," the mayor said, continuing after the crowd quieted. "This is a singularly special day. Each and every one of us is a part of it—and a part of history itself. We are privileged to be here at this time and place...a time of peace and prosperity. We are fortunate indeed to be part of this County of Hampden, in the glorious Commonwealth—"

A noise, a strange mechanical chugging, had begun. It

grew louder, and the crowd began to murmur. Mayor Kallen turned his head and cleared his throat.

"This glorious Commonwealth of Massachusetts holds a unique place in the Union, and our beloved Eastfield . . ."

"Look!"

"Did you ever?"

"What in the name—"

"Dear Father in Heaven!"

There was no use in trying to continue, the mayor knew. The crowd was on its feet, and the dignitaries and guests sharing the stand with him were all looking too.

There, in the center of Front Street, it was—a carriage the likes of which the town of Eastfield had never seen before. It was not the shape of the thing that was so unusual, for it was, in fact, much like the Phaeton, the most popular model the Buggy Works turned out. More than half the men staring at it worked on carriages like it, attaching fittings, mounting seats, setting hitches. But this carriage had no hitch. It was pulled by no horse or beast. There was a large metal box mounted where the horses should be, and a wheel of some sort instead of reins. Behind the wheel sat Paul Hazeltine. Beside him sat his wife, Olivia, with Constance, her youngest daughter, in her arms. The boy, Paul, Jr., sat in the rear seat, with his sisters Francine and Margaret, and a frightened Brigid.

"Look! A horseless carriage!"

"Did you ever imagine—"

"I read something in the paper, but—"

For once, and for what some would later recall as the only time it had happened, Mayor Kallen was speechless. He stood unmoving as the vehicle came to a stop in front of the reviewing stand, with a bump and a series of quick, loud noises. Paul Hazeltine sat motionless as the carriage shook, and then, when it had come to a full and final rest, he stepped out, walking around the front of the thing to open the door for his wife. Olivia handed little Constance back to Brigid, and Paul helped his wife down, his blue eyes holding hers as she opened her parasol and lifted the hem of her white lace dress. Still looking at him, at him alone, she took the arm he held out, walking slowly to the edge of the Common. The children, guided by Brigid, followed.

As if frozen in a tableau, the Hazeltines stood motionless. There were muffled noises from the crowd, many a "My word!" and, "I never!" Nervous coughs came from some of the men and sighs from some of the women. Paul Hazeltine's unyielding stare slowly silenced them then, as if he were a mesmerist able to work without words, made them take their seats again.

Mayor Kallen, rubbing his hands and not even trying to mop the sweat that fell from his scalp and face like nervous rain, started down from the reviewing stand, cautiously, then more quickly, wiping a palm on his coat at the last possible second before extending it to Paul, who shook it quickly and without comment. The Hazeltines followed the mayor up the steps to the stand.

All the eyes of Eastfield were on the Hazeltines, Paul and Olivia and the children, as they took their seats while Mayor Kallen hurriedly concluded his welcoming remarks and began to introduce the Celebration's keynote speaker. Then, all eyes turned upward, where with no warning a thick gray cloud had appeared in the blue, bright sky, covering the sun and discoloring the day.

# - 5 -

"...ONE DAY, one day that will come sooner than we can know or judge, we will look back at this day as a modern version of ancient history. The world will be the same, or rather in the same place, but different. So different! It will be a world of wonders!

"A world—an entire world—of which we are part...a vital part. Our homes will be powered by electricity. Not just for lamps, but for all our daily tasks. It will open and close our doors. It will heat and cool us, allowing man mastery over the elements. It will churn butter and press our clothes—even cut our hair and shave us. It will iron our clothes and sew them."

Had his voice been less fervent, more titters and smirks would have been exchanged. As it was, the visions of the future propounded by Paul Hazeltine, who had been hastily introduced by a nervous Mayor Kallen, were amusing the crowd more than informing it. As always, Olivia Hazeltine was oblivious to the reaction of others, not even seeing the crowd sprawled on the Common under the darkening sky. She sat, her back a straight line in her seat on the reviewing stand, her body turned at a slight angle that enabled her to stare, transfixed, at her husband's profile.

He gripped the lectern with both hands, pitching himself and his message toward the audience.

"In the coming years, in just a decade perhaps, we will celebrate not only ourselves and our isolation, but the greatness of being part of the world! In Italy, a Mr. Marconi has just discovered the radio—a way of sending messages through the air without wires, my friends—"

"Without wires indeed!" someone called from the rear of the crowd.

"What does Italy have to do with us?" another voice asked.

"Can't you see?" Paul Hazeltine asked, his veins throbbing. "A hundred years ago, would our ancestors have believed that we would have the telegraph or streetcars? Our children—we ourselves—will be able to send our own voices through the air. Distance will be no matter. And after voices, there will be pictures as well, in our homes! Italy, France, China—all the places that seem so far away will no longer be distant. For we will travel! Travel to them with an ease and speed that will dazzle us. Ships, ships bigger and faster than any we can imagine, will cross the ocean in the blink of an eye—"

"Like the *Utopia!*" a voice shouted.

"And the *Regina Regenta!*" another chorused.

Both of the vessels, the first a British steamer and the second a Spanish cruiser, had sunk off Gibraltar. There had been four years between the disasters, but the death tolls of each, five hundred seventy-four dead when the *Utopia* went down and at least four hundred gone when the Spanish vessel sank, were the kind of news that few who heard it forgot.

"True," Paul Hazeltine agreed, unwilling to lose the audience before him to its own ignorance. "But man will master the sea! Science will show him how to avert storms and perhaps alter them. New ships will be built that will travel under the water instead of on it—" He paused, reluctantly, for the gasps and exclamations. "—and there will be airships that will cross continents and oceans like huge mechanical birds—"

"And just how is that, may I ask, sir?" Willie Stammond rose unsteadily to his feet in the center of the Common. As usual, he'd been drinking, and though he made a show of removing his hat as he posed his question, his wavering made Lily, his wife, blush and lower her head while her neighbors chuckled.

"How? How you ask?" Paul Hazeltine leapt down from the platform, and both the dignitaries and the crowd on the Common stirred. Would he knock Stammond down on the Celebration day itself? But instead of moving toward the Common, he ran toward its edge where the vendors, their sales temporarily suspended, stood idly observing. From the startled balloon man, he grabbed a sheaf of brightly colored balloons and ran back to the platform bounding into place.

"Like this!" Paul Hazeltine cried, releasing them. Children clapped as the balls of bright red and blue and yellow rose in the darkening sky, their eyes following them as they drifted higher and farther. "As simply as that, sir!" the speaker continued. "Mark my words, man will master the air and the universe as well! The planets! The stars! The very heavens! It is not our capabilities that limit us—only our vision. What the mind can imagine, the hand can build! What man can conceive, what he can dream, he can realize!"

The simple demonstration stilled them. Olivia beamed, half-hearing her husband's words but certain, certain in all the bones in her body, that his every word was as true as the white of her gown or the gold of her wedding ring. In the house, it was common for him to lock himself in his study for hours, to pore over his books and the scientific papers—some in French or German or Italian—that came to him in envelopes with strange, colorful stamps. At dinner, seated at the head of the table, enjoying Brigid's roast of lamb and the chutney that Olivia herself had put up, he'd speak of names like Taintor and Duncan and Daimler, Edison, Marconi, and Stanton. The inventors, she'd come to understand, were like friends to him, like Springfield's Everett Hosmer Barney, one of the rare guests they'd entertained, who'd made advances in guns and locomotives and, finally, a fortune in roller skates and a process for the perforation of bank checks.

Engines and carburators, talking machines and the wireless—electricity itself: they were mysteries to her, certainly, but what did it matter? Paul understood them, her beloved, adored, adoring Paul, and by the strength of his faith and her faith in him, she came to believe fully. The details didn't matter really, nor did the complex diagrams he studied.

They, Olivia had decided, were not unlike the illustrations in the garden and botany books in which artists attempted to depict the internal nature of a flower or plant. In her mind and her heart, it was the beauty of the garden that mattered: the experts, men like Paul, could concern themselves with internal workings.

"The world is a place of change," he was telling them. "And on this day, it is fitting to note that change will come faster than ever in the pages of history that have yet to unfold themselves. As we look back, we must look ahead. As we recall Eastfield's past, we must look to its future, to the prosperity that progress will bring to each of us—"

"Mr. Hazeltine, sir?"

"Hush!" Lily Stammond implored, already mortified, but

it was too late. Her husband had once again risen and stood, weaving, demanding to be recognized. "If I may ask—"

"Go ahead then," Paul Hazeltine said.

"What of progress at the Works, sir? Seeing as how you did arrive in a horseless carriage of some sort..."

There were murmurs of agreement from the crowd, from the men and women whom, from the moment of the vehicle's appearance, had wanted to know the same thing. One read in the papers of such things, of course, but like the other inventions and discoveries, like the dreams Paul Hazeltine was spinning on the speaker's platform, they were remote, even amusing. The Hazeltine carriage, quite suddenly, had become another matter.

His Buggy Works was their livelihood, and for him, the owner, to arrive at the Celebration in a carriage drawn by no horses at all surely meant something.

"A good question, sir," the speaker responded with something akin to a smile. "Very good indeed. The times, as I've said, are changing, and we must change with them or be left behind. We will continue to make buggies and carriages, to be sure. On farms, on coutnry roads, away from towns and cities, many will continue to ride them.

"But I have chosen today to demonstrate the new Hazeltine Electric Car—" he paused, letting them stir and settle again. "The prototype—"

"What's that again?" a voice called out.

"The model," he answered, trying to contain his annoyance. "The first of its kind. The Hazeltine Electric Car will be built here, in Eastfield. The Works will be enlarged, of course. There will be new jobs and a new future for Eastfield. For all of us!"

On the Common, they looked at one another, not knowing whether to rejoice or to worry. New jobs, he'd said, but what of the old ones? What of the work, the familiar work, they already knew? And which of them had the vaguest of ideas about turning out electric cars?

"What's to happen to us, then?" a man called, speaking for them all.

"Yes! What about our work?"

"We don't understand. We'll be fired—"

"How are we to live?"

"Please!" he implored them, splaying his hands. "Please believe me, you have no need to worry. When I bought the works from Mr. Palmer, I introduced new methods. Changes and improvements were made, weren't they?"

The crowd was quick to affirm it, remembering the raises and the cousins and kin taken on at the Works under his management.

"What I'm speaking of now is another change—a matter of learning a few new simple skills which I can easily teach you. Just as the first changes resulted in more work, the Hazeltine Electric Car will bring a new prosperity. Not only to the Works, mind you, but to all of us. There will be more workers with more money to spend in the shops. There will be jobs for all who want them. The Hazeltine Electric Car will carry Eastfield into the twentieth century! It will make this place the center of the very industry that will change our entire nation.

"To change, in conclusion, is to grow, and grow we must. For at this time in our history and the history of man, to stay the same is to stagnate and decay."

His final words were drowned out by the thunder of their applause, and Paul Hazeltine stood stiffly as the photographers' flashes exploded. Mayor Kallen was at his side, posing with him, pumping his hand in the hope that the press and the townspeople would think that he'd known about the electric car well ahead of time and that it was he, perhaps, who had convinced Paul Hazeltine to announce it at the Celebration.

The crowd surged toward the speakers' platform. A calliope, silent during the speech, began to play, and several of the members of the bands that had marched earlier struck up another Sousa march.

The reporters and the curious pushed for a better look at the new vehicle, while Paul tried to answer the questions that were being fired at him in rapid succession.

Did he really believe that the horseless carriage would be the coming thing, and how soon would production begin? Would there be new jobs? New people moving to Eastfield?

The townspeople pressed closer and closer still, hanging on his every word. Their spirits, already heightened by the day, soared. What could make the Celebration more complete than the wonderful news; and what reason could their be, given the day and man, to doubt it? Paul Hazeltine had changed their lives; now he would change them again, make them better still.

The doubt and skepticism passed like the clouds in the summer sky. Horseless carriages? Why not? Moving sidewalks, flying machines, all manners of convenience and pleasure that the mind, the mind of a man like Paul Hazeltine, might imagine—of course!

They listened and hugged one another, their bodies moving in time to the music, smiling as their children danced. The promise of new prosperity, of a future brighter than the already brightened present, spread through them like an epidemic.

Their eyes moved from Paul Hazeltine to the horseless carriage to the sky. And, sometimes, to Olivia and her children, sitting motionless on the reviewing stand, strangely immune to the spirit infecting them all.

## - *6* -

"OUT OF THE QUESTION, my dear," Paul told his wife as he helped himself to one chop, then another, from the platter Brigid offered. When he'd taken peas and summer squash, she moved silently to the opposite end of the table, where Mrs. Hazeltine would serve the children, then herself, as was her custom. "It makes no sense whatsoever, as I'm sure you'll realize on further consideration."

"Of course, Paul," Olivia answered, feeling her face flush.

"I assure you we're far better equipped to teach the children than is some public schoolmarm."

"Yes, you're quite right," Olivia agreed readily. The idea of sending Paul, Jr., and Francine to the Eastfield Public School had been a mistake: for the life of her, she didn't know why it had crossed her mind in the first place. Perhaps, she thought, it was the lack of companionship she remembered, distantly, from her own childhood. Or perhaps it was simply that Miss Herrick, the librarian, had inquired earlier in the week when she'd been shopping in town as to whether the children would be enrolling for the fall term. Education, by law, was compulsory, but certainly nobody would press the issue. If Paul Hazeltine, as the leading citizen of Eastfield, chose to educate his son and daughters at home, it was his affair; a right that came with his power and position.

"I'm sure the company of the local children would bore

Paul and Francine, not to mention inhibiting their progress—"

"I think I'd like it," Francine interrupted. The outburst was so unusual that even Brigid, who'd learned from the first to serve meals in silence, concentrating on prayers that none of them would stain the heavy linen tablecloths and napkins, stared at the girl.

"Francine, your manners!" her mother corrected.

"I'm sorry," the child answered.

"And why do you think so, may I ask?" Paul said.

His daughter, as she'd been taught, blotted her lips and placed her silver carefully on her plate before speaking.

"I—I thought it would be nice to have playmates, Father. Like the other children do."

Paul smiled gently at her. "But you are not at all like the other children, my dear. They simply don't have your advantages, Francine. You have nothing—aside from age— in common with them at all, any more than I have anything in common with my employees. Do you understand that?"

"Yes, Father," she answered.

"I would be very pleased, Francine, if you might realize how fortunate you are."

The girl moved her eyes away, glancing across the table at the quick smirk that flashed over the face of her brother. There was, beside a mocking, a deeper, darker, cruelty that she could not understand, but which frightened her all the same. She dropped her eyes to her plate.

"Quite out of the question," Paul Hazeltine said to them all, before addressing Olivia. "I have some business matters to attend to, my dear. You won't mind if I don't take dessert?"

"Of course," Olivia answered, secretly wanting him to stay another few minutes, hoping her voice didn't betray her.

He rose at the head of the table almost ceremoniously,

lingering before leaving, surveying the room with its heavy
Persian carpet; its gleaming Waterford chandelier. The buffet, Italian like the table, a masterwork of inlaid woods,
shone and smelled of lemon oil. The walls, covered in a
deep rose moiré, were accented by a series of oils—hunting
scenes he'd found in London.

His possessions, as always, pleased him, and, as always,
in taking stock of them, he noted his family among them.
Paul, his son . . . the boy was bright, a natural heir to his
father's domain. Francine . . . spirited perhaps, though out-
bursts such as the one at dinner were certainly rare. Time
would temper them in any case. Young Margaret, and
Constance, in her highchair . . . both placid children, with
a nature like their mother's.

And Olivia. *Olivia* . . .

He'd asked her to excuse him, as he always did, out of
courtesy rather than an interest in her wishes. Never before
had she been anything but agreeable: were she, once, to say
anything but "of course" when he announced his plans, he'd
have been startled, shocked. It was her passivity, Paul
thought as he crossed the room at last, that had in part
attracted him, the obviously malleable nature and disposi-
tion. These, to be sure, has struck him as keenly as the fine,
perfect line of her nose and the high rise of her cheekbones.

More than anything, though, it had been a sense of a
quality beneath her docile, almost timid exterior that had
taken him. He'd found it odd, the initial attraction he'd felt,
having resigned himself to a life of solitude (partly of choice
and partly as a circumstance of his drive). There was about
Olivia Langley, he'd observed from the first time her uncle
introduced them, an unworldliness. It went beyond simple
innocence, into the fiber and fabric of her being; if she was
shy and sheltered, she was also the sort of person who was
incapable of imagining the world's despair. If she longed
for "experience," the kind of experience she savored in the

romantic fiction he so often found her absorbed in, what she *needed* was protection, guarding, shielding.

Her uncle, Paul thought, might have known this too: the business that had been transacted between them was certainly not bad enough to have so enraged the man.

For his part, Paul had been enraged by the uncle's taking his niece so for granted. He was protective, to be sure, but the guarding was heavy-handed. Like a rare orchid, Olivia had been confined to the house in Boston as if it were a bell jar. When he'd decided to take her (and he'd decided at once) he'd vowed to create a secure space for her in which she might not simply bloom, but flourish. The idea, as soon as he'd thought of it, became a consuming passion.

He'd felt a sense of mission, for who might be better suited to the task of guarding a woman so unaware of the common cruelties of the world than a man who had experienced them in his first memories? He'd never spoken of the day he'd left Eastfield, or of the fire, or the few lean and unhappy years he remembered before that, but he'd never escaped them either, no matter how far he'd gone.

In China, trading, in London, on business, in Boston, at his bank—as a man, young at first and now older, he'd often been overcome by moments of anguish, feelings so intense that he'd needed all his strength to withstand crumbling under the weight of them. The knowledge of the world's sadness and random pain, Paul Hazeltine felt at such times, was his special and private burden.

At the Buggy Works, as he'd done on the streets of cities all over the world, he studied the faces of his workers, searching for a sign he could not describe, but was certain he would instantly recognize. Was it possible, he wondered, that they, too, these "common men," despite their apparent lack of complexity, shared his awareness of the true horrors of life, horrors worse by far than any the imagination might conjure up? Were they able, through some gift denied him, to keep this awareness at a comfortable distance, to lose themselves, perhaps, in the monotony of routine tasks and simple pleasures?

He had not fully closed himself to the possibility that this might be so, but increasingly he found it almost impossible to believe that other men, most other men, shared his concerns. The burden would be too much: most men would break beneath it.

No, he thought, he had been given—through fate, if there was such a thing, or at least through circumstance—a special and dreadful gift, a vision that set him apart. He'd come to think of it as both a burden and a kind of glory, a singling out. On the bookshelves on the walls in his study there were volumes, exquisitely bound in fine leather, of the writings of the great thinkers. The philosophers, the men of science, the visionaries . . . in the company of their words, Paul Hazeltine felt something close to companionship. He perceived himself in a chain, a fellowship first forged at the world's beginning, when one man in some remote, uncharted cave established himself as a leader, a man whom other men followed.

It was not his intention nor his purpose to walk in steps that had been marked out before, but rather to use his mind to make new paths. That was why he had, after so many years, come back to Eastfield; why he had bought the Works from Mr. Palmer and modernized them; why he was now going to convert them to the production of horseless carriages and, in the process, change the historical landscape of the place in which he had been born.

Sitting at his desk, the double oak doors drawn closed behind him, Paul Hazeltine looked at the rose marble fireplace and wished that the evening were cooler. In spite of the summer temperature, a not-unfamiliar chill had come over him, or rather up through him. He had felt it often enough, but had never learned to fully accept it. It was a kind of melancholy, a longing for things that might have been different but could not be changed.

Sometimes, times like this one, the mood suddenly overtook him. A particular piece of music in a concert hall, a passage in a novel by Hardy or one of the Russians, was capable of making it stir. Coming back to Eastfield, something he'd never planned to do, had been a measure of self-protection. There would be no symphonies to churn his feelings. He'd given up reading fiction, and poetry as well.

The deep green desk blotter and the brass desk set from the Louis Comfort Tiffany studios in New York were the landscape in front of him. Paul's hands moved over them, over the smooth, shining mahogany of the desk itself, as if to anchor himself and steer his thoughts away from unpleasant things.

What, after all, did he have to complain about? he asked himself. He had seen the world—all he wanted of it—and made his place in it. Like the prodigal son, he had come back to the very town from which he had fled, returning in triumph. He had chosen a woman on whom he could focus his attention and desire; with whom he had had children who, like their mother, he could shield and protect from a world that seemed, the more he thought about it, quite mad.

And if there were to be times when his own emotions were more difficult to control than the behavior of his family or the work of his employees, if there were moments when a part of his heart that he wanted to deny longed to share the strange aches he felt... well, he could afford to lock himself away, behind the high hedge, behind the heavy stone of the house, behind the doors of his study—and wait for the moment to pass.

## - 7 -

"Wait here for me," Brigid told the children. "I'll just be a minute—"

"Why can't we go in with you?" the boy asked her, his eyes challenging.

Brigid felt her face flush, though she told herself that the thought crossing her mind was silly. Paul was far too young to know about the "unmentionables" she had to pick up at Mr. Smith's Apothecary and Pharmacy. Still, he'd sensed her uneasiness, the embarrassment and the hope that Mrs. Smith would be at the counter and wouldn't have to be summoned from the back room. The boy's face was the very image of his father's, Brigid told herself, down to the defiant set of his jaw.

"Because I said so," she told him, hoping her voice sounded stronger than she felt. "Stay with your sister and watch our packages." She hurried inside before he could answer her, turning only when she'd safely closed the door. She peeked at them through the gilt lettering on the paned windows.

Paul, though she didn't know why, frightened her. It wasn't just that he looked like his father or had his father's coldness. There was more to it than that, something she sensed in him—an evil, a deliberate cruelty—that alarmed her.

The girl, poor thing, was so different. Poor Francine, such a sweet child, so good, but so lonely, too. Only the week before, when she'd had a rare Sunday off and had taken the train to her sister's house in Hartford, she'd talked about it.

"She has such a sad look about her, that Francine," Brigid had said over a cup of tea in the kitchen. The dishes had been done and Kate's husband had gone to the parlor to read the newspaper, leaving the two women alone. "It's enough to break your heart—"

"My heart won't break for any of them, living so high on the hog," Kate had answered. "Of course you always had a way of making a tale all the better for the tellin'—"

"I'm not! It's just the way I put it to you. Nothing but the best for them. Fresh linens at every meal, and the finest clothes—"

"Then where's the pity of it?" Kate had asked.

"It's . . . they're so shut off, is the thing—from everyone about them. The mister, he has the Works and those electric carriages of his. And the missus, she's a kind enough soul. Quiet, don't you know, and likes to keep to herself—"

"And who wouldn't?" her sister interrupted, making light of it again.

"It's the children, Kate. All to themselves. It's not right—"

"And it's not for you to judge. Be glad you have a position with them, Brigid, and leave it go. Linens and all, they pay a fair wage, those Hazeltines of yours."

"I suppose," she'd agreed, not at all satisfied, but willing to move on to news of friends in Hartford and the latest letter from the Old Country.

In the drugstore, the image of the children standing on

the sidewalk made her sigh. As bad as Paul, Jr., might be in his heart—and she was sure he was very bad indeed—his sister was good, Brigid told herself. The boy, in his knee-panted suit, looked perfectly comfortable: Francine, in her starched sailor-blue dress with its lace collar, looked unnatural and uneasy, as if she'd be more comfortable putting on any old thing and running with other girls her own age.

On the drive to town, and particularly once inside the more populated center of Eastfield itself, Francine had kept her eyes from the road, focused on Brigid's hands on the reins of the horse. Where Paul, Jr., seemed to take pleasure in the stares of curious unlookers, Francine felt that eyes had a way of boring into her very soul...

"May I help you?" a voice asked.

"Good day, Mrs. Smith," Brigid answered, relieved and turning away from the window, going about her business...

"Why are you doing that?"

"Doing what? I'm not doing anything—" Francine protested.

"You keep looking at the ground," her brother challenged.

"I'm watching the packages. For Brigid."

"You're afraid!"

"I am not—"

"Yes you are! You're afraid. I'm going to tell Father—"

"No!" she pleaded, meeting his eyes at last. They stood like hostile strangers, Francine fragile and frightened, her brother aware of his self-assurance and its effect on her, enjoying it all.

"Pete!"

"Where ya going?"

"Wait—"

The intrusion of voices changed things. The two Hazeltine children who, moments before, had seemed locked in a tableau of private distance, quickly came to life, pressing close to one another, taking each other's hands. Across the street, a group of children watched them from the sidewalk, pointing and whispering behind their raised hands.

*If only Brigid would hurry and come out,* Francine thought, squeezing her brother's hand with all her strength.

But it was not to be. He returned the pressure as one of the children, a boy older and bigger than the rest, separated himself from the group and began to move toward them, looking back over his shoulder every few steps to the friends who watched him in awed silence.

Francine felt the panic inside her. She tried to pull free of Paul, to run to the protection of Brigid and the drugstore, but he would not release her.

"How come you don't go to school?" the boy asked, in front of them now. His pants were dirty and patched at the knee, and his shirt collar strained at his thick neck. The strap of brown leather wrapped around the books he dangled over his shoulder was scratched and worn.

"We have lessons at home," Paul answered.

The boy scraped the stone walk with his heavy, scuffed shoe. "Yeah? Well I think it's because you're stuck up."

"We are not!" Francine said to her own surprise. In order to avoid him as he approached, her eyes had traveled across the street to the group of children, wishing she were one of them. The desperation of her answer was so clear that the boy's cheeks flushed. He turned his full attention to Paul.

"How come you never come to town, then?"

"We're here now," Paul Hazeltine, Jr., answered calmly.

"Yeah, because your nurse is shopping, that's why. We seen her go inside. Tied to your nurse's apron strings! Tied to your nurse's apron strings!" He turned to his admirers on this sidewalk, urging them to join him, to take up the taunting chant. A few did, the bravest of them venturing into the street, the rest giggling in place.

"You'd better stop!" Paul told them.

"Why?" the boy who'd started teased. "What are you gonna do about it? Gonna fight?"

Paul Hazeltine, Jr., shook his head. Instead of the reaction of fear his tormentor had expected, his face was set in a superior smile.

"What then?"

"I'm going to tell my father," Paul said. "And then your father won't have a job. And you won't have any food. And you'll die."

The boy was taken by surprise. He shifted his weight from foot to foot, nervous now. "Aw, who needs them?" he asked the group of his friends, whirling suddenly. "Come on," he called, and they followed him, running down the street.

Francine watched silently until the flock of them disappeared around the corner of State Street.

"You shouldn't have said that," she told her brother as he let go of her hand.

"Why not?"

"They could have been our friends," she answered wistfully.

He shook his head. "No they couldn't. We're different from them. Remember what Father said?"

The door of the drugstore opened before she could answer. Brigid came toward them, her hands full of wrapped packages which Paul dutifully took from her. "Having a visit, were you?" she asked. "I saw from the window. That's nice, but we'd better be getting back..."

The three of them walked the half-block to the waiting

buggy, passing stores and shops and strangers on the street. Paul held his head high. Francine looked down at her feet, feeling the watchful eyes on her, frightened, yet longing for the group of children who might appear at any moment.

Once all the purchases were gathered up, Brigid and the children mounted. With the reins in hand, Brigid turned to Francine. The poor child looked so unhappy.

"You should smile, dearie," the servant girl said.

"Why?" the little girl asked.

"Why? Well . . . because you're young. And if you don't laugh and smile now, when will you?"

For an uncomfortably long moment Brigid would always remember, Francine's sad eyes held hers, as if asking the same question.

part two
*1903*

## - *1* -

FALL CAME EARLY that year. There was no Indian summer at all: by the second week in September, people were lighting fires and expecting the first frost. Farmers cursed the short season and nature itself seemed to resent the abrupt change. Overnight, the trees had turned from green to a sickly brown, with few of the usual shades of red and orange and yellow.

The weather had gone out of control, out of control like the rest of life, Paul Hazeltine thought in the quiet of his study. The sounds of the house, of the children playing and dinner being served, were distant, muffled by the oak doors he'd drawn closed. The account books, the ledgers of the Hazeltine Works, were open on the desk before him, but the room itself was dark except for the fireplace.

From time to time he moved from his chair, poking at the logs, adding more wood. The gargoyles on either side of the fireplace looked grotesque in the light, their wide-mouthed grins mocking him. And the fire, flaring and dying and flaring up again, did no more to warm him than the blood-red brocade smoking jacket that had come to be his uniform.

He tried to remember the last time he had felt warm, but could not. Nor could he precisely recall the moment when the coldness, a chilling of the heart and spirit, had first come upon him.

"The New Year," he said aloud, trying to place it. But it was the birth of the new century, three years before, that he was referring to. Time itself had become harder to keep, little more than a chain of disappointments that had varied only in magnitude.

Eastfield had ushered in 1900 with unrestrained joy. There was gold in the Klondike, and in the future as well. The Spanish-American War had been won. There were jobs at the Works for all who wanted them. On the Common, a giant bonfire burned. The Hazeltines hadn't attended, but they'd gathered in Paul's study, at his rare invitation, to watch the glow in the night.

*Then* he'd been warm, Paul thought, remembering the smiles of the children (all except Francine, who'd wanted to join the crowd on the Common) and the pink cheeks of Olivia, her belly full and rounded under the white lace gown and the white shawl he'd insisted she wear. Her delicate condition became her, he remembered thinking: her term was nearly over.

He'd held her hand that night as they stood at the window, while the children talked about the baby who would soon arrive. Margaret, seven then, had learned to knit. She was making a blanket. Paul, Jr., was certain that the child would be a boy, a little brother whom he could teach to fish the river. Constance, at five and a half almost four years younger than her brother, said that it would be a girl, she was sure.

"And you, Olivia?" Paul asked his wife.

Her laugh was young and girlish. "Whichever," she answered, for the child would be an extension of him, and that was all that mattered.

On the first day of the New Year, her labor began. Arrangements had been made for a nurse, an acquaintance of Brigid's sister, to come from Hartford, but she wasn't due until later in the month. The servant girl and Francine did

their best to make Olivia comfortable while Paul went into
town for the doctor. The roads were packed with snow. Dr.
Worley, the elderly physician, had refused to ride in the
Hazeltine Electric Carriage, insisting on using his own
buggy.

By the time the two men reached the house, Francine
was at the door, sobbing. The other children sat in the
parlor, Margaret and Constance comforting each other as
they whimpered, Paul, Jr., looking on dry-eyed.

"Oh, Father," Francine wailed, reaching for him. But he
pulled away from her embrace, bounding up the stairs. The
sight in Olivia's room made him weak: the blood, and her
pallor, and the misshapen and lifeless thing.

"Dear Jesus, you've come!" Brigid cried. "I did what I
could—"

"It's all right," Dr. Worley told her, calmly taking
charge. He sent Paul from the room as he opened his bag.
There were hours of water being carried from the kitchen;
of sheets being changed; of glances that spoke volumes and
eyes averted. When, at last, it was over, the physician left
Olivia sleeping. He gave Brigid strict instructions regarding
his patient's rest and medicine and left a powder for a
husband whom he believed to be so distraught he could not
speak. Brigid gave the children some semblance of a meal.

When they were asleep, when the servant snored in ex-
haustion, while Olivia dreamed or didn't, Paul Hazeltine,
his jacket long since off and his white cotton shirt stained
with sweat and sadness, walked through the quiet house.
He had not noticed the icy gust that blew around him, angrily
circling the kitchen as he opened the door the tradesmen
used. Walking past the barn, he was unaware of the heavy,
soaked snow.

Dr. Worley had left a lantern burning in the icehouse,
and Paul's eyes were fixed on it. He paused at the door,
his hand trembling on the latch, wanting to be able to turn

away but too certain that the force that had driven him to this point had already driven him beyond it.

*It*, the stillborn thing, lay bundled in a white sheet.

The nerves of his fingers quivered as he forced them to the bundle. Beyond that first, tentative touch he stroked the lifeless bundle that might have been a son or daughter. Slowly he began to unwind the sheet, twisting and rolling it over the cake of ice on which the physician had placed it, so as not to have to raise it in his arms.

When it was nearly done, the last layers stuck: it had been wet, he realized, silently wretching. The sheet had soaked and frozen to it. He pulled and stepped back, gagging. The creature that had died inside his wife was hideous and deformed. Its mouth and nose were one. There were gill-like slits at its throat and rigid flaps of skin where its arms and feet might have been. And worse, worst of all were its eyes, big and pale gray and staring at him, staring—

He screamed that night, choking on his fear and the outpouring of his guts. Rage and disgust spewed out of him, covering the monster he had conceived, making it all the more repellent. There was a set of heavy, spiked tongs on the wall of the icehouse. Seized by hatred, Paul grabbed them and lunged at the thing on the ice as though it were a strange reptile that might, at any moment, attack. Forcing the handles of the tongs together, he felt the spikes pierce the skin, the frozen tissue and bone.

Dragging the impaled thing behind him, he pushed through the snow to the drive alongside the house. He followed it to the Way, then crossed the woods in an unbroken rhythm, not hearing sticks break beneath his feet, not hearing the small game scurry away. The Connecticut River was high and fast. As he swung his burden, tongs and all, commanding it to the water, he felt a jagged pain in his chest and knew, as never before, the pain of a heart shattering.

From the shore, in the dark stillness of the night, he

watched the current carry the sinking thing that had spoiled his home and his life forever. The heavy iron tongs weighed it down as the current took it, fast but never fast enough.

When he came to look in on his patient the following morning, Dr. Worley made a discreet inquiry about arrangements. "I've taken care of that, thank you," Paul informed him. The subject was never mentioned again.

But in the town of Eastfield, eyebrows were raised. Old Mrs. Cheyney, who kept house for the widower doctor, was known for the raisin cake and gossip she dispensed at her table. "Poor Olivia," they said as they heard the story of her misfortune. Clearly, the pity of the women was with her, not only as one of their own sex, but as the unfortunate wife of a man whom God, in His own good time, had come to punish. And on the first day of the first year of the new century: plain as the nose on your face, it was a sign.

In time, the house found its rhythm again, but the beat was slower and changed. Olivia took a tonic to build her strength, and drops of the morphine tincture the doctor had given her for her nerves. In her bed jacket, she sketched on canvas the flowers she planted in the summer, and worked them in petit point. In her robe, she joined the family at table, rarely eating more than a few bites of food, often unaware of the conversation, always smiling a faint and distant smile. The scene before her might have been an illustration in a book, or in one of her magazines.

Paul, for his part, tried to pretend that nothing had happened. He set books out for the children each day, volumes about botany and nature, and at night, he discussed these subjects and others, which he deemed important to self-sufficiency, with them. But each night, later, alone in his study, he wept. For fate had taken that which he'd made perfect and destroyed it. Decay had invaded the polished perfection of his domain.

As if it were contagious, Olivia's distance from life began to accompany him when he went to the Works. In Eastfield, enthusiasm was high for the electric horseless carriages. The Works had been enlarged and the pay raised to two dollars and fifty cents per day, and there was work for all who sought it. Paul, however, found himself thinking of his former competitor in the carriage trade, Gene Walter Vincent Smith in Springfield. Smith, his fortune made, had turned from business to art, traveling to the Continent with his wife Belle, bringing treasure after treasure home, so generously sharing the gifts that the city of Springfield had built a museum to house them.

*And I?* he thought. He had tried to give Eastfield a future, a piece of his own vision. Slowly, unwillingly, he came to see that his vision had been clouded.

There had been a time when he'd had to make a choice in terms of the engine for his motor car. N. A. Otto's gas engine had been invented in 1876. Sixteen years later, another German, Rudolph Diesel, had invented an engine that was fueled by oil.

He had made his choice, banking the future of his automobile, and his fortune, and Eastfield itself on Edison's marvel.

In Springfield, the Duryea brothers had experimented with the gasoline engine. When they went their separate ways, Frank Duryea had merged with an arms and tool manufacturer to form the Stevens-Duryea Company. They were working on a six-cylinder gas-powered machine. The Knox Automobile Company, like the Atlas Motor Car Company, was located in Springfield, as was the home of the Bailey. In 1901 the area's first automobile club had been formed, and by 1902 the gasoline-fueled motorcycle was in production at the Hendee plant on Springfield's Winchester Square.

Paul had followed the progress of the industry, both at home and abroad. The reports from foreign capitals were encouraging: at the Paris Exhibition of 1900, automobiles had dominated the Champs Elysées. The French, the Germans, and the Italians, like the English, were more receptive to the idea of motoring, it seemed, than were the Americans. Still, the Glidden Tour of 1903 had attracted attention in the newspapers, with readers avidly following the progress of the thirty-four "horseless carriages" as they made the eight-day drive from New York City to Pittsburgh.

For many, Paul had known from the start, the automobile would be viewed as an extravagant toy for the upper classes. The finest and fastest cars were imported. Americans were put off by suspicions of both foreign products and a technology they did not understand. If the mechanical process could be simplified, he'd reasoned, if the principle that had produced the electric light and moving pictures and the Edison disk could be brought to individual travel as it had been to the trolley cars, all would change.

Not for lack of trying, the principle hadn't worked.

He might have changed, converted to the gasoline engine, but he hadn't. And now there was news of a man named Henry Ford in Detroit, planning the mass production of a sturdy machine that could be sold cheaply because of the reduced costs of its high-volume manufacture.

"Lost," Paul whispered in the darkness of his study.

Lost. There was the money, which didn't matter all that much since there was more of it: most of his fortune was in the names of his family, Olivia and the children. There was chance, the opportunity to have made his name, his presence, and enduring thing—for the man, Ford or whoever, who made the motor car an institution would be assured of a permanent position among the men of greatness.

The thought of making changes had occurred to him, of

altering the engine of the automobile that he'd hoped would carry his name into the future, into history itself, and making changes in production. But in doing so, Paul thought, he would be a follower rather than the leader he'd seen himself as. His purpose had already been defeated.

The future that had once been so securely in his control was lost to him forever, the dream gone.

The men at the Works looked upon him as their bene-factor. The town of Eastfield had rallied around him, caught in the web of progress and prosperity he'd spun. His wife and children respected him and more, believed in him fully. Yet he had failed them, failed them all, and soon, inevitably, they would know it. He would be, at that moment, fallible and worse, foolish, no different from the ordinary men who sweated away their long hours at the Works.

There was a wrenching in his heart as Paul Hazeltine considered the moment when he would look into the hazel eyes of his wife and see, instead of the total devotion they'd always held, something else: a sadness that reflected his own. Or worse, a despair, a shame, an accusation of having been failed—

"No!" he said, banging his fist down on the desk with tremendous force, not feeling the pain, for the image in his mind's eye of Olivia, her love in part lost, was far more painful. No, he might face the creditors, and his employees, and the town, but he would not be able to confront her.

Her faith had been a kind of fuel for him, a sustenance. In a matter of time, depending on how long he continued the deception, it would be used up and depleted.

He felt older than his years, consumed by a sadness that knew no depths. A coldness of spirit froze him, numbing him so that it took all his strength to push away from the desk, to rise from his chair and walk the short way across the study to his shelves of books. The titles of the volumes, many of them etched in gold leaf on the leather bindings, reflected the dancing light from the fireplace as if teasing him. There in those pages was the bulk of the world's wisdom, Paul thought, or rather the myth that the world was a place of wisdom at all.

For how could there be wisdom where there was no reasonable pattern, where a man might flourish for a time, as he had, only to fail, and where empires rose only to fall?

*It was chaos,* he thought, the idea emblazoned with the force of a sudden insight. It was all madness, all cruelty. Without wanting to, he thought of the long-ago day when he'd stood in the cemetery of the Trinity Church yard, staring at his parents' graves. He remembered the empty words about "infinite wisdom" and a "divine plan."

Then, as a boy, he'd found them hollow and he had run from them.

In his study, as a defeated, breaking man, Paul thought that perhaps there might be a perverse truth to them after all. Perhaps there was a God, but if so, He was no kindly provider. Instead he was a cruel jester, a master sadist.

*Yes,* he thought, convinced. Yes, it could be true. Proof abounded all around him! For all the complaints about the early autumn on the farmers' parts, the River Road was crowded on Sundays not only with families from Eastfield, but from Springfield and Hartford and even farther away, come to admire the supposed beauty of the dead foliage. They were fools, Paul realized, who spent the morning in their churches, praying to the God who ruined their harvest, then mocking themselves, hours later, as they stood in admiration at the spectacle of His destruction.

Perhaps in decay there was a curious, dreadful beauty; a fierce yet strangely delicate unfolding of destruction that caught the unwary eye and held it, spellbound, even against the will of the beholder. Hadn't he, as a young boy watching his parents' farm burn, *wanted* to run beyond the sight? And hadn't he been rooted in place, unaware of the cold, transfixed by the blazing flames and the sticklike figures writhing and twisting and only then, after a time, falling still?

When he left Eastfield, he'd made his way to New London. Crossing Massachusetts and Connecticut, the worst part of it hadn't been the shame of asking strange women at strange kitchen doors for something to eat, or even foraging for food. The nights had haunted him.

In barns or in beds it made no difference. Like an animal who has watched a foreign specie of hunter kill one of its number, his senses had become more keenly tuned. His guard had gone up more quickly, triggered by a flash in his mind's eye of the fiery image that had so totally and forcefully absorbed him. He had sought, without realizing it, to protect himself from any recurrence, unaware in his youthfulness that the world is a wild place where horrid and gruesome things occur all too often, and where as random a factor as proximity determines whether one will have to bear unwelcome witness.

In the houses where he'd sought a night's refuge, he'd noticed the occasional crucifixes, or the samplers so meticulously stitched beseeching a blessing on the home. There were horseshoes over the barns where he slept in the hay, and later, when he left New London and went to sea, men carried all manner of amulets and talismans.

They were no safeguard, he realized now. There were no safeguards at all. Heavy draperies, closed eyes, and even the hedge around his house was ineffective. At any moment a cry might come, a scream so sudden and sharp that before even being aware of having done so, a man had leapt from his bed, swept the curtains aside, thrown the door open.

By then, it was too late to turn to heaven with a quick thought for mercy——if there was a heaven at all.

More likely, he thought, the sky at the moment would rain blood, or frogs, or something even worse. Gasoline engines . . .

Well into his manhood, he'd isolated himself, not realizing that isolation was a useless defense. As he'd prospered, he'd come to think of himself as immune. Then and only then had he taken Olivia, not wanting a companion with whom he might share the vision of destruction—too frightening a thing to view alone—as some men did. He had, with time, put the memory of that vision behind him.

He had thought of himself as the kind of man who did not need to lean on his wife in the privacy of the parlor; the kind of man who could, within himself, summon the courage to kick over the rock beside the stream without fear of the sight of the salamander that might have been a dragon.

Instead, Olivia had been someone, *something* for him to cherish and protect. He'd had enough strength for her as well as himself.

But his strength was gone, and resting his palms against the scalloped surfaces of his finely bound books, Paul was quite certain that it would never return. Like the future he'd planned, it was lost to him forever. He studied his books again, as if one of them might hold a last and desperate answer. His finger slid over a shelf of poetry: Sidney invoking sleep; Herrick writing of the prime of life, forever lost; and Pope longing for a final solitude.

A crackling log made him turn away. The blaze reminded him of the fire so many years before. Watching it, his hand took a book from the shelf. As he'd chosen it, he decided, he would open it, searching for a random message. It was Wordsworth.

*What though the radiance which was so bright*
*Be now forever taken from my sight . . .*

The words moved him as they never had before, and he had to struggle back to the chair. It was true, too true, he knew, placing the book on his desk. Nothing could bring back the hour when life for him had bloomed full. It was gone forever . . .

He opened the top drawer of the desk and took a sheet of linen paper, holding it to the light of the fireplace, studying the swirls of fiber. Then, placing it on the blotter, he dipped his pen in the Tiffany inkwell Olivia had given him. His hand trembled as he wrote; his tears fell on the paper like his words.

> *My darling Olivia,*
> *The Bank will not fail you as I have. For-*
> *give me if you can. Forget me if you must.*

He signed his name and read what he'd written over and over again. It was better this way, better to do it rapidly in one stroke than to make her suffer with him, to force his weary mind to attempt to continue the deception that he was master of his fate and hers. There were ways of doing it that might be quick or relatively painless, but what mattered was to do the thing and get it done.

He took the brass well with its glass lining and brought it to his mouth. The ink was bitter. The thick black drops dripped from his chin to his jacket.

Replacing the inkwell, centering his final note on the blotter, Paul Hazeltine leaned back in his chair, the fire moving from the grate to his stomach.

The words in the book shimmered and danced, and as he died, he considered that it is indeed the certainty that the flower will fade and the grass parch or freeze that makes their shining hour so glorious and so splendid.

## - 2 -

Sleep, as Olivia had known it, had changed.

It had always come easily for her and deeply. After dinner, when Paul withdrew to his study as was his custom, she would spend time with the children, reading to them, playing Chinese checkers, kissing them goodnight as they went, accompanied by Brigid, to their rooms. When their doors were closed, she would climb the stairs to her own bed, walking carefully and quietly so as not to disturb—even through the heavy closed doors—her husband at his work.

In the bedroom, she would wind one of the music boxes that delighted her, the tiny enameled bird that fluttered in its gold filigree cage to the tune of "The Last Rose of Summer," the porcelain pin box that played "Plaisir d'Amour," when the lid was lifted. Changing into her nightclothes, she'd lie in bed with a magazine or novel, not reading, but turning the pages in anticipation of the sleep that would come, soon and surely.

Giving herself to it, she would smile, knowing that at some point in the night she would stir, dreamily, at the knock on the door that she need not answer; that she would turn to the familiar echo of Paul's breath in her ear and the comfort of his body sleeping beside her own.

With what she had come to think of as her infirmity, her habits had changed.

The strange feelings had unsettled her, and though the drops the doctor had prescribed restored her former calm, it was a semblance of relaxation rather than what she had known before.

The medication had become part of her nightly ritual, the amber bottle with its glass dropper a fixture on her bedside table. Three of the drops, carefully stirred in a glass of water poured from the pitcher Brigid set out for the purpose, would make her drowsy. But instead of the deep and uninterrupted sleep she was used to, she would drift in and out of consciousness. Sometimes, when she glanced at the Venetian clock on the dresser, the gold balls moving back and forth under their glass bell, she'd be surprised to discover that what she'd thought were moments of rest were hours. Sometimes, it was exactly the opposite. The sensation, while not unpleasant, was confusing, made all the more difficult by the time of year.

Often over the summer, she had taken to her bed while the last light lingered outside the window. Waking, she did not know if it was still twilight or dawn.

Her eyes had become strained, and Paul's increasingly late hours downstairs had taken away another measure.

There had, in addition, been another change, an after-effect of her confinement, she thought. The drops made her sleepy at first, but during the night she would wake fully, surprised by her own energy. Moving almost in slow motion, so as not to disturb Paul or the rest of the household, she would put on a robe and quietly make her way to the door, carefully turning the brass handle. With no particular sense of destination, she would wander through the halls, down the stairs, and through the silent rooms.

Her eyes, accustomed to the darkness, would be like a

stranger's. She would stand before the china cabinet, admiring the Crown Darby plates and the Waterford goblets not as possessions that were hers, but as if they were objects in one of the museums she had visited in Boston. In the parlor, her fingers would brush the polished wood of the tables with a new awareness of their smoothness.

From time to time she caught herself humming a tune that one of the music boxes had played, or a song unexpectedly recalled from her childhood. Giggling, she would bring her hand to her lips to quiet herself. Taking care not to wake Brigid, who slept in a room off the kitchen, she would open the door that was never locked and secretively steal into the night. Barefoot, raising her robe, she'd feel as if she were dancing instead of walking, the moist lawn a cloud tickling her legs.

Though she had never told Paul, for fear of angering him or more likely, having him think her foolish, there had been a time, early on, when the remoteness of the house and the surrounding grounds had frightened her. In those first months, the call of an owl or the scattering of animal feet over the lawn had unsettled her, even from the safety of her bedroom.

The things that had once caused her to turn away from her window had come to make her smile. The moon, Olivia believed, was her friend. Nature itself knew her. Sometimes on her night walks, she came upon rabbits. Startled at first, frozen at the sight of her, they seemed to sense that she meant them no harm, and soon went about their business. There were deer on some nights, crossing the lawn from the woods behind the house to the Way and the river on the other side of it, and once she'd seen a fox.

It had not occurred to her to be afraid; only to move, to float, to dance across the cool grass, to laugh at the moonlight, when the moon was full, on the sundial Paul had had set near the beds of flowers she'd planted, and at the mockery it made of time.

The house, outlined against the night sky, was like a magic castle in one of the children's books, a place apart from everything around it and where all who dwelled within would be forever safe and protected.

She would walk for hours, her energy mounting. Only when it crested would she make her way back to the house, her movements more contained as she entered the bounded world of the kitchen. Then, silently climbing the stairs, she'd go to bed and almost instantly fall into a sleep that lasted well into the morning.

If her feelings were new, they were so pleasant that she did not question them. The haze she drifted in and moved through during the day was a joyous secret tempered only by the fact that there was no one to share it with. Sometimes, playing with the children, entering their games, Olivia felt that there was a special bond between them, though Francine, the eldest and quietest of them, would sometimes look at her strangely.

Paul, Olivia was certain, would understand, providing she could find the words to tell him. And find the time as well, since he was working so hard and so late. He was such a kind man, so considerate, she thought, sleeping on the sofa in his study so as not to disturb her. He'd told her so when she asked him why he was so rarely in their bed.

True, as he reminded her, the doctor had told her to rest, but that seemed to have been ages ago. She felt so much better now, better and younger than she'd ever been. He mustn't stay away, no matter how late he finished his work. For what would he think if he were to come upstairs and bind the bed empty? That she'd gone? Been captured by Indians who, according to the old wives' tales, still lived in the woods?

The drops, in recent days, had lost some of their power. The bottle might have been too old, Olivia had thought, but Brigid had gone to town for it only two weeks before. Perhaps the pharmacist had made the solution too weak. In any case, she'd managed to solve the problem by trying four drops at a time instead of three. The effect was even better than before, her sense of well-being more complete.

But it was a shame that it should be hers alone. Paul, when she saw him, looked tired, or at least she thought he did. She couldn't be sure, since the drops sometimes made her eyes play tricks on her. She'd begun to feel a kind of guilt, a sense that perhaps she was failing him. In his concern for her, he'd come to overlook himself: it was her duty to restore the former balance of things, to offer him what wifely comfort she could.

For several nights, she'd forced herself to stay in her bed, drifting in and out of dreams, imagining him beside her only to find, when she was fully awake, that he was not there at all. Without her walks, a restlessness had begun to grow within her, directing her to a willfulness she had not known previously. Perhaps, she thought, he was waiting for her.

Yes, that was it! She had never before disturbed him at his work, but maybe that was the very thing he wanted, an unmistakable sign of her recovery. She would lead him upstairs to the bedroom, pour him a glass of sherry, perhaps, or fix him a glass of her own medicine. Then, together, they would lie and love, or perhaps even walk together in the night, sharing her newfound joy in all that was theirs.

Even if he was at his work, she believed, he would not be too angry. And not too busy to leave his papers and come to her. For when had she ever really asked him for something that he had refused her?

The moon was full as Olivia Hazeltine left her bed and

seated herself at her vanity table. There was no need for a lamp. She smiled at the brilliance of her eyes, her hands catching her hair, more bronze than copper in the moonlight, at the nape of her neck.

The movements were automatic, a habit. Her fingers turned the loose strands into a coil, swirling it and pinning it to the top of her head. Her skin, pale as cream, was smooth and cool to her touch. Dabbing a touch of lavender water to her throat, she admired herself for a time.

There was no sound from the children's rooms, though she knew that if she listened at their doors, she'd hear their steady breathing. On the stairs, she had to still her own laughter as her step faltered—how clumsy of her, she thought, how silly. She slid her hand along the smooth banister as if it were an anchor, guiding her and holding her.

The space between the edge of the parlor and the Persian rug that was almost the size of the room reminded her that she'd come downstairs barefoot. Paul would scold her for forgetting her slippers. Still, she smiled at the hint of light under the heavy oak doors, touching her hair, steadying herself.

"Paul?" she called softly, whispering his name so as not to wake the children. "Husband?"

There was no answer, no response as she knocked, over and over again, at the doors of the study.

She smiled, knowing that he was involved with important papers, totally involved in some piece of men's business. Rapping and calling, rapping and calling, she waited for the moment when she would succeed in distracting him.

But there was no answer, and she drew her hand back, wrestling with a moment she was completely unprepared to contend with. She'd never done this much, let alone more. Imagining the scene, as she had done in her bed, she'd heard the sound of his chair turning, the sigh as he placed the pen back in its stand, the crossing, softer then louder, of his step as he came to the door.

Waiting for these anticipated and expected sounds, her agitation grew.

"Paul?" she called in full voice, pressing her mouth, then her ear, to the place where the sliding doors met, suddenly desperate for him. She gasped for air, swallowing it like a drowning woman, then fought to regain the normal rhythm of her breathing, and with it her composure.

Olivia stepped back from the door, smoothing her hair, touching her cheek, smoothing her nightgown as if she had just come to stand in front of the study.

When at last she parted the doors, when they slid quietly in their perfect grooves, she did not scream. For a small eternity, she stared at the body of her husband, fallen from the desk chair to the rug. Ink and blood spilled down his chin, over the stubble of his beard, staining his jacket.

In that small eternity, there was an instant in which something within her, something shaping her nature, something already pitched in a definite direction, snapped forever, fixing or unfixing her for all time. There was a moment when she quite understood that he was dead, but it was a moment that would and did pass with such speed that she brushed the tears from her eyes, not knowing why they were there.

When her vision cleared, she saw a piece of paper on his desk and recognized her name.

Olivia smiled back at the gargoyles on the fireplace as she held the note, not reading it.

"Have you been writing to me again?" she asked, her voice a girlish titter. "I so look forward to your letters, Paul. They make me feel as if I'm there with you in Eastfield instead of here in Boston...so far away. But we'll be together, won't we? Just the way you said. In Eastfield, together forever..."

She smiled as she folded the unread note and surrendered it to the smoldering fire as if handing it to a lover.

Turning to the thing on the floor, its arms akimbo, its face contorted in a final agony, she considered the widening spot of ink and blood in which its head rested.

"White vinegar, I think," she said, studying it. "Yes... white vinegar and perhaps a bit of soda afterward." With the same sigh she might heave if the children made a sudden mess that unexpectedly demanded her attention (a spilled box of her dusting powder; a jar of preserves dropped on Brigid's day off), Olivia began to clean, deciding first how to approach the problem.

She knelt, brushing the matted hair from the dead thing's forehead, her hand loving and tender.

Then she pulled at the smoking jacket, pulling till it tore at the sleeve, which she stuffed into the open mouth so that there would be no more dripping.

She grabbed the body under its arms, making a noise as she raised it to a position that allowed her movement. Starting, stopping, then starting again she pulled the heavy and stiffening corpse through the parlor and the dining room, through the dark kitchen, out into the waiting night.

"I've been so hoping that you'd join me one of these evenings," she said, the tenderness of her tone jarred by the effort of hauling him. "It's..." she paused to catch her breath, "lovely, isn't it, dear?"

She leaned him against her knees, unwilling to let him fall completely to the ground because it would make raising him again all the more difficult. Pausing, Olivia glanced at the lawn and the barn, so still in the hour before dawn.

"I've wanted to share this with you, Paul," she said. "And now we can have it together."

She took hold again, dragging him over the grass, back toward the barn and the icehouse beside it.

"Don't . . . don't you leave me, now," she cautioned, her breath ragged. "I'll only be a moment, dear . . ."

Propping him against the wall of the icehouse, she looked inside. There was no shovel, but she remembered something that made her laugh, having caught herself in a foolish mistake. The barn, of course! There were her garden tools, and the heavier equipment as well. She looked at Paul's body.

"I'll be *right* back," she promised. In the barn, she surveyed the spades and rakes and shovels, choosing one that was relatively small. "Oh dear," she said as she carried it back to the icehouse. "I've forgotten my gloves . . ."

It didn't matter, Olivia decided as she forced the spade into the damp earth. The oak handle was smooth, the ground accepting. With the intense force that every human is capable of at such moments, she dug in a steady rhythm, speaking to herself and the body she'd pulled into the icehouse.

"You've needed a rest, dear," Olivia scolded. "You've been working much too hard. I should have said something, I suppose, but you are always so concerned about me . . ."

The dirt rose around the narrow hollow she was creating.

"You'll rest now, Paul. The children won't bother you, I promise. It will be cool . . . and quiet . . ."

She'd unearthed a foot and a half of dirt and dug another six inches. Then she outlined the shape of a body, deeper still. Sweat and dirt soaked her face. Her hands were raw, but she did not notice.

"It's ready, Paul," she whispered at last, setting the spade down. She didn't have the strength to lift him again, but pushed him until his body fell, face down, into the bed of earth. Pushing his arms, adjusting his legs, she made him conform to the shape she had prepared.

"Rest," Olivia Hazeltine told her husband as she began to cover him with the dirt. "Rest, Paul..."

An hour later, it was done. There was the problem of the dirt he'd displaced—the floor had to be flat and even, after all—but a solution came to mind. From the barn, she took a burlap sack, scooping the extra dirt into it. She piled the rest on the spade, then scattered it over the lawn. It would be good for the grass, she thought. She packed the floor of the icehouse down, then pulled the heavy sack of earth outside.

Her nightdress was stained and soaking as she returned the spade to its place on the barn wall. The early light filled the sky as she walked back toward the house, pleased with herself, not noticing the second-story windows where Francine, her eldest daughter, looked down in horror, and where her son, the son named after her husband, watched her as he had from the start, with a smile as strange as her own.

# - 3 -

"OUR MOTHER IS MAD," Francine whispered behind the
closed door of her room. Saying the words aloud made her
feel even more guilty than when she only thought them.
The idea, at first, had struck her as impossible, unimag-
inable. Looking down from her window, watching her
mother on the night when their lives had changed, she had
longed to find herself in a nightmare.

Stepping aside, letting fall the curtain she'd held back
with her hand, she'd struggled to contain the scream that
had been on the verge of forcing its way out of her. Her
body had been seized with a panic that made her want to
run; instead, she'd made herself go back to bed, made her
eyes close in the hope of being overcome by sleep from
which she might awake to find everything as it had been.

But she hadn't slept for all her wanting to. She'd waited,
her heart pounding so loud she was sure it echoed through
the whole house. After a time, familiar noises had lulled
her into a false hope. Her brother and sisters were getting
up. Brigid was in the kitchen, preparing breakfast.

She was the last to go downstairs, taking her time as she
washed and dressed. She'd lingered outside the dining room,
soothed for the moment by the usual sounds of silver against

dishes and the voices of Margaret and Constance, chattering to each other.

"... Your egg will get cold, Margaret," her mother was saying as Francine made her feet move. "Why can't you follow your brother's example—Francine, dear!" her mother had exclaimed. *"There* you are. We were beginning to wonder, weren't we, children? I was almost going to send Brigid up."

Francine had gripped the back of the heavy oak chair, feeling the edge where the velvet material met the wood cut deep into her fingers. She was falling, she thought, about to fall—

"I—I was asleep," she heard herself say.

"Well, no matter," her mother announced, holding out her arms.

Each step toward her was an effort. Her sisters continued their talking and giggling, but Francine felt her brother's eyes on her. Her mother had changed into one of her white dresses, Francine noticed, but her hair was disheveled, and the once-flawless hands were red and scratched. Her cheek was flushed. Kissing it, Francine felt as if her lips were burning.

As Francine took her place at the table, Olivia rang the crystal bell.

"We're all here now, Brigid," she told the servant. "Francine has joined us at last."

"Yes, missus."

Was she imagining it, Francine asked herself, or was Brigid purposely avoiding her eyes?

"I'd like my medicine, I think," her mother added. "Yes, I'd like my drops now, if you please." When Brigid left, Francine watched her mother's fingers dart from the lace at her neck to her disordered hair.

"Your father has been called away on business, Francine," Olivia Hazeltine said calmly. "I was telling Paul and your sisters." She smiled at her son, seated at her right, and patted his hand. "But we have a man of the house all the same."

"Mother?" Paul had asked, his eyes fixed on Francine, who in turn watched the plate of food Brigid had silently set before her. "If Father is gone, and if I'm the man of the house, may I sit in his place. Until he comes back?"

Olivia had considered the question briefly. "I think so. Yes, I think that would be fine."

She'd nodded, smiling her approval, as the boy summoned Brigid, instructing her to move his plate and glass to the head of the table, opposite his mother.

"Yes," Olivia observed, measuring her drops into the tumbler of water the servant had brought her, "yes, I'm quite sure your father would approve..."

Francine had tried to catch Brigid's eye, but it was no use.

A moment of truth, of recognition and admission, would surely come, Francine thought. When it came, as it was bound to, it would set the thing gone wrong to rights. Her father would be missed in town, at the Works. The story about his going away on business might deceive Constance and Margaret, Paul and Brigid, even, but there were others who would ask questions and demand answers.

That first day, the rhythm of the house had gone along relatively unchanged. Francine had tried to keep herself at a distance, afraid to mention what was so obviously unmentionable, but unable to totally ignore it. The others— Margaret and Constance—played happily. Paul, Francine felt, or thought she did, for she was no longer as certain of anything as she'd been the day before, watched her more than usual. Her mother fussed over her sisters, took her medicine, and went about her day as she had gone about all the days before it.

Reluctantly, desperately longing for some sign that would renew her hope, Francine had come to realize that the impossible was possible after all. Hours, then days had passed. The meals were taken at the table in the dining room, with her brother in the seat her father had once occupied. Otherwise, there were no visible changes.

Rather than remorse, her mother appeared to feel lighter in spirit than she had previously, more content and calm. She took her medicine at the table now, often as not, and frequently napped in the afternoon. But the house, Francine began to understand, was like a castle in one of the fairy tales she read to Constance and Margaret when their mother rested; a place unto itself, separate from its surroundings, in which life, of a kind, went on unaltered by circumstances that might, in the absence of magic, create changes of devastating consequence.

Over the years, the Hazeltines' separateness from the town of Eastfield had been a thing of which she had been acutely aware, but until those first days after The Night, Francine had never understood the fullness of her family's distance from those who might have been neighbors. She'd both dreaded and looked forward to her trips to town with Brigid. The strange glances, some hostile and others envious, made her uncomfortable, as did the whispers behind carefully raised hands. But the sight of girls her own age, and the sense of the life that they led, extended so far beyond the strict perimeters of her own, filled her with excitement.

Her father had told them all how fortunate they were to be Hazeltines, how much better off they were than the people of Eastfield. Yet Francine, in the privacy of moments alone, imagined what it might be like to be one of the girls she saw walking hand in hand on the Common, carrying their schoolbooks, giggling about boys and teachers. She imagined the pleasure of having a friend her own age, a girl named Jane, she decided, who would have dark blond hair that would, depending on the day and occasion, be worn in braids or tied back with a blue-and-white checked ribbon.

When she was a child, Francine had been given a dollhouse. It had come from London, her father had explained, and was fashioned with great detail. The chandeliers, the patterns of the wallpaper in the various rooms, the miniature tables and chairs and sofas were exact replicas of classic pieces. Reluctantly, Francine had passed the toy along to Margaret and Constance, and often she played at it with them, or pretended to.

Sitting with them, going along with their improvised games, her imagination would follow a separate course of its own. It wasn't a dollhouse, but rather a house in Eastfield—Jane's house. Instead of being populated with its resident collection of her brother's toy soldiers and assorted dolls and animal figures, it was a special and secret place in which Francine and her friend spent long hours discussing themselves, dreaming their futures.

One afternoon, a week after her father's disappearance, Francine took the dollhouse from Margaret's room and brought it into her own. Her sisters were having their naps; her mother, too, was resting. She sat down on the rug in front of the dollhouse and lost herself in imaginings.

Jane, in the space of a few days, had been transformed from friend to something more, half sister, half extension of herself. Francine pictured Jane in one of the second-floor bedrooms in the dollhouse. She saw herself there as well, the two girls sitting on the floor of a room she'd come to think of as her own, despite the differences in colors and furnishings.

"Our mother is mad," she whispered to Jane. "She is. Mr. Kelton from the Works called today, and Mother sent us outside. She gave him some paper that she said was from Father, but I know it wasn't. I saw her the day before yesterday in Father's study, copying the way he signed his name. There was a paper she'd written with his name over and over. Jane, it's true. Our mother is mad—"

It was a feeling rather than a sound that made her turn, and she was startled by what she saw. She'd been careful to close the door, hadn't she? She was sure she had, but now it was open. Paul, her brother, was standing in the doorway, staring at her. Francine felt sick with a fear beyond reason.

"I—I was playing," she heard herself explain, wondering why she felt the need to explain herself at all.

"You said it. You said that Mother—"

"I didn't!" she insisted, frantic as he leaned back, the door closing surely this time. "I was playing. I was making believe..."

Her words stopped as he slowly moved toward her. Unable to rise, Francine crawled back cowering to the edge of her rug, to the rose-printed spread that hung from the bed. She want to run away, to look away at the very least, but she could not. More than the menace of his movements, Paul's eyes held her, frozen and afraid. They were her father's eyes, Francine realized in panic, cold and penetrating—

"Never say that. Never ever say that again." His voice was without inflection, and as he spoke, his hand moved back. Francine watched, unable to shift her position or raise an arm in her own protection as his hand came down, striking her full in the face. Before she could cry out, his entire body was on her, forcing her back on the rug. Paul's hand covered her mouth, then his face was pressed against hers and his hands were all over her at once, along her legs, under her dress.

When she tried to pull away, he pinched her, butting his head against her face. He forced his hand between her legs, laughing to himself as she shook with terror. Then, as suddenly as it had begun, the attack was over.

"I'm the man of the house now," Paul told her, standing up, smiling, leaving.

Francine brought her knees to her chest, wishing that she could have come into her home where it was greeted like and find herself across the rug, inside the dollhouse with Jane. She clenched her eyes and fingers, the muscles of her body, and the will of her mind in a frantic moment of hope and longing. For if her mother could go mad, if madness could have come into her home where it was greeted like a guest or taken for granted, why was magic impossible?

"Francine, what *are* you doing—" Brigid's surprise turned to concern. Her words hung, and the ironing seemed to hover in her hands. She put it down on the dresser and knelt to the child. "What is it? Your stomach?"

The tug at her skirt was so strong that Brigid nearly fell over. Steadying herself, she brushed the damp hair back from Francine's forehead.

"Where—where are they?" the child asked.

"They?"

"Everyone else—"

"Why, your mother is resting, and your sisters are outside with little Paul. They were 'helping' me, as they call it, but thank the dear Lord they—"

"Are you sure?" Francine asked. "He's not in the house?"

"Who? Your brother?" she paused. "What is it?"

"Make sure. Look out the window. *Please*—"

Sighing, the servant girl rose and went to the window. "There they are, playing in the icehouse, of all places—"

A sob of anguish made Brigid turn suddenly. She crossed herself. "Saints preserve us, don't frighten me that way! You sound like you're dying—"

Francine shook her head slowly. "It's worse than dying."

The sadness in her face was too much for Brigid to take. "Rest a while, and you'll feel better. I'll put the things I carried up away later on—"

"No! No please, don't go!" the girl begged her as she started for the door.

Brigid licked her lip nervously. "All right, but I can only stay a minute. I've got a chicken in the oven, and there's—" The tears in Francine's eyes interrupted her excuse. Brigid's voice softened, though she knew she'd be sorry. "What is it, then?" She sat on the bed, and Francine sat close beside her, like an animal working for warmth.

"Something is wrong, Brigid," she began. "Some . . . thing is wrong."

"Go on," Brigid told her, given to it now for better or worse.

"It started—I don't know when it started, really," Francine realized. "When Mother was sick, I think. Or last week. And then today—"

Brigid covered the girl's trembling hand with her own. "Do you remember what I told you, what your father asked me to tell you when it happened that first time, when your mother wasn't well enough to tell you herself?" Francine didn't answer, but her blush, matched by Brigid's own, was sign enough. Of course she remembered the strange feeling in her stomach, then the terror of the blood.

"Sometimes," Brigid continued, ill at ease, "before it comes, you feel queer—"

Francine shook her head. "It's not that."

"What then?"

The words came out in a rush, disjointed words, trans-
lations of things Francine had seen and felt, imagined and
dreamed. Everything had gone crazy suddenly, didn't Brigid
see that? Her father was gone and dead and her mother was
mad. Paul was evil, the whole house was evil, and the
fullness and shape of that evil hadn't taken complete form.
There was a world so close and so far away—Eastfield, and
normal people, Jane—and now they were cut farther off
from it than ever, they would never be part of it. Her mother
was mad and the house was a prison and her brother had
touched her—

Spellbound, Brigid listened, her lips moving slightly as
she invoked the names of the saints and the Blessed Mother
herself. The child wasn't well. That had to be it. A fever
or worse. For it couldn't be true, none of it, even if the
mister had gone off suddenly and the boy was sitting in his
place.

"It's true," Francine whispered when she finished, clutching at Brigid's arm. "I *know*."

The servant girl was flustered. "You . . . you musn't say
such things, Francine. It's a sin to even think them—"

The girl began to cry again. "Please!"

"Please what?"

"Save me," she begged, her hand on Brigid's arm like
a vise.

Brigid pulled away, turning back the bedspread and the
covers. "You rest now, dearie. You can have your dinner
on a tray, I expect—"

"Save me," Francine pleaded again.

Brigid hesitated, looking over her shoulder to make certain that all was quiet in the hall. Reaching behind her neck,
she unfastened the silver chain, kissing the crucifix it held
and slipping it under Francine's pillow.

"Don't tell anyone."

"I won't. I promise I won't. But will you help me?"

Brigid guided Francine to the bed, tucking her in. "I'll pray for you," she promised.

Then Brigid turned and hurried away, not wanting to see the desperation in the young eyes again, wishing that she weren't simply leaving the room, but that she'd never come into it.

Francine's soft weeping followed her as she closed the door, and she tried to tell herself that maybe the girl was wrong, maybe it was the monthly after all. For that, miserable as it was, was far better than a curse of another kind.

# - 4 -

THE ROOM OFF the kitchen was clean and white, and as homey as she'd been able to make it. Mr. Hazeltine had made it clear, when he'd hired her, that he had no use for religion, but the room was hers, and Brigid had hung a crucifix over the bed and set her Bible and rosary on top of the oak dresser. She'd sewed her own curtains, a soft yellow, to hang at the windows that looked out on the back yard and the woods beyond. Her sister Kate had crocheted an afghan as a Christmas present, and Brigid used the multicolored square as a throw at the end of the small bed, carefully folding it each night and removing it to the straight oak chair, then draping it over the brass footboard each morning.

It wasn't a terribly spacious room, certainly not compared to the rest of the house, but that had made Brigid all the more comfortable. The parlors and study, the dining room and the bedrooms upstairs had intimidated her with their spaciousness and their riches. She'd been afraid to dust at first, worried that she might accidentally break or disturb one of the delicate knickknacks—*"objets,"* the missus called them.

She was more at ease in the familiar territory of the kitchen and her own room, and they had recently become a retreat from the rest of the house and the puzzling, disturbing changes within it. Exactly what the changes were, Brigid didn't know.

From the start, the Hazeltines had struck her as an odd lot. Their money, for one thing, set them apart from everyone else, just as the house was set apart from town. All the rich, she supposed, were odd: after all, they had the means to let them indulge their ways, no matter how strange. Kate had agreed with her, and for a time, the family's wealth had been a comforting excuse.

Standing at the sink or bending to the oven, washing or hanging the wash out to dry, Brigid struggled with the thought that it had become more than a matter of money. She tried not to think it, but the thought was always lurking in her mind, waiting to catch her by surprise.

The talk with Francine had scared her. The poor child was sick, she'd told herself as she hurried from the room. A fever had gone to her brain, surely, and, coupled with her usual moodiness, had made her think all kinds of strange things.

For a time, a brief time, she'd considered the idea of telling Mrs. Hazeltine that the child wasn't in her right mind. It wasn't at all the thing to do, Brigid had decided, mentioning only that Francine didn't seem to be feeling well. Even if she'd told the missus only a part of what the girl had told her, it would be embarrassing all around.

Olivia herself had supervised the tray and taken it up to Francine's room that night. She'd gone so far as fixing the cup of tea for her daughter herself, adding tonic drops which she assured Brigid would bring Francine around. Brigid had smiled and nodded, a course of action that had been proven successful over the years she'd been in the household. She was suspicious of doctors and medicines herself, but the medicine she picked up regularly in Eastfield for the missus had certainly improved things, bringing back her employer's spirits even if they did make her a bit lightheaded at times.

Francine, for all appearances, had recovered.

She took her meals at table, and spent time with Margaret and Constance. But she was quieter than she'd been before, Brigid noticed without wanting to, and kept her eyes and her distance from her brother. She hadn't talked about the things she'd mentioned that day in her room, but whether it was because she was better or because she hadn't had the opportunity, Brigid wasn't certain. She hadn't avoided Francine, which wouldn't have been possible, but she'd taken care to keep busy and keep the little girls close, thereby limiting Francine's opportunities to seek her out alone.

Yet as much as she wanted to dismiss the whole incident, to chalk it up to fever and the strange feelings she herself had had when she was Francine's age, coming into her own, there were things that gave her pause, making her wonder about things that weren't, after all, her business.

It *was* queer that the mister had gone off in the night without so much as a by your leave. His business trips weren't all that frequent, and when they were necessary, he was in the habit of preparing well in advance, giving her detailed instructions about packing his clothes and the running of the household in his absence.

Stranger still was the visit from Mr. Kelton, manager of the Hazeltine Buggy Works. It wasn't that she'd meant to listen, but, serving tea as the missus had instructed, she hadn't been able to help it.

And if the missus was surprised that Mr. Hazeltine hadn't told his foreman about his trip, she hadn't let on. Instead she'd laughed, as if it was a private joke between the two of them.

"Paul has been so busy of late," she'd told her guest. "His trip was urgent and very sudden. He left this note

putting you in charge of running things in his absence, Mr.
Kelton, and I'm sure he knew that the Works would be safe
in your capable hands."

The visitor had cleared his throat, embarrassed by the
compliment. "Thank you," he'd told the missus, "but . . ."

She'd urged him on when he paused. "Yes, Mr. Kelton?"

"Well, this letter I received, ma'am. From the First Bank
of Boston."

The missus had sipped her tea. "Which letter was that,
Mr. Kelton?"

"Why, the closing of the Works, ma'am. Surely you
know—"

"Ah, yes," she'd answered, glancing at the piece of paper
he held out. Apologizing for her eyes, she'd asked him to
read it aloud.

Brigid had had to step into the dining room itself to catch
the words, and even then she'd missed some of them. Mr.
Kelton's voice had been soft, and his speech fast. But she'd
heard enough to understand that the bank, acting on authority from Mr. Hazeltine, was instructing Mr. Kelton as
manager of the Works to sell them at once; the property,
buildings, all machinery and inventory. Work would continue until such a sale was made, but the banker expressed
the hope that terms would be finalized as soon as possible.

The news had startled Brigid, but the missus had acted
as if it were no more important than a report of weather in
some distant place, and no more complicated.

"Surely the instructions are clear enough," she'd said
politely.

Again her guest cleared his throat. "Begging your pardon, ma'am, I'm not—not experienced in this scale of
business. Mr. Hazeltine himself would handle something
of this sort, I'd expect."

"But Mr. Hazeltine has left you in charge, and he is not here."

"Yes, ma'am. Or no, no he's not. I...I wondered if perhaps I should wait for him to return—"

"I don't think so, Mr. Kelton. More tea?"

"Thank, you, no."

"My husband doesn't discuss the details of his business with me, but he did say that this—this matter—was quite important to him. I'm sure he intends you to undertake the instructions outlined in the letter as soon as you can."

"But *how,* ma'am?"

"Why don't you consult with the bank, Mr. Kelton? Perhaps that would be best. Naturally, all of your expenses would be met by the Works."

Brigid had heard the relief in his voice as he told the missus that it was a fine idea, and no doubt what Mr. Hazeltine had had in mind.

"There is one more thing," Mr. Kelton had said. "If the Works is to go up for sale...well, the men are bound to hear, aren't they?"

"I suppose," Mrs. Hazeltine said, offhandedly.

"Then...what am I to tell them, ma'am? They'll want to know why, I expect. And about their jobs."

The missus laughed for a moment. "It *is* Mr. Hazeltine's business, after all, Mr. Kelton. And it is his decision to sell it. I would expect that the purchaser of such a business would endeavor to keep it going, and would need men to do so, don't you think?"

"Yes, yes of course. Certainly..."

He'd thanked her for her time, and asked her to convey his respects to Mr. Hazeltine, which she'd promised to do. Brigid had made sure to busy herself in the kitchen as the missus showed him out, then the missus had joined her.

"That Mr. Kelton is the most nervous man," Olivia observed. She'd opened the oven door. "Baked apples! A pity Mr. Hazeltine isn't here. He's so fond of baked apples." And with a smile, she'd gone to her room.

If Olivia discussed the sale of the Works with the children, she'd done it when Brigid wasn't nearby. The subject had never come up again, though Brigid had noticed correspondence between the bank and Mrs. Hazeltine in the mail she took to and brought from the post office in town. And while the Hazeltines themselves ignored the matter, it became the principal topic of conversation among the citizenry of Eastfield.

Not a tradesman stopped by who didn't mention it, though Brigid answered, honestly, that she knew nothing about it and kept such conversations short, as was her habit. On the streets of Eastfield, it was even worse. Manners made it impossible to bring inquiries to an abrupt end. Bold as brass they were, Mrs. Putney and Mrs. Tremont and the rest of them who fancied themselves gentry of some sort. They came right up to her in the street, and didn't mind at all what they said, even in front of the children.

"Still on her medicine, is she?" Mrs. Putney had asked when Brigid picked up the missus's drops. "Poor Olivia!" as if they were the best of friends. "And him so sick, too. Tuberculosis, isn't it? He's gone out West, I understand—"

"The Hazeltines are quite well, thank you," Brigid heard herself answer, mindful of little Constance holding one hand and Margaret holding the other.

*"Really?"* the woman asked with a knowing look. "But I did hear that he was sent away—"

"With due respect, Mrs. Putney, I don't discuss my employers' affairs." With that she'd turned and led the children away, secretly pleased with the realization that, like it or not, Mrs. Putney couldn't do a thing about it.

There were times, particularly on those visits to town, when Brigid felt more like one of the family than she ever had before. She was protector of a secret, even if the specifics of that secret were as unknown to her as they were to the rest of the town. Within the house, too, her sense of position grew.

Mrs. Hazeltine had stopped consulting with her about menus, leaving the matter entirely to her except for an occasional special request. The children's supervision, on the whole, attracted less and less of Mrs. Hazeltine's direct attention, Brigid observed. At fourteen, and given her quiet nature, Francine seemed older than her years. It was she who supervised Margaret and Constance, eight and six years old, teaching them the lessons that her mother had taught her. Paul, like his sister, acted older than his twelve years. He'd taken his mother's words about being the man of the house to heart, and spent much of his time alone, which was fine with Brigid. Sometimes he went to the river with his fishing pole, or into the woods with a rifle he'd been given by his father on his last birthday. Cleaning fish was unpleasant, but dressing the small game, in Brigid's opinion, was even more distasteful. It was just as well that Paul took to it with a strong, if somewhat unnerving, relish.

With Mr. Hazeltine gone—no, *away,* Brigid reminded herself, only *away*—the atmosphere of the house had relaxed somewhat and her own workload lightened. It would, of course, have been all the better if the children were in school, and better for them as well, if anyone asked her opinion. But they weren't, and no one had asked, and so she went about her daily tasks, with one autumn day following another so quickly that you had to look twice to notice it was nearly winter.

Certainly a body would never know by looking at the

missus, who still wore white, whatever the season.

There were, however, changes in the appearance of her employer that Brigid had observed but discreetly pretended not to see. Once so careful about her person, so fussy and particular, the missus hadn't become untidy so much as unaware. Often her hair looked as if she'd made a mistake in pinning it. Her chignon came undone, or loose strands strayed from her formerly careful coils. Her skin, always pale, had become pallid, it struck Brigid, and though her copper hair had lost some of its sheen, her eyes always gleamed. But her hands, poor thing, were not all that steady in spite of her medication. Her dresses and nightclothes had become increasingly spotted and stained, sometimes with the wine she'd begun to drink more and more regularly.

In what Brigid had come to think of as the old days, the missus had occasionally sipped just a single glass of sherry. But with Mr. Hazeltine gone—no, *away*—the missus had begun to sample his stock of spirits, finding his cellar of wines particularly to her liking. Once, when Brigid had come upon her pouring a glass of wine in the pantry, Olivia Hazeltine's face had flushed with unexpected color.

"The doctor suggested it for my condition," she explained. "It helps the medicine work."

"Of course," Brigid had replied, knowing full well that it had been ages since the doctor had come by, and wondering why, if she was going to take to drink, the white wine wouldn't do just as well, since it would no doubt be easier to get out.

With the weather getting colder, Brigid consoled herself, at least the children's clothes would be less a problem. Paul would no doubt spend as much time out of doors as he liked; he'd always done more or less as he pleased, and now with the mister gone—no, *away*—he did it all the more. Francine was no problem, really, but the little ones were forever making a mess of themselves and everything they wore.

Thinking of them as she washed the last of the dinner dishes and rinsed the sink reminded Brigid that it was time to check on the two girls upstairs. The missus had felt tired after the meal, and had announced that she was going to rest in her room. Francine was working on a piece of embroidery in the parlor, and Paul was who knew where.

Brigid herself had filled the tub, taking care that the water was neither too hot nor too cold and that the window was shut tight so the girls wouldn't catch a chill. She'd set them in the water, then gathered up their clothes and taken the things downstairs to the laundry room. It was time enough to get the girls out, she decided, passing quickly through the parlor so as not to afford Francine a chance to engage her in conversation.

She heard the familiar giggles from the other side of the bathroom door as she opened the linen closet to get the towels. Their pleasure made her smile, in spite of the mess she knew there'd be to clean, the splashed water all over the floor. Her hand reached for the brass doorknob, but an unexpected voice made her stop in mid-motion.

"Go ahead," it said.

"Like this?" Constance's small voice asked.

"No, silly!" Margaret answered. "Here, like the picture. See?"

"That's right," the voice agreed.

"I told you!" Margaret shrieked, pleased with herself. "And I go like this..."

Brigid opened the door and reeled at the sight before her. The two little girls sat facing each other in the half-filled tub. Margaret's fingers were pressed between Constance's open thighs. On the edge of the porcelain tub, his shoes and socks and pants off, sat their brother. His feet dangled in the water, and his hand was guiding his sister's to his swollen erection.

"Holy Mary, Mother of God!" Brigid said, not knowing if it was a cry or a whisper. The three of them looked at her, the girls in innocent enjoyment and Paul in amused defiance.

"We're playing French ladies," Margaret told her.

"Like in the book," Constance added.

Brigid's eyes moved from the tub to the book on the bathroom floor, near Paul. It was a large volume, and the tinted illustration, revealing three adults in a facsimile of the scene before her, added to her embarrassed anger.

"Where—where did you get such a book?" she managed to ask.

"Paul got it—" Margaret began.

"—from Father's study," Constance added.

Paul himself said nothing, and made no move to disengage himself.

"Get dressed," Brigid told him, telling herself that it was ridiculous to be frightened by a twelve-year-old boy but frightened all the same.

Instead of following her instructions, he smiled at her. "I got something else, too," he said.

"Show her!" Margaret said.

"Yes, let Brigid see," Constance exclaimed, giggling.

Without taking his eyes from the servant, he reached into the pocket of the shirt he wore.

"No, no don't! It's a shame and a sacrilege—" Brigid begged as she recognized the gleaming silver object that swung from the chain in his hand.

"Do it!" Constance urged, delighted.

The girls laughed and splashed as Paul slipped the chain over his penis, so that the cross dangled from it.

"Let's play the game again, please?" Margaret asked.

Obligingly, Paul moved his hips so that the cross and chain swayed back and forth, back and forth, while the girls, like hungry fish, tried to catch it in their mouths.

She dropped the towels and fled. The laughter of the children, of Constance and Margaret and Paul together, followed her down the hall, making her move faster and faster. A thought raced through Brigid's mind, the thought that it wasn't madness that had infected the Hazeltine family but something worse. It was a darker thing, darker and even more deadly.

"Come back, Brigid!"

"Come and play!"

"Brigid?"

Were they calling to her, she wondered, or was it in her mind. It didn't matter: the only thing that mattered was that she get away. With every step she took, a piece of a plan came to her. There was no organization to it; instead it was like a random pile of bricks. Kate, her sister. Francine, the poor child! Running away. Telling a priest—

"Brigid, where are you?" a voice called, or she thought it did.

The priest would know what to do.

"Come back, Brigid."

She turned and Paul was there, the cross dangling from the organ he stroked with his hand. He was coming closer, closer, smiling like the devil himself, ready to profane her as he had the symbol of Our Lord—

Brigid's hand was on the round finial atop the banister; she was eager to escape. The boy continued to move toward her.

Her room. The door. The lock. Something flew at her—

Then she was falling, her head knocking on the stairs and railing. By the time Francine reached her, just a few seconds later, her broken and battered body lay in a heap.

"Brigid! What happened? Brigid?"

The woman's lips were moving, but Francine couldn't hear the words. She bent closer, till the faint breath pressed against her ear. "...I am heartily sorry...for having offended Thee..." The whisper turned to short, irregular gasps. It was then that Francine saw the crucifix on the floor, a few feet from where Brigid lay.

Had the servant taken it from under her pillow, where she'd kept it since the day in her room? How else could it have come to be next to her? Francine picked it up and tried to place it in Brigid's hand. With the last of her strength, the woman resisted, clasping her hands as if it were some foul, ungodly thing that Francine was attempting to force on her.

"God...save us," Brigid whispered, choking on the words. "God...save us all."

Her eyes rolled back toward the top of her head, which pointed to the stairs, and to the boy, softly laughing, who stood at the top of them, savoring the spectacle of his sister as she sobbed over the body of the one person who might have been her salvation.

# - 5 -

"POOR OLIVIA," they said in the town.

"Poor Olivia," what with one thing coming right after the other, but then when it rained, didn't it pour?

"And don't think the last cloud has passed over *that* house, mark my words!" Mrs. Putney told Lucy Tremont as they chatted in the Eastfield post office. "But 'as ye reap,'—"

"All the same, I feel sorry for her," Lucy confessed.

Mrs. Putney's glance conveyed her disapproval of the sentiment. "It's not as though she's going to have to pack it in and go to the County House, is it?"

"No," Lucy agreed, since it was common knowledge that Olivia regularly received checks and correspondence from the First Bank of Boston. "But all the same, in her condition. And Mr. Hazeltine taken sick—"

"Taken off is more likely, if you ask me!"

"Mrs. Putney!"

The older woman was in short temper. The subject of the Hazeltine misfortunes was interesting enough, but Lucy had yet to face the facts. Then, too, her shoulders were hurting the way they always did when the cold came, even worse this year than last. Nothing to do but learn to live with it, Dr. Worley had told her, dismissing the latest tonic she'd asked about as a waste of money. She'd pressed him for a few details about the accident at the Hazeltine house, hoping to play on his sympathy, but the physician had been curt, suggesting that she worry about her own aches and pains.

"You can't teach an old dog new tricks," she told her companion. "Didn't he run out of here like a bat out of you-know-where when he was a boy? Who's to say that he didn't get the urge and up and go again? Probably living the high life in New York or even farther."

"Oh, no! I heard he went to Detroit. He had a heart attack—"

Mrs. Cheyney, who'd been standing by, taking it all in without comment up to that point, felt obliged to interrupt. "He's in the mountains is what I hear. For his health."

Mrs. Putney sighed. "I say good riddance to him wherever he is!"

"Still, it would have been so much easier for poor Olivia if he were home. With that unfortuate girl breaking her neck... why, it gives me a fright to even think of it!"

"It was a sign," Mrs. Putney observed, triumphant.

"Or a loose runner on the stairs," Mrs. Cheyney responded.

"The Lord works in mysterious ways," Mrs. Putney told her. "Not so high and mighty are they now, our Hazeltines! Remember him at the Celebration? Talking about this and that and so sure of himself. Going to put Eastfield on the map, he was! It's a lucky stroke about the new company, is all I can say. Or who knows if we'd have supper on our tables?"

"Lucky for Frank Kelton, too," her friend agreed.

The news that the Hazeltine Works were being sold had swept through town like a wind. Frank Kelton had done his best to reassure the men who worked under him that he'd do all he could to see they had their jobs under the new management, but there had been a panic all the same. Some of the men had decided to leave and get while the going was still good, while there were jobs to be had in the mills and paper factories in Holyoke and Springfield.

The facts at hand and the season had cast a gray pallor over the town. At night, the men who spent their days at the Works came home sullen to women who wanted reassurance and were unused to worry about their futures.

Had the Works been sold? Was there any news?

Spoken or unspoken, these questions dominated the attention of the town. Instead of answers came rumors that made the waiting all the worse. And with the waiting, with the passing of weeks that became months in which the future Paul Hazeltine had so glowingly outlined hung like a darkening curtain, came a resentment, more felt than discussed.

Eight years before, at the Celebration, Paul Hazeltine had promised them something. He had given it to them, or begun to; then suddenly it was being taken away, out of his hands, and theirs as well, to be thrown up in the air and to land where it might. It was fine and good for him and his in their fancy house by the river, but what of them? How would they pay the grocer and the butcher? How would they pay the landlord? If he cared at all—and what man wouldn't?—he'd be there, reassuring them, guiding them, taking the responsibility of the position that his money gave him instead of merely the profit or loss that wouldn't affect them one way or the other.

Frank Kelton was a fine manager, and fair enough, too, but seeing that quotas were met and the day's work done was one thing, and giving reassurance was another; a thing for which Kelton himself would be the first to admit he was unprepared.

The accident at the Hazeltine home, in its way, had been

a kind of relief. It provided something to talk about that related to the subject immediately at hand, while at the same time offering a distance. The Irish woman who'd been a girl when she went to work for the Hazeltines was known in the town, if only by sight. She'd been aloof and even rude at times, in the way of her employers, but with her death, one and all agreed that Brigid hadn't been to blame.

She'd been loyal and protective, poor thing, and what had it gotten her except a ride in the baggage car of Wednesday's three o'clock train to Hartford, where her weeping sister and brother-in-law would bury her.

It was a tragedy onto which the town could project its collective emotion: the sendoff at the station attracted a number of onlookers—Mrs. Putney, Mrs. Cheney, and Lucy Tremont—who, while they hadn't known Brigid all that well, as they told her sister, felt obligated to pay their respects. And who, as the train departed, noted to one another that a final goodbye was a deal more than the unfortunate Brigid got from any of the Hazeltines, even if Olivia had received the sister and brother-in-law, along with Dr. Worley, who had been summoned after Brigid's fateful fall and obligingly took care of the medical details.

If Olivia Hazeltine had paid for the arrangements with the Calhoun Funeral Parlor, what did that mean? What was the price of an embalming and the rest—or even the check that it was rumored Olivia had bestowed on Brigid's survivors—compared to a life?

Brigid's death was still hot on the tongues of the town when the news came that the Works had, in fact, been sold and the sale finalized. Spirits soared, but the initial elation was tempered by the details. Contrary to what everyone had expected, the Works would no longer make horseless carriages, or carriages of any sort.

The new owner, a Pittsfield man named Spikney, had

bought the plant with the intention of converting it at once to the making of coffins and caskets. Paul Hazeltine and his electric carriage had promised to lead Eastfield into the future. The arrival of Harold Spikney, and the news of his plans, gave the town a reminder of the futility of dreams and the finality of death.

The macabre combination of circumstances was noted by many—the wags who made jokes about going from carriages to coffins but riding all the same; those with a leaning toward spiritual matters who insisted that it was all part of the Lord's plan for Paul Hazeltine and a fitting reminder of His power; and those who fell into neither of the other two categories, but who felt none the less that it was as if the servant girl's death was a misfortune of which they had, needlessly, to be daily reminded as they went about their work.

"Between us," Mrs. Putney told the women in the post office on that day in early winter, "I'm just as glad my Aaron isn't working down to Spikney's and coming home with death on his hands each night."

"But it's not like that, do you think?" Lucy Tremont asked, thinking of her own Ralph, and the metal bindings he hammered at his bench. "It isn't as though they put them into the things, after all—"

The opening of the door cut her short, and they all turned to see the new arrival.

"Speak of the devil," Mrs. Putney whispered, ignoring Mrs. Cheney's attempt to hush her.

Feeling the eyes she was reluctant to meet, Francine wished that her navy wool coat, wet with the snow that had begun to fall as she came to the outskirts of town, were bigger, a tent in which she could totally enclose herself.

After Brigid's death, and the sadness it held for her and her longing for the restoration of some sort of normalcy, she'd dreaded coming to Eastfield. Brigid had been a buffer between the town and her family, Francine understood: it had been Brigid who spoke for the Hazeltines, holding off the curious, making sure that the distance her father had dictated between his children and the local citizenry was kept.

Even as Brigid's sister and her husband sat in the parlor, the question had begun to gnaw at Francine: how would she manage?

The house, in comparison, had become a minor problem. There was the drudgery of it, the physical work of the cleaning and cooking, the washing and dusting and the rest. But the daily repetition of the dreary tasks was a pastime if nothing else. Margaret and Constance, given simple jobs and instructions, were willing and even eager to help. And as long as there was something to eat, as long as things had a semblance of order about them, who was there to complain?

The trips to town were something else again, and when the first one became inevitable, Francine debated how to take it. Her sisters had been insistent, and so she'd taken them, secretly pleased that Paul had stayed at home. The stares and whispers had, as she'd expected, been naked as they'd walked through the streets, the unspoken questions evident in almost every face they saw.

But the shopkeepers, aware that the Hazeltines, whatever else one might say about them, always settled their accounts promptly, were courteous, and if her sisters had sensed the reaction they provoked, they hadn't shown it.

The second time, it had been different. It had been a Tuesday and one of her mother's good days. While her mother read to the younger girls, Francine had dressed and announced her departure. She had several stops to make—the pharmacy; the post office; Mr. Emergy; the butcher—

it would be easier and faster if she left the younger girls at home.

Walking down the Way, then along River Road, Francine had been filled with the same mixture of fascination and dread she felt when she looked at illustrations of the exotic specimens in the botany books her father had collected. Eastfield held a forceful, though threatening, attraction. The trip itself was a rare opportunity to be on her own, to chart her own course, albeit a predictable and circumscribed one, without fear of her brother suddenly appearing the way he did in the kitchen or in her bedroom, nefariously enjoying the startling effect he produced by catching her unaware, waiting and watching silently until she noticed him.

Her chance to be alone was itself worth the stares, the whispers or sudden silences.

But to her astonishment, then her delight, Francine found that they were fewer than she'd expected, fewer by far. The tradespeople noticed her, of course. So did the regular customers in their shops, and the women in the post office. Without Brigid or her sisters, though, it was possible to lose herself, to be just another girl who lived in Eastfield . . . a girl who was visiting.

The loss of her identity as a Hazeltine, if only for minutes at a time, was a joyous and freeing discovery. Her senses heightened, Francine began to rush not the trips to and from town, but the actual errands themselves. For years, she began to realize, she'd made the same predictable stops.

Now, for the first time, it was possible to extend her route, to explore Front Street, and State, and Water and High as well. Eastfield, it struck her, had grown without her even seeing it. West of High Street, there'd been an influx of French from Canada. They had their own bakery and grocer, and walking among them was like going to France, or so she imagined.

Even Front Street had changed. There were stores that offered "Specialties," "The Latest Ladies' Wear," and the like. There was the Bijoux, featuring "The Greatest Personalities in Vaudeville and the Music Hall Art Forms." Just off Front Street, there was the Commercial Hotel, with its Bar and Grill.

Once, released from the constant fear of being watched— though well aware that there were those, like the women in the post office, who would, recognizing her, watch her— Francine discovered the new pleasure of observing rather than being observed.

Like a novice collector who has been given his first postage stamp album, Francine savored the commonplace, the newness of it making it strange and exotic. The faces she watched—women with children; couples; young men— were frozen in her mind. In the same way, snatches of overheard conversation were savored and replayed later, at home, while she cooked or did the dishes.

It was not, of course, always possible to make the trip to town alone. Every few visits, Francine included her sisters, grateful that her mother had given up any interest in Eastfield. There were times, too, when her brother accompanied them, and those were the worst of all. Instead of trying to blend, as she'd come to think of it, Paul took pleasure in standing out. Rather than avoiding a prying eye, he met it defiantly, staring the onlooker down. Francine took care to guard the pleasure of her solitary visits to town, knowing that even though Paul would not share it, having inherited or absorbed his father's disdain for the "common" place and people, he would begrudge her and destroy it, or somehow use it against her.

In their way, the trips she had to make with her sisters made the trips alone all the more exciting.

At Setley's Books and Stationery, Francine would pore

over the new novels, drawn by their brightly illustrated jackets. Outside the Bijoux, she'd study the posters heralding the singers and dancers, the magicians and jugglers who had "entertained Heads of State throughout the Continent." With envy, she'd peek at the girls who waited for the entertainers at the stage door on matinee days. If the time was right, though she never knew exactly what time it was, she'd watch as the men (their husbands? lovers?) met them, and, offering arms, escorted them to the Grill of the Commercial Hotel.

The sounds and the sights of the streets of Eastfield had become something close to the secret gardens into which the children in the stories her mother read to her sisters were always wandering. Somehow, Francine thought, things had gotten turned around. It was home, the place she came from, that was like a garden: enchantment lay not in the peace and quiet surrounding it, but here in town.

At times, the oddest thoughts came to her. What if she didn't go home, Francine asked herself? What if she were to take a meal at the Eastfield Tea Shoppe on the Common, or a room at the Commercial Hotel? What if she were to wander through the streets, not trying to hide in her coat as she did when recognition struck, but smiling, pleased with herself like some of the girls she saw?

Anything might happen, any form of wonder, or enchantment, or escape . . . yes, *escape*. She and Margaret and Constance, she'd take them too. She'd rent one of the places advertised in the *Eastfield Crier*, and eventually they would come to fit in. People would forget who they were and who they had been—

"Nine cents, Miss Hazeltine." It startled her, making her aware of where she was and instantly putting her at distance from the things she'd tried to think about in order to keep from remembering.

"Yes?" she said, the old pounding in her heart.

"Nine cents, miss. To post your letters."

"Of—of course," Francine replied, reaching into the inner pocket of her coat, remembering that she'd crossed the floor and taken the letters out already. She counted the coins out and turned around, then turned again, knowing the man was clearing his throat for her attention.

"Don't you want your mail?" he asked, aware of the appreciative audience.

"Yes, please," she answered, thanking him quickly as he handed her the envelopes and two magazines, which she slipped inside her coat.

The old boards squeaked as she made her way to the door, not wanting to hurry but unable to slow down, knowing that the women, frozen as if they were in a photograph, would come to life as soon as she left, and that the silence would be filled with conversation.

She felt better as she closed the door after herself, leaving her fear and anxiousness behind along with the warmth of the place. Her breathing became normal as she crossed the Common, her boots sinking into the snow. Taking a last look around her, a look at Eastfield, Francine sighed and started for River Road, secretly dreaming of the day when she might come to Eastfield, or some place like it, and never, never have to go home.

# - 6 -

THE LAST NIGHT'S snow had been heavy, and it had formed a thin frozen crust. Paul had been up early, before his sisters and almost before dawn itself. In the kitchen, he'd taken the stock and barrel of the Winchester "Take Down" Repeater from their case, oiling and polishing the pieces separately before fitting them together and loading the .32 cartridges.

Paul worked silently and slowly, glancing up every few moments to the window, smiling to himself. They would come, he knew: the brook three quarters of a mile up in the woods behind the house would be frozen still, and they'd come as they had for the better part of a week to the river.

He'd watched them, lulling them into a false sense of safety, following their tracks when they'd come and gone, and now he was ready.

Waiting, he glanced around the familiar room. The dishes were washed and put away, the kitchen table cleared except for the cup of tea he'd made. He was finished with it, but Paul didn't consider taking it to the sink. That would be for Francine to do. He was the man of the house, the master.

There was his mother to be looked after, but her needs were few. As long as she had her drops and her drink, she was no trouble at all.

Things had changed, and in the beginning the change had worried him. For a time he'd feared that with his father gone, someone would come to change it all around, to send them away, to his mother's relatives in Boston, perhaps. It hadn't happened, and with every day that passed, he'd felt safer, more sure of himself.

The Works had been the first test, but he'd been pleased to find that his father's relationship with the First Bank was such that the instructions from Mr. Hazeltine were followed without question. Outside of Kelton, nobody had even sought his father out.

The business with Francine had been a challenge, but the answer had come to him easily, and it had kept her in his control. She'd been easy, as easy as Brigid. Lately, ever since Brigid was out of the way, she had even given up struggling when he came to her in the night. She liked it, but she tried to pretend she didn't. He felt it in the way her nipples hardened under his fingers, in the way her thighs trembled and the wetness when he took her.

The thought of Brigid made him smile. He'd nearly laughed when her sister came and the doctor told her about the accident. He'd been unable to feel pity for either of them, the dead fool or her stupid cow of a sister, though he'd put a suit on and sat beside his mother with a solemn look on his face.

All the while, he'd thought that his father had been right. Most people were sheep, followers, gullible idiots who would believe anything they were told as long as they were told with authority. He'd known, then, why his father despised the simple-minded townspeople.

*"Fool!"* he'd wanted to say, but he'd kept silent, amazed that it didn't occur to Brigid's sister to question the circumstances. Finally she'd left with her watery-eyed husband, and the doctor had gone, and things had been right again.

They were all fools, all of them. Brigid, and Eastfield, and even the First Bank. It had been his idea that his mother ask for money to be transferred into her account; she'd agreed at once and copied the letter he wrote for her. Before he gave it to Francine to mail, he'd had Margaret copy it over. She had a gift for drawing and such; it had been impossible to tell the copy from the original. And now it was locked in the desk to which he had the key, along with the checks and the account books.

Money, his father had said, was security. The statements from the bank showed that they were secure. They would stay as they had been, safe and in the house, away from the town—

A movement caught his eye at the line where the snow-covered lawn met the bushes beyond it. Paul stood, staring through the window. The doe's head didn't move as her eyes scanned the smooth ground. She came forward, her steps hesitant at first, then quicker, and the adolescent fawn followed, his trail broader as he ran from her and toward her, from her and toward her, playful and teasing.

They passed the barn and the icehouse. Paul turned to the window of the door, watching them cross the side lawn and make their way down to the brush and trees, covered with glittering ice in the early light.

*They're near the Way,* he thought, reaching for the jacket he'd hung on one of the pine chairs around the table. *They're crossing it now, through the brush and over River Road. They're down the bank and at the river...*

He opened the kitchen door, pleased with its silence: he'd oiled the hinges the day before.

*They're drinking,* Paul thought, watching the pattern his breath made in the frozen air. In his mind's eye he could see them foraging in the bushes, checking the damp ground for whatever growth there might be where the snow was light. He raised the gun and aimed it at a point near the edge of the cleared yard and waited. The sky was lighter now. There was no sound but the crackling of the bushes in the distance. The sound became louder and suddenly they appeared, scampering out of the brush.

Paul held his breath.

He fired. The shot was an explosion in the stillness of the morning. It caught the doe in the neck, and she fell. Paul started toward her, then stopped as the fawn, bewildered, nudged its dead mother then turned its head this way and that. Paul heard the footsteps coming down the stairs, through the dining room. He turned and raised his hand, motioning for the girls to stand back.

The rifle still raised, he moved out of the doorway, toward his prey. The fawn took a few steps backward and moved to its mother. It sniffed the air, uncertain, and advanced toward Paul. They walked toward each other, the animal drawn, perhaps, by the wide blue eyes and the deceptive calm.

Paul waited until there was only twenty feet between them and fired again.

"Fool," he said.

"You didn't have to do that!" Francine called from the doorway. He turned to her. "You didn't let it have a chance—"

She stopped as he grabbed the fawn's hind legs, bringing them together in his left hand, raising the tail end of the body off the ground. With his right hand, he pulled his knife from the sheath that hung from his belt and made a quick cut. He laughed as the blood and intestines spurted out, over the white snow, toward Francine. And, as she vomited into the snow, he laughed all the more.

# - 7 -

THE SECRET WAS inside her, as constant as her heartbeat. It pounded steadily, threatening at times to break free in spite of Francine's awareness that she had to keep it to herself. It was her comfort, her companion, the anchor she clung to when her brother came to her room at night, when the touch of his hands and the roughness of his taking aroused her. It was there when he left, and when she cried silently, ashamed of her response, feeling betrayed by her body.

There had been a period of time when she'd feared that her body would make her a prisoner of the house, against her will. Then the secret had come, and with it an excitement she shielded behind a veneer of calm as she went through the regular routine of her days.

Sitting in the parlor, listening as the music started and stopped and began again, she was torn between the awareness of what was to come, and the desire to hold the moment that would soon be a last memory.

"My hands won't reach!" Constance whined, pouting at the keyboard.

Her mother smiled. "Of course they will, dear. It's all a matter of turning the wrist."

"But my wrist isn't *big* enough," the ten year old protested petulantly.

Olivia stroked the child's long blond hair absently, then seated herself beside her in front of the Knabe.

"Like this," she said, and Francine bit her lip as her mother began to play. The strains of "The Spinning Song" filled the parlor and the early afternoon. As she played the first bars, Olivia, with the winter sun behind her, was as beautiful as the music. Then, as Francine had known it would, it all changed. Her mother's fingers faltered; her rhythm broke. She continued, but the notes and chords became increasingly dissonant, the meter of the piece out of time.

Olivia stopped suddenly, and Constance tried again, starting a scale. Francine glanced at Margaret, but the twelve year old was intent on the doll's dress she was sewing. She didn't appear to notice as her mother slid from the bench, standing at the window and lifting the wineglass she'd set on the octagonal rosewood table. She saw her eldest daughter watching her and her face took on a wistful expression.

"I did such lovely work, once," she said. "Your father always complimented me on my fancy work, you know."

"Yes," Francine replied, seized by a surge of sorrow that came as suddenly as the surge of sound that had begun several weeks before, when her mother had rediscovered the piano. From a distance, the distance of the doorway, the figure of the seated woman, remembered from her childhood, had held a promise. But the promise had been broken. She'd listened as her mother tried the familiar pieces, "Für Elise," and "The Spinning Song," and "I'll Take You Home Again Kathleen." More awkward that the mistakes she'd made had been her apparent inability to recognize them. She'd played the same things over and over, hitting the same wrong keys or notes that were equally cacophonous.

Now, Francine wondered if perhaps her mother, even in some small way, had known all along; if perhaps she hadn't simply been trying to fool the younger children, who went along with all she said and did as if it were a game of her devising in which they, too, were included.

"It's different now," Olivia said, observing her fingers as if they were a stranger's that had been mysteriously appended to the ends of her arms. "They don't do quite what they should."

"They will," Francine promised, wanting to cry without knowing exactly why. "In spring, Mother. When the warm weather comes."

Olivia Hazeltine parted the lace curtains with her hand, looking out over the frozen white lawn to the trees beyond it. "Perhaps," she said. "It seems so far away, though." She lifted the glass to her lips. Droplets fell on the bosom of her dress; she smiled at them as if they were jewels, rubies instead of spots of red wine.

The snow magnified the sunlight, throwing it back in her face. To Francine, it looked like a magic light, bathing her mother in a beauty that could only be found in photographs and memory. The blotches and discolorations that had begun to appear on the once-perfect skin were gone. The lips, colored and moistened by the red wine, were young and healthy, instead of pale and dry. Even the tangled hair seemed to catch the light and hold it in a bright copper web.

At the piano, Constance began to practice the piece her mother had been trying to teach her. Each time she made a mistake she went back to the beginning, and after several attempts, she banged at the keys with her fists.

"I can't, I can't, I *can't!*" she whined, banging once more.

"I don't suppose it matters," her mother observed, still looking out the window.

"I want to go find Paul," the little girl said.

"No," Francine answered firmly. "He's fishing on the ice. It's no place for you."

"But I *want* to—"

"It's dangerous," Francine said.

Olivia began to hum softly to herself the child's piece Constance had been trying to play. "They used to skate on the Charles," she said to nobody in particular. "In Boston. When I was a girl. I'd watch from the window...the bay window. Back and forth, back and forth...the turns that some of them used to do!"

"Did you skate, too, Mother?" Margaret asked.

Olivia laughed softly and turned. With the movement, the illusion of beauty was gone, and the familiar image of decay and neglect had returned. Francine felt herself shudder.

"Me? Oh no, not me. It wasn't...suitable. Under the circumstances..."

"What circumstances?" Francine asked gently.

Her mother considered the question carefully. Her head tilted and her hand went to her hair. "I...can't quite remember, dear. It was all so—so long ago, you see..."

"Yes, Mother."

Constance jumped off the piano bench. "I want to go outside. I want to play in the snow!"

Margaret put her sewing down, ready to go along. They looked at Olivia, who in turn looked at Francine.

"All right, go ahead. But put your mittens on, both of you. And stay where we can see you—no going to the river." The Connecticut River was frozen, but the currents were swift and the ice weak in spots. Without another word, the two younger girls hurried to the closet in the foyer where they kept their coats. There was a gust of cold air as they opened the front door, slamming it behind themselves. Moments later, they were examining the snowman they'd been working on for the past few days, then packing more snow onto its round body.

Francine and her mother were alone.

"I feel a chill coming on," Olivia observed.

"Would you like something, Mother? A cup of tea?"

"Tea..." she repeated. Then, with delight. "Yes, that would be lovely. I believe it's time for my medicine. You know how cross the doctor gets with me if I don't take it on time—"

"I'll make a cup," Francine offered. Leaving her mother, she went to the kitchen.

The Wedgwood cup and saucer, the wooden handle of the teapot, the long, red-and-white-tipped match she struck to light the burner of the stove... she held them each a beat longer than usual, lingering with the special awareness of the secret that was hers and hers alone.

She would never again do these simple things that had become habit, never again touch these objects that were as familiar as her own body.

Waiting for the water to boil, she put a pinch of tea in the fat little pot, memorizing the pattern of small blue flowers, and set it, along with the cup and saucer and the sugar bowl, on the silver tea tray. Her fingers traced the ornate pattern of etched swirls.

Who would polish the silver, she wondered? Who would make the tea and do the dishes, wash the clothes and do the ironing? Brigid was gone, and soon she would be gone, too—

A current of guilt struggled against her joy.

It had happened! It had happened to her! It had been like a story, but not a story made up in the mind of a stranger for other strangers to read or hear, but rather an adventure tailored to her most secret wishes. And to think that she'd almost missed it!

Looking at strangers, watching them, was a pleasure. Talking to them, however, was something else. Coming home from town the week before, she'd heard the carriage following her down River Road. She hadn't turned, not even when she began to think that it had slowed and was following her. It was some acquaintance of her father's, perhaps, someone who was curious and would, given the slightest encouragement, ask questions that she'd be unable to answer.

"Miss?" a male voice had called. She'd pretended not to hear, and he'd called again, this time pulling up beside her.

"Could I offer you a ride, miss? You shouldn't be carrying those packages with the road so icy. You might slip."

Before she knew it, he had fastened the reins. He was lifting the packages from her hands, then lifting her onto the seat beside him. He talked as he rode, about himself and his job. Listening to his words was difficult; Francine had found herself watching the wind toss his dark curly hair forward and back, forward and back.

His name was Ned Tanley. He was twenty-four years old, and a traveling salesman, dealing in yard goods and notions. He'd arrived in Springfield by train from Albany, and had rented a carriage to call on merchants in the nearby towns and the farm wives in the outlying areas.

He'd seen her shopping in Eastfield, he told Francine. He'd watched her as she made her way through the streets. When he saw her heading away from town with her packages, he'd followed; he'd hoped she wasn't frightened.

Once it had been established that he wasn't one of the locals, all fear had left her. She'd been pleased, with him and with herself, mesmerized by his words and his smile and the attention she'd never been allowed from an outsider and had never allowed herself.

"You're sweet," the man had said, patting her hand.

She'd continued to smile at him, saying little as they rode. It was only when he asked her how far she was going that she realized they'd passed the Way and the house. They were farther down River Road, in the westerly direction away from town, than she'd ever been before. She'd wished that they could keep going and going.

"I guess we'll have to turn around, huh?" Ned asked, not angry that they'd gone out of the way. "Would you like to stop and walk a bit? Do you have the time?"

Riding was faster than walking, she'd thought; the time could be spared. He'd led the horse to a clearing off the road, hitching it to a birch tree. From the back of the wagon he'd taken a heavy blanket, putting it around her shoulders like a cape.

They'd walked into the woods, and when he tried to kiss her, Francine had not resisted. The blanket had fallen from her shoulders. As the stranger spread it, she joined him on the frozen ground. He'd opened her coat and felt her body through her dress.

She'd grabbed at him as if he were a last, desperate hope. He lay beside her as she unbuttoned his pants, drawing him out, stroking him. When she caressed him with her mouth, he'd been surprised.

"Well I'll be!" he'd said. "Where did you learn that?"

She'd wondered if he wanted her to stop the thing that her brother had taught her to do, the thing that was shown and written about in the books Paul had found in the study. But Ned's hands on her head told her he didn't; that he was pleased with her.

Then she'd lain back as he lifted her skirt. Out of habit, her body had tensed; her brother, in his visits to her room, had taken his pleasure and made her suffer. But this time, it was different. Instead of pain, there was only pleasure, gentle at first and building. Her hands, her mouth, her whole being had ached for him, reached for him.

"I ought to get you home," he said, moments after they had finished. "You must be freezing."

"Not really. Not at all," she answered in a voice not quite her own as he gathered up the blanket, shaking off the snow.

"Know what I'd like to do?" Ned Tanley asked her. He told her before she could answer, or even guess. "I'd like to keep you with me all the time." He winked and slipped his arm around her shoulders, guiding her back to the waiting horse and carriage.

"Yes, I'd like that, too."

Stopping in place, he turned to face her fully, his mouth a wide grin. "Should we do it then?"

"Do what?"

"Go off together."

"Yes, oh yes!" she told him.

He'd thought she was kidding, but by the time they'd been riding for a few minutes back the way they'd come on River Road, she'd half changed his mind. In spite of the questions he'd begun to ask, sh 'd given him as little information as possible. A story in a book she'd read came to mind, and she claimed it. She was an orphan, Francine explained, living with a spinster aunt. Her aunt would be glad to see her go.

"And you'd do it? Go off with a man you hardly knew?"

Her enthusiasm and hopes had mounted. "Yes! Oh, yes!" she'd insisted, knowing that she couldn't tell him that anything she got would be better than what she had. He dropped her off, as she asked, a half mile past the Way, toward Eastfield. Francine had thought it wiser to walk back, in case Paul was in the woods.

"I think you're teasing me," he told her.

"No—no, I want to go away—"

He thought it over. "Tell you what. Let's see...it's Thursday. I'll be finished by Tuesday. I'll make my calls and be back here on Tuesday. And you'll meet me?"

"I promise! You'll take me—we'll go away?"

He nodded, smiling, sizing her up. "To Albany. On Tuesday."

"At the train. I'll meet you in the afternoon," she offered.

Reaching into his pocket, he'd pulled out a schedule and consulted it. "I can get the eleven-thirty in Springfield. I'll be here a little after noon. The train to Albany comes at half past two."

"I'll be there!" she vowed, gaily.

"How about a kiss on it, then?"

Calculating and innocent, she'd kissed his lips again.

That had been on Thursday afternoon. Coming up the Way, then inside the house, the joy of the secret had briefly been replaced by an oppressive dread. Having never been so happy before, Francine was sure that one of them, Paul, most likely, would notice something had changed. But dinner passed, then Friday breakfast, and the rest of the day. Even Friday night, when he came to her bed, her brother hadn't known. She hadn't tried to deny him, knowing full well it would only lead to trouble.

Tuesday, it seemed, would never come. Now it was here. Now, in the kitchen, with the kettle whistling and the tray set for tea, with her mother in the parlor and Paul fishing. With the girls outside, and Ned already at the station, where she'd be joining him soon, so *soon*.

She poured the water and looked at the kitchen clock. It was twelve-thirty. His train would have arrived. She lifted the tray.

Olivia was where she had been. She didn't react to the sound of Francine returning to the parlor.

"Mother? I've brought your tea."

"Tea?" she repeated, apparently confused. "Oh, yes. How lovely." Olivia took a place on the sofa beside her daughter. "Aren't you having any?"

"No, Mother. I have to go into town and do the errands."

"Errands. Will you take your sisters?"

Francine touched her chest, half-convinced her heart would leap out. "I don't think so. Not today. They can come next time. Besides, I think Constance looks a bit flushed."

"Really?"

"Yes," Francine answered, pouring the tea from the pot into the cup. She handed it to her mother, who took the familiar bottle from her pocket. *Tincture of Morphine,* it read. She added several drops to the tea, then sugar, stirring it well.

"Mother?" Francine began. "Do you think it might be a good idea..."

"Yes, dear?"

"Constance and Margaret. They—they haven't been keeping up with their studies, you know."

"They haven't?" Olivia asked, surprised. "I had no idea."

"Things like reading, for instance."

"Constance is only ten, Francine."

"But Margaret is twelve, mother. And she has such a hard time with even the most simple words. I thought that perhaps they could..."

"Yes?" Olivia asked pleasantly, sipping from the cup.

"Well, have—lessons. Go to school—"

"School?" Olivia echoed, laughing. "Why, you know how your father feels about that subject. Surely you can't have forgotten already!"

"No. Of course not," Francine stammered. "But it wouldn't have to be school here, would it? In Eastfield, that is. They could go away—just to Amherst, perhaps, or

Springfield. The MacDuffie School is supposed to be excellent—"

Her mother's laughter made her stop. "Wherever *do* you get such ideas?" Olivia asked, putting her cup down. "Eastfield or elsewhere, I know your father. He wouldn't hear of it. Besides, what would that do to his plan?"

"Plan?"

"Yes, dear. For us. To all be together here. Always together. Imagine, if he were to come home and find your sisters in school!" She laughed again, as if the very idea of it were too preposterous to even consider.

"It was just a thought," Francine said softly.

"A foolish one, dear. But I won't tell Father when he comes home." Olivia beamed, then whispered as if another presence in the room might overhear her. "It will be our secret."

Francine's sudden embrace took her by surprise. She returned it, but there was little strength in her hold.

"I . . . I should get started for town."

"A good beginning makes a good end," her mother observed, watching as the girl took her coat. "Be sure you get back before dark."

"I will, Mother."

"Francine?"

"Yes?"

"Are you shaking?"

*She can see it,* Francine thought, panicked. "Me?" she made herself say. "No, Mother—"

Olivia's laugh was soft and sad. "It must be my eyes."

"You've been looking at the snow. It's too bright for you."

"The snow," her mother repeated. Francine ran to her and kissed her. "Goodbye."

"Hurry home," her mother answered.

She would always remember the sound of the heavy door as it closed behind her.

She would remember Constance's whine in the yard. "But I *want* to go with you!"

She would remember kissing her youngest sister, and hugging Margaret, and the confusion of emotions as she began to walk down the Way, her pace increasing until she was running along River Road, running to Eastfield and her future. She was free, finally and forever! But what if Ned wasn't at the station? The world, the sane world, was waiting. But she'd brought no clothes and no money from the house. She had escaped! But she'd left the others.

Even when Ned met her on the platform and lifted her into the coach car, even when she was seated beside him and he was telling her of the times they'd have together, even when the train began to slowly pull away from the station, Francine Hazeltine found herself thinking of the others.

*Margaret and Constance,* the track said as the train moved, *Constance and Margaret . . .*

There was an unexpected ache in her heart as she thought of them and of her mother, and a tear in her eye as she turned in her seat at the window, watching till Eastfield and all in and around it were out of sight.

"Goodbye," she said silently. "I would have saved you, too . . . if I could . . ."

*part three*
**1929**

## - 1 -

"CAN I HELP YOU?" the young woman asked from her position behind the counter of the Chelsea Yarn Shoppe. She naturally addressed the question to the woman in the fitted gabardine suit with the sheared beaver lapels, but the man in the blazer and bow tie answered, tipping his wide-brimmed hat.

"Actually, little lady, I'd like a word with the proprietor," he said, flashing her a smile.

"I'm the proprietor," she responded, toying with the collar of her hand-knit pink chemise dress.

The man feigned astonishment. "You are? Why, I'd have sworn you were just a high-school girl, Mrs. . . . ?"

"Millman," she replied, aware that the regular customers—Mrs. Spano, and Mrs. Silverman, and Mrs. Goodwin, who spent a good portion of their days sitting in the brown straight-backed chairs, their needles clicking away as they made sweaters and conversation—were taking it all in. *"Miss* Rose Millman," she added.

"Rose, huh?"

*"Miss* Millman," a voice behind him said. The man had never met Sarah Spano, but the combination of her tone and the maternally protective glare in her eyes were enough to

make him reconsider. "Of course," he said, tipping his hat once more. "Miss Millman," he said, turning back to the woman who stood in front of the bins of brightly colored wool, then turning again to include her customers.

"Harry Johnson, ladies," he told them, bowing to introduce himself. "And let me introduce none other than Miss Francine Le Faye, one of the stars of the hit show, *Midsummer Madness,* that is opening tomorrow night at the Court Square Theater in your fair city of Springfield. Direct, I might add, from an outstanding run on Broadway—"

"Oh, Harry, stop," Francine said, blushing, aware that the women were looking at her in a new way.

"See how modest she is, ladies?" the man asked. "The hallmark of a true star. No wonder she's charmed all the critics, is it? *The Globe, Mirror, Variety*—"

"My part is very small," Francine told the women. "But the play is good—"

"Good?" Harry Johnson echoed. "It's great! Sensational! An evening of entertainment you won't forget—"

"Ever since they opened the Paramount, we like the vaudeville better," one of the women said.

"Vaudeville?" the dapperly dressed man asked, amazed. "My dear madam! How can an obvious connoisseur of the arts such as yourself even *think* of comparing jugglers and second-rate magicians with an outstanding drama such as *Midsummer Madness?* Particularly as performed with a cast including artists of the stature of this lovely young lady."

"Harry, please," Francine said, embarrassed.

He ignored her, snapping open the leather case he carried. Producing a cheaply printed cardboard poster, he held it delicately, as if it were some rare work of art.

*The New York Stage Hit!*
*MIDSUMMER MADNESS*

With All-Broadway Cast
One Week Only!
Sept. 30—Oct. 4
COURT SQUARE THEATER
Springfield, Mass.


When the women had all seen it, Harry Johnson turned his attention to the proprietor.

"*Miss* Millman," he began pointedly, "I know your lovely shop attracts the patronage of some of your fair city's finest people. I myself was struck by that beautiful sweater in your window—and I couldn't help but notice that there'd be room, a small corner is all, for this announcement.... You'd be doing a cultural service to the community. And there'd be two free passes in it for you—"

"Four," Mrs. Spano corrected him, her knitting needles clicking.

Harry turned to her. "Isn't that what I said? *Four* passes."

The petite, pretty young woman behind the counter smiled in spite of herself. "I suppose it would be all right," she allowed.

He bowed. "Thank you, *Miss* Millman. I know you won't be sorry." He hurriedly maneuvered his way around a bin of discounted, odd skeins of yarn and put the poster in the window, as if afraid she might change her mind. Then he counted out four passes and gave them to her.

"Well, see you folks," he said, taking Francine's arm. "We've got to be getting over to the theater. Rehearsals, you know—"

"I'd like to buy some yarn," the woman said softly, refusing to be led out the door. She turned to the proprietor. "I'm looking for a pattern for an angora beret—and the angora, of course—"

"I'll write it out for you. Everyone's making them. Did you have a particular color in mind?"

"Something in a brown, I think," Francine answered. "Not a dark brown, but something more..."

The proprietor reached beneath the counter and produced a box. "Take a look at this. It's a new shade. 'Mink,' they call it."

"Oh, yes! That's exactly what I wanted—"

The man cleared his throat, and she turned to him.

"We really should be getting to the theater. We don't want to be late," he reminded her.

Francine looked from him to the woman behind the counter. "Would it take long to get the instructions?" she asked.

"Not really. But if you like, I can write them up for you and set them aside with the yarn."

"Would you, please? We're stopping just across the street at the Bridgeway. I can pick it up after rehearsal."

"Could I have your name again?" Rose Millman asked, writing up a sales slip.

"Francine Le Faye. L small e, then a space, capital F-a-y-e," the man answered, spelling it out.

"He's a press agent," Francine explained. "Thank you. I'll be back for it."

"Ladies," Harry Johnson said, saluting them as he escorted Francine out of the Chelsea Yarn Shoppe. Only when the door was closed behind them, when they were walking down Broadway, did his manner change. "What do you want to bother with balls of yarn for, Frannie? She took the poster, didn't she? I gave her the passes—all four of 'em?"

"I want the beret."

"So you want one? Buy one. Hell, I'll buy you one!"

Francine smiled in the early October chill.

"I like to knit. It's something to do."

"Yeah, while you wait for the customers to buy tickets. Did you catch the gal in the store. 'We like vaudeville.' And if those talking pictures they keep writing up in *Variety* ever get off the ground—"

"But they won't, Harry. Will they?"

He shrugged. "Search me." His arm moved from her elbow to her waist, and he felt her body stiffen. They were in front of the district courthouse at Elm Street, just about to cross Court Square to the theater. "What is it?" he asked.

"It's nothing, Harry," she answered.

She began to walk away from the municipal buildings, toward the green park, but he didn't move.

"Come on, Frannie—what's eating you?" he asked again.

"Really, Harry. It's nothing. I just feel..."

He shook his head. "Honey, it's *something*. Ever since Albany you been acting funny. Last week in Hartford, and now here it's worse." He lowered his voice, though no passer-by was close enough to overhear them even if he'd been listening. "How about last night, Frannie?" he asked.

As was often the case when the company played a new town, the cast of *Midsummer Madness*, all of them staying at the Bridgeway, Springfield's most popular theatrical hotel, had gathered in the dining room for dinner. Later, the group broke up into smaller contingents, partying in someone's rooms or tipping the bell captain for the name and password of the nearest speakeasy.

Harry loved the gossip and the camaraderie, Francine knew, and she'd thought that he'd hardly miss her when she excused herself.

"I—I had a headache last night," she explained. "I wanted to get away from the noise."

"I'm not talking about dinner, Frannie," he said. "How about when I came up?"

There was no recrimination in his voice, but in his eyes, Francine could see the wound of her rejection. It had been the first time in how long, she asked herself? The towns and theaters, the layovers and layoffs, blended together, and she had to struggle to make her mind compute them. It had to be nearly a year, she realized, since they'd been working together, and almost as long since they'd started going together as well. And once, only once in all that time, had she refused him her body.

His question hovered in the crispness of the late morning. Wanting to answer it, sincerely sorry for having hurt him, Francine held back, wary that even a half truth or the hint of one might somehow turn into a sliver of the whole truth.

"I'm sorry," she apologized. "We'll make up for it. I promise."

Reassured, he smiled, and this time when his arm encircled her, she let it mold itself to her body without resistance.

"That's my girl," Harry said, squeezing her.

*It's another part*, Francine told herself, *it's a play, and I am Francine Le Faye* . . .

But in spite of herself, she shivered as she looked beyond Broadway to Columbus Avenue, and beyond that to the Connecticut River. Did the dark water flow toward Eastfield, she wondered, or from it?

"Cold?" Harry asked, aware of the trembling of her body.

"It must be whatever I had last night," she answered quickly. "Maybe it's a touch of the flu."

He stopped, and, putting his hands on her shoulders, turned her to face him, studying the high color in her cheeks.

"You'd better see a doctor, Frannie. I know you've got something—"

"I'll be fine," she assured him. They were in the center

of the square, so much like the Eastfield Common that it made her feel dizzy. Another few steps, she reminded herself, another few seconds, really, and they'd be across it, inside the theater, rehearsing the play. In its illusion, the dual illusion of the character she played and her identity as Francine Le Faye, the actress, a protective safety waited.

"I don't know," Harry said, considering the matter. "You're not yourself, doll."

"My . . . self," she repeated.

"Know what it is, Frannie?" he asked.

She knew, and knew he didn't know, so she didn't even try to answer.

"We're both getting too damn old for this grind, kid," Harry Johnson told her. "Maybe when this tour is done, we ought to get out, huh? Settle down, get hitched, and have a couple of kids. Whaddya say?"

"Maybe," she allowed, smiling at the familiar offer. They'd been going together so long that it felt like a marriage, and everyone in the company treated them as an established couple.

"Right now, you go back to the hotel. See a doctor or something about that flu. Okay?"

"But the rehearsal—"

"Forget it. It's just for lights, anyway. When that's done, I'm gonna hit the newspapers and see what I can do. That advance man stinks." He kissed her cheek, promising to see her later at the Bridgeway Hotel, and Francine watched him hurry across Court Square, into the theater.

The moment Harry was out of sight, her heart began to pound wildly.

"I am Francine Le Faye," she whispered into the autumn wind, trying to anchor her identity.

But the feel of the breeze and the smell of it, heavy with

pine and the scent of the river, stirred a part of her that she'd hidden beneath the name and persona she'd taken.

As if in a trance, she turned, walking down Elm Street to Main, where the stores were. But instead of shop windows or passers-by, Francine saw glimpses of her own life, visions of her history.

There she was, a young girl leaving home, meeting a man who was really no more than a stranger on River Road. A girl, so desperate and so naive that she'd actually believed a stranger could take her away, rescue her, make a life for her.

There she was eight months later, alone, her would-be savior gone back to the wife he hadn't mentioned. She'd been in Albany, with no friends and no money except the few dollars he'd given her to get "settled." She wouldn't go back to Eastfield, she'd promised herself; she'd *never* go back. But where she would go, where she *might* go, she'd had no idea. Then, as now, she'd wandered aimlessly through the city. A theater marquee had caught her eye, and without being aware of it, she'd walked around to the stage door, remembering the fascination she'd had with Eastfield's Bijoux. In Albany, however, it had been different. She wasn't watching from a distance—a man was at the stage door, and he was talking to her, asking her if she'd come about the part.

"Yes," she heard herself answer. Then she'd been led inside, told to take off her coat. Had she had any experience? someone asked her. "Still, she's pretty enough. And the part isn't big enough for it to matter," someone else said.

"But you're free to travel, aren't you?" the man who had been at the door asked. "We play Pittsburgh next week, then Erie. And I don't want an actress who's going to leave me stranded like the one you'll be replacing!"

"Oh, I won't. I won't," she promised.

So quickly it had happened! She was trying on a costume, being handed a script and told what passages to memorize. It was a story about a man who became a drunkard, a melodrama, and the woman who played the character of her mother went over her lines with her, showing her the gestures and facial expressions Francine copied. They were rehearsing her scenes in the room that wasn't a real room at all, but a stage set. She was a fast study, someone said— she'd learned her lines in only a few hours—but she had to speak up, project.

The older actress was painting her face. She was led onto the stage, aware of the audience that was settling into seats in the theater that had been empty earlier. The heavy velvet curtain parted. The bright lights blinded her, shutting out the audience, and the past, so that the only reality was the play.

It was over, and there was the applause, then the other members of the cast congratulating her.

She moved from the furnished room she'd been staying in to the theatrical boarding house where the rest of the company stayed. Without question or hesitation they accepted her, believed the answers she invented for the questions they asked. She was twenty years old, she said. Her name was Francine Le Faye. Her family had lived in Boston, where she said she was born, then moved back to Canada, where they'd originally come from.

*I am an actress,* she realized, amazed. And with her amazement came a tremendous relief, for she was safe. Was twenty-five dollars a week a lot of money? Never having earned any, she had no idea. But more than the money, the thing that mattered was the security of her identity and the safety of her newly discovered future.

There she was, Francine thought, seeing images of herself in the glass of the stores on Main Street. On trains, on stages, in melodramas, and thrillers, and comedies. The towns and cities she'd played merged into a series of hotels and boarding houses. The parts she'd played fused into a single fantasy that was more comfortable, far more comfortable, than the past she'd managed to escape.

She had learned quickly the craft of the stage—the moves, the timing and delivery of her lines. And she had learned, too, the art of calling on the managers in New York when she was between engagements, of playing the part of Francine Le Faye, the woman she had invented and become, and elaborating on the threads of the past she had woven.

Where many of the actors she met aspired to stardom, thinking of the road as something to do until the right part in New York came along, or until one of the casting directors for the new motion picture companies discovered them, Francine had never sought stardom. While other actresses competed for roles in the new plays, she was content to remain a featured player, touring in proven successes that would guarantee her a full season's work. It was not the applause or attention that she sought, but the escape, the movement, the endless illusion that was so much easier and more comfortable to live with than her memories.

There they were, she thought, the years passing, and her youth with them. She observed it, in memory, as she'd lived it—not with regret, but with a detachment that had become more natural to her as one season followed another. The other Francine was gone, all but forgotten, a character in a play that she'd once performed. She—the new Francine, Francine Le Faye—had been born on an Albany stage.

For a time, Francine had resisted the flirtations and attention from men. They were betrayers all, she'd been convinced, dangerous and best avoided. But as she discovered her talent, she found, too, the full power of her own body and the beauty that others said she possessed. There'd been affairs on the road, more convenient pastimes than anything else, and some romances as well over the years.

There'd been offers of marriage, and the idea had appealed to her. But always, she'd pulled back, warned by an instinct that told her she would have to provide more than surface answers to questions about her past and family.

But perhaps Harry Johnson was right, she considered. She was no longer a girl, but a woman of forty. It was time, perhaps, to settle down, and Harry was a kind man, a good man. Early on, she'd told him that she did not care to talk about her girlhood, and to his credit, he'd let it go at that. He was in his forties too, and as a couple on the tour, they'd tended to one another's comforts as a husband and wife would care for each other, both of them aware that most of the members of the *Midsummer Madness* company were younger.

The movies were the coming thing, Harry had said. He had some money put aside, and so did she. They could find the right location and buy a movie theater, he'd told her. Their futures would be assured.

At the corner of Main and Vernon streets, Francine stopped stock-still. *If only we hadn't come here,* she thought.

She'd carefully managed to avoid coming even close to Eastfield over the years, usually signing for tours that took her to the South or Midwest. Twice she'd played Hartford, and she'd thought, not wanting to, of Brigid. Was her sister in the audience? Francine had wondered, afraid to scan the faces beyond the footlights. Was someone else who'd known Brigid sitting out there in the darkness, watching the actress Francine Le Faye impersonate a flapper in *Wild Daughters?*

The possibility, no matter how remote or irrational, had made her uncomfortable. She hadn't wanted to experience it again, and she'd nearly turned down the *Midsummer Madness* tour because it meant playing Springfield. But Harry had persuaded her to join him, and not being able to tell him why she didn't want to take the offer, Francine had agreed. All summer, in theaters from the resorts of Pennsylvania and New Jersey to Maine and down to Cape Cod, she'd struggled to shore up her defenses. It was only one week at the Court Square Theater, after all. And it was Springfield, not Eastfield.

For all she knew, her sisters and brother, and her mother, too, were gone—moved away, perhaps. She'd had no contact with them for years, then one day, in New York City, she'd taken a second box at the post office under her former name. She'd gone back to her room with the idea of writing a letter in mind, and to her surprise, the task had kept her up all night. What to tell them? What to ask? What secrets to keep? And, above all, why? Why even try to affirm the tie she'd been so grateful to break?

In the end, the note she'd written had been short, only a few lines telling them that she was well and working, without specifying the kind of work she was engaged in. They could write to her, she added, at her post office box. She signed the letter *Francine Hazeltine*, and for a long time, she'd stared at the strangely unfamiliar signature.

There'd been no answer to that letter, or to the others she'd sent inquiring after her mother's health. There was no response to the cards she sent at Christmas, and on her sisters' birthdays, as best she remembered the dates. But she was always careful to affix her return address, and the clerk at the post office assured her that if the addressee had moved, the letters would either be forwarded or returned to her.

In spite of the lack of response, she had maintained the

post office box for more than a decade. It waited, an unopened and unfilled part of herself, a dark tunnel that connected her with a past far more terrifying than any of the thrillers in which she'd performed.

Had they disowned her? She wondered. Did they hate her so—after so much time? Or had they simply forgotten her? In her mind's eye, Francine saw her family like characters in a play, actors so engrossed in the scene they were playing that they were totally unaware of the audience. Was the action still the same? Had they continued in their strange way, not even aware that their lives, in the context of the world just beyond them, was off-kilter? Or had someone or something intervened?

Strangers were staring at her, Francine realized, shivering with the memories of being a curiosity piece on those long-ago excursions into the town of Eastfield. She'd been an actress even then, she thought as she continued down Main Street, a performer for the interested and amused onlookers.

*And them . . . what of them? Did Constance do the shopping now, or was it Margaret? Was her mother better, or worse, or even still alive? And Paul, Paul the damned— did he still hold them all in his spell, in the unnatural grip of superiority their father had passed to him like an inherited disease?*

"I must know," Francine said aloud.

The sensible thing, she realized, would be to tell Harry, to explain it all as best she could and have him go back with her. But if he knew of the madness, might he not be afraid of her? If she went alone, if the house were sold or burnt down, yes, *destroyed!*—she would press it no further. She'd forget it and them and be Francine Le Faye, only Francine Le Faye Johnson, for the rest of her life.

She passed Worthington Street, then Fort. Then she

crossed Main at the Paramount Theater, her eyes and feet following the dark stone arch that supported the train tracks that led to and from Union Station, such a sad and short few steps away.

# - 2 -

SHE WAS DREAMING a dream she had dreamt before, not often or recently enough so that it conformed to a regular pattern, but the sort of dream that makes such a strong impression that it is fixed forever. On recurrence, one is more aware of the differences from rather than similarities to what one thought was remembered.

It had to be a dream, Francine thought, settled against the heavy red velvet head rest of her seat in the parlor car. For this could not be the place she remembered. Perhaps Eastfield was farther than she thought—otherwise, she'd have seen the factories (so *many* factories!) when she'd stood on the other side of the Connecticut River that had fronted the house.

There'd been the river, then the woods, then River Road...a *different* River Road. It was impossible that it was the same placid road that she could see across and beyond the churning violet water. There were buildings—*what* buildings?—she wanted to know, surprised by her anger. Perhaps she'd taken the wrong train and come to a place like the place she remembered, but not the same place at all. One like it: after all, she'd traveled enough to know that so many places seem so much the same.

But, "Eastfield, Eastfield next," the conductor was calling. A man across the aisle was taking down suitcases for himself and his wife, and the train was crossing the railroad bridge over the river. "Eastfield station," the voice called again as the train slowed.

Francine closed her eyes, hoping that when she opened them again she'd be in her bed, in any bed. But when she did, the conductor was coming toward her down the aisle.

"Eastfield," he said, matter-of-factly. "Your stop."

For an instant, she panicked. How did he know? How could he? Then he walked by, and she felt between her fingers the ticket he'd punched only a few minutes before. She slipped it into her purse, laughing at herself.

*I'm being silly,* she thought. *Harry would laugh at me if he knew. He'll laugh when I tell him about it . . .*

But standing on the platform, the fleeting moment of good humor was over before the train had departed for Holyoke, farther down the line. In its place was confusion as Francine surveyed the scene before her. The quiet town she remembered was gone, replaced by something so totally different that it made her senses reel. The stores—where had they all come from? And the people—so many people!

In her memories, Eastfield had been a place so small that she couldn't walk down the streets without being recognized and stared at. But that Eastfield, the town of her childhood, was gone. In its place was a city of strangers, more of them than she remembered or might have imagined.

She was used to being watched: in that sense, she'd considered from time to time, Eastfield had prepared her for the stage. She'd anticipated, in a dark corner of her mind, having to deal with questioning glances as she made her way to the house off River Road; possibly with recognition if any of the old-timers, accustomed to the physical signs of age in familiar faces, were still around.

Not once had it occurred to her that she could, as she had, find Eastfield preoccupied with the lives of its own, or that she was no longer one of that number. For years, all the years until she'd left, she'd longed to be apart from the town, to be part of someplace else. Then, when she'd gone, her memories had tied her to Eastfield all the same, for all the distance of time and travel. Alone on the platform, watching the men and women and children go about their business around her, Francine felt the cord she'd imagined binding her vanish into the October air. It was a sensation she experienced with a mixture of relief and a vague sadness. *I am a stranger here,* she realized, thinking of all the years she'd longed for anonymity. *Now, they move around me as if I were a ghost . . .*

Like a ghost, a shadow, she moved, unobserved and unnoticed, down the once-familiar streets—Center, and Market, and Front. Had the Common shrunk, she wondered, remembering the long-ago Fourth of July when she'd sat in the reviewing stand, a frightened child, while her father spoke.

The statue of Mathew Wyndham that had been unveiled that day had seemed to dominate the Common with its gleaming newness. It had tarnished to a whitish green, and its patina gave it the illusion of blending in with the dry grass and foliage.

Across the Common, Francine's gaze went to the skyline of Eastfield. It, too, had changed. The business that had been her father's, for a time, had once been the dominant building of the town. A large sign atop the building her eyes found out of habit read EASTFIELD CASKET COMPANY, but there were bigger and newer buildings in town, factories, offices, and apartment houses that caught her eyes and held them, telephone polls and trolley tracks, street lights and alleyways that were either new or that she'd forgotten.

Without realizing it, Francine's hand went to her hair as her mother, Olivia, had touched her hair so many years before, then to the skin of her cheek. Whirling, she caught a glimpse of herself in the window of what she'd remembered as a bookstore—what *was* the name?—but was now a Kresge's Five and Ten Cent Store.

I've changed, too, she realized.

Those first years, her figure had thinned and stretched as she attained her full womanhood. She worked hard to keep it, not gorging herself and letting her body go its own way as some actresses did between engagements. The past few years in particular, sensing a natural thickening, she'd taken special pains to avoid bread and desserts. She cleansed her skin carefully after each performance so that not as much as a trace of greasepaint remained to clog her pores, and she creamed it faithfully each night, just before brushing her hair.

But, as if to spite her, a web of fine lines had woven itself around her eyes, and there was a sagging under her chin. Sleep was no longer an adequate guarantee against the puffiness that might or might not form under her eyes. And more and more often when she brushed her copper-colored hair (her "best" feature, more than one man had told her in compliment), Francine found herself plucking out the wiry random gray strands.

The changes were slow and subtle, or so it had seemed to her. So slow, in fact, that they'd lulled her into nearly ignoring the process, in spite of the vanity her profession demanded.

Standing there, at the edge of the Eastfield Common, Francine understood that the face and body she took for granted had deceived her. Her eyes filled with bitter, unexpected tears for the youth she'd been so busy escaping from and that she hadn't, until that moment, realized she'd

lost long before. She was like Eastfield, or she had been—
a thing that had been unaware of the changes taking place
within it.

Her face might as well be a street map of the town, her
features, the familiar intersections of streets. For all the
times she'd looked in her mirror with hardly more than a
detached eye, the subtle alterations had compounded one
another until her appearance was restructured, another image superimposed over the deceptive image that was more
a memory than a reflection.

Without knowing exactly why, she was overcome by a
sense of betrayal, and with it, an intense though unfocused
anger. What had she imagined? That Eastfield was some
magical place, untouched by time? That her sisters and
brother and her mother, if they were still there, had somehow managed to defy the basic laws of nature?

She forced herself to walk. Automatically, her steps took
her away from the Common, west toward the outskirts of
town and River Road. Her mind wasn't on her movements,
but on the visual images of her memories. Her mother,
Constance, Margaret, Paul . . . *no,* Francine wanted to cry!
They weren't like that at all, not any more. No matter how
hard she tried, she could picture them only as they'd been
in their youth, and in her own.

Imagination was her talent, the core of her work. Reading
a script, envisioning a character for the first time, she had
discovered a natural aptitude to form a picture in her own
mind, then to make that picture a superficial reality with
her tubes of greasepaint, her pencils and sticks and powders.
Yet for the life of her, and the love of them, such as it was,
Francine couldn't "see" the brother and sisters she'd left as
they would look as adults, any more than she could picture
her mother as an old woman.

A chilling gust of wind made her shiver: she should have

worn a cape, she told herself, as Harry had suggested when they left the hotel that morning. Or perhaps she should go back, Francine considered—not for the cape, but for the safety, the *certainty* of the hotel.

What madness, what impulse had brought her back to the very place she'd so dreaded?

Her emotions, those of the moment and those of the years that had built to it, were a whirling confusion, and they encircled her like the oak and maple leaves that blew around her feet.

Teasingly, almost purposefully so, it struck her, they brushed against her consciousness, as variegated as the foliage.

There was the dull, dead brown of the way Eastfield appeared to her in dreams and the way it looked now that she was back. She'd walked farther and farther away from the Common, noticing that the most obvious and jarring changes were those closest to town. Away from the clustered buildings, her disorientation had given way to moments of melancholia. Instead of feeling as if she'd come back to Eastfield for a short visit, it was as if she'd never left. She felt like the girl she'd been instead of the woman she'd become; a girl frightened of being sentenced, forever, to a doomed existence in an eternally autumnal place.

Her step slowed as she retraced the route that had fixed itself into the fiber of her subconscious so many years before. She wasn't Francine Le Faye, come back on a lark for a family visit, but Francine Hazeltine, who hated both the trips into town and the home they took her from and led back to.

*I should have hired a taxi,* she told herself. She'd walked the route often enough when she had to: there'd been cars at the station, and in town. It was foolish to make the journey by foot, by herself.

"I'll call one to take me back to the station from home," Francine said aloud. Then, "from the *house...their house,*" correcting herself.

For they had to have a telephone, didn't they? Why hadn't she asked the operator for the number, why hadn't she called instead of visiting?

She was out of Eastfield proper now, the town behind her. But what was ahead, past or future or both, she didn't know—only that she had come too far to turn back.

## - 3 -

RIVER ROAD—the River Road she remembered—was gone. The weathered surface, the packed dirt that had frozen in the winter cold and been topped with a fine layer of dust in the summer months, had been paved. Instead of the single lane she remembered, there were two lanes now, a white stripe dividing the traffic.

And the traffic! So *much* of it!

There was no possibility of making her way down the center of the road as she'd done when she was a girl, stepping aside at the distant, occasional sound of a carriage or horse and rider. Coupes, sedans, and trucks passed in either direction, almost in nonstop succession. No sidewalk had been laid, but there was a curb, and in widening the road, the trees and heavy brush closest to it had been cleared.

Once, years before, when she was appearing in a drawing-room comedy that had toured the Midwest for several months, Francine had played her part in spite of a cold complicated by a fever. An understanding doctor, summoned by the theater manager in Chicago, had given her some lozenges that had allowed her to overcome her hoarseness, but the combination of the medication and her temperature had made her feel giddy and strange. When she

stepped on stage, she'd had the sensation of having wandered onto a set that had been altered. The props had seemed
misplaced; the lines, so familiar, struck her ear as strange.

The memory of that feeling came back as Francine
walked along the edge of the road.

There was the river itself as a bearing. There were trees
and the same autumnal smell in the air.

But River Road had been out of town, a thoroughfare
that led to or from Eastfield. Hadn't privacy been her
father's compulsion? He'd purposely chosen land away from
town for his house.

In the years since she'd been gone, Eastfield had spilled
out of itself. On the side that followed the line of the Connecticut River, the land looked much as she remembered
it, the willow and oak and brush and the gentle slope of the
ground down to the rushing water. But on the other side,
the side she walked along, it was different, all so different.
There were houses here, small saltbox affairs for the most
part, and clusters of them in some places. What had been
a solid stretch of thick, wild wood that had run from the
outskirts of town to the house that had been her home was
now interrupted by occasional streets that ran at right
angles from River Road.

Standing at these new corners, Francine's eyes searched
the streets and the houses that dotted them. Dogs ran in
yards; wash hung from clotheslines. What did the people
who lived in these places know of her family? she wondered.
She could ask of course, simply present herself at a door
and introduce herself as someone who had once lived in the
town and was seeking to renew an old acquaintance. Did
they know, by chance, a family called the Hazeltines? She
could sound casual, asking for directions—

ROADHOUSE MOTOR COURT

Francine's body stiffened as she hurried by the squat,

ugly building and the cluster of bungalows behind it. Whatever else they had been or might have become, the Hazeltines had been the most prominent family in Eastfield. The surge of pride surprised her, and she felt affronted. What would people in a place like *that* know of her family? Certainly, the Hazeltines, whatever their fate, hadn't been reduced to mingling with their new, no-doubt unwelcome, neighbors.

Quickening her pace, Francine saw that the intrusion of new buildings tapered off. Farther down River Road, they were few, then there were none at all. The traffic, of course, was as heavy as it had been nearer to town, but that, in view of things, was to be expected. She moved farther from the curb, as close to the trees as she could, collecting herself and trying to compose herself.

Her hand went to her stomach, pressing against the hard ball of fear. Ridiculous, she told herself—this was no different from the feeling that occasionally took hold of her before she stepped on stage, and it was even less justified. This time there weren't even lines to be raced through in her mind, no mistakes or missed cues to be anxious about.

They were her *family* after all—her brother, her sisters, her mother. What was the use of trying to compose, in advance, the words she'd say if they were at home . . . if they were even living in the house after all these years? She rejected the explanations and apologies that swirled through her mind. She was a woman, a grown woman!

Perhaps the family had been angry when she left without warning or word, but they'd be happy to see her, to welcome her for a visit. And, too, they'd be more surprised than she, having no idea that she was coming. It would be pleasant, a pleasant visit, Francine told herself, thinking of herself as if she were a character in a play.

There was nothing to apologize for—she'd made her

own life, and a different one from theirs. What harm or fault could they find? What cause for judgment?

"I should have brought them presents," she said to herself. But no matter: she could send them something from one of the stores in Springfield. She'd shop for it the next day. Perhaps she'd go back to the little yarn shop and buy some wool to make them each a sweater or a scarf after she'd seen their sizes—

She stopped suddenly, aware that she'd come to the place where the Way led from River Road to the house. Or at least she *thought* it was the place. The single tin mailbox, mounted on a post, hadn't been there—they'd collected their mail in Eastfield, at the post office, back then. The Way itself seemed different. Had it been that narrow all the while? Had the birch and oak leaned so markedly toward one another over the dirt path, as if their upper branches were hands reaching for one another? There were spots, Francine saw, where they met. The leaves that were left and the bare branches themselves were intertwined so that the Way took on the appearance of a dark tunnel. Only here and there could one glimpse the clouded gray sky.

Maybe, she considered, she should open the mailbox. No name was written on it—perhaps there'd be a letter, an envelope with the name of whoever it was who lived in the house now. She'd feel foolish, certainly, going to the door if it had been sold.

A low, sudden wind flicked the leaves around her feet, and Francine turned with it, toward the road. *Someone is watching me,* she thought, her eyes darting around her. But there was no one and nothing nearby, only the ribbons of cars on River Road and the woods and brush that led to the river on the other side.

"I must look the fool!" she said aloud, calming herself, even if none of the drivers or passengers in the automobiles noticed her. And what could be more embarrassing than if someone were to come along, observing a stranger at his mailbox. If her family had moved, she'd best find out the simplest way, and besides, she'd come so far to see the house again.

The Way had not been cleared in a straight line, but at an angle from River Road. After only a few steps, the sound of the traffic faded. Several yards later, the Way had become a world unto and of itself, detached from the road and the town and, in its manner, even time.

The wind seemed to race forward and back, as if trapped. One moment Francine felt it forcefully propelling her forward. The next, it was like a physical power she had to struggle against. It didn't whistle or sing, but seemed rather to moan at a variety of animal-like pitches, punctuated by the clatter of the trees. Like a caged creature, she thought, battling against its confinement. Or, having long since accepted confinement as a condition of its existence, reacting to the sudden presence of an intruder.

"I belong *here*," a voice inside her said. "I *did* belong here, once..."

She hurried, eager to be through the Way, anxious for the remembered sight of the hedges and lawn and the prized flowers her mother had loved so. Like an unseen stranger, the wind tugged at her sleeve as she neared the end of the Way, holding her back. She was breathless as she emerged from the narrow path. A vine, hidden in the fallen leaves, caught her foot, Francine stumbled with a stab of pain; then pain was replaced by fear.

If the Way had seemed dark and confining from River Road, from this view it looked like a funnel. She was at the widest end, and could barely see the dot of light at its entrance. *The time and the light,* she reminded herself. They were playing tricks on her.

Rubbing her ankle, catching her breath, she turned at last to the view etched so strongly on her memory. Her eyes blinked, then closed for a long moment before reopening.

"Oh . . . oh, my," she whispered as the wind caught a strand of her hair that had come loose, lashing it into her eye.

She flicked it away, and her vision was obscured again, this time by tears as she absorbed the shock of the sight before her.

The formal hedge, once so perfectly cut and trimmed, so uniformly evergreen, had grown unchecked. Menacing, spiky branches extended like arms, as if the hedge was a series of guards, pushing visitors away from the house itself. It no longer was topped by an even, ordered line, but had been left to grow its own way, nine feet tall in some places, thick rather than tall in others. There were spots, too, in which some blight had been given full rage and reign. Here, the hedge's green had given way to a sickly yellowish brown. There were patches—holes, really—where there were no leaves at all, only a thorny web of brittle, dead twigs.

These spaces were like windows, and Francine's gaze was reluctantly drawn to them.

The hedge presaged what could be seen through it; the rest of the grounds, and the house itself, had fallen into neglect. Something worse than neglect, she thought, for the combination of nature and disregard would have made for a prettier picture. What Francine saw through the hedge, a window in her memory, was ugly—so ugly that it struck her as violent and deliberate.

Where Olivia, her mother, had so carefully tended her roses, low, dark weeds spewed in strangling configuration. There was something about their solid, impenetrable mass that held her eye, and she shivered as she recognized it. It

wasn't possible, she told herself, it couldn't be...yet the
snarl of brush, from the angle at which she stood, seemed
to have grown of its own accord into the shape of a single,
giant blossom as if to mock her memory.

But her eyes didn't linger long.

The lawn had once been painstakingly manicured, the
grass soft and cut, the weeds pulled from the edge of the
fountains and sundial. Even as a girl, when she'd thought
the house a prison, she'd been able to find some pleasure
in looking out the window or in walking around the grounds.
But care and order had long since been lost. Francine heard
her father's voice echo in her mind, reading aloud the Latin
names from the botany books in his study.

The rare, the beautiful, the cultivated was gone from all
but the images in her memory; there was no lawn now at
all, but a parched and dried patchwork of wild grass and
weeds that had flourished in the warmer months...in *years*
of warmer months, Francine thought. The fountain and sundial were all but obscured, overgrown by strangling vines.
The stone paths were cracked where they could be seen at
all: something small and dark scurried along one of them,
just ten feet in front of her, and she turned her eyes away,
startled and frightened.

*It's only a squirrel or a chipmunk,* logic told her, but
Francine trembled from her vantage point, unable to look.
Was it the animal she didn't want to see, she wondered, or
the house itself? It was there, still standing, but she'd focused on the yard, or what was left of it and what it had
become.

*"Run!"* a voice inside her cried. *"Go back!"* it pleaded.

But she had come far, so very far to turn around now.
Something more stirring than fear or revulsion made her
force her eyes open. Something she didn't fully understand
and couldn't define or explain, even to herself, but which

she knew she had to complete now or else be haunted by for the rest of her days.

Trying to steady herself, trying to think of the beads of perspiration on her face and the trembling in her limbs as a kind of stagefright, Francine concentrated all her strength.

"The house...how could they?" she whispered, her eyes burning now.

The line of demarcation between the land and what was built on it had long since disappeared. The house, once so striking that visitors had traveled from Springfield, from Pittsfield, and even farther for just a glimpse of it from River Road, appeared to have grown out of the ground, or the ground was growing over it. Thick vines curled and twisted their way up along the façade, winding over windows where they met other vines that grew from the roof.

The limbs of those trees nearest the house were fat and gnarled, and close upon the house now, as if reaching for it.

The wind whistled, and something ran nearby, but Francine continued to make her way forward. Dried oak and maple leaves swirled around her, so brittle that their points and stems cut her legs. Her eyes were fixed on the front door, on a point above the ornate knob that had once been polished and gleaming brass but was now covered with streaked, sickly green tarnish. Her eyes ignored the paint that was rolling off, it's curved edge now a landscape of blisters and shards.

Instead, she focused on the small pane of stained glass, remembering the way the foyer had been filled with the wondrous blue and red light that had poured through it when the sun shone.

"Oh dear," she said when she was at the door at last, close enough to see that the pane had cracked. It was so covered now with dirt and dust that the colors could no longer be distinguished. Light, she knew, would no longer shine through it, no matter how bright the sun.

Her hand trembled violently as she raised it to knock. Francine found it impossible to master her body. Her right arm shook from side to side instead of forward and back; her tightly clenched hand was a numb ball rather than the fist she'd tried to make. With her left hand, she clutched her right wrist, not frightened any longer, but horrified.

Was it a force, as strange an evil as the place she had come to, that kept her arm from moving forward to knock on the door to her past? Was it something else that made her body fail her?

There was only a moment in which to consider these and other questions, then the moment passed and the door, ever so slowly, began to open without Francine's having knocked at all.

# - 4 -

IT WAS ONLY the wind, she thought. Perhaps the house was deserted after all. She wasn't going out of her mind, Francine observed, letting her arm fall. The door *had* opened, if only a crack at first. It groaned and creaked. Her nostrils were assaulted by a gust of something for which she was totally unprepared. She'd remembered the smell of the house as a combination of cut flowers and lemon oil and the scent of her mother's perfume. Instead, she was struck by a mixture of mustiness and something more raw.

She tried to speak, but her throat was dry and her lips parched. For a time, it was all that she could do to stare into the darkened sliver of foyer, trying to make her eyes adjust.

"It's me," she managed to say at last, hoping that her high-pitched nervousness would pass for gaiety. "It's Francine, come back to visit . . ."

There was a noise (footsteps? human, or those of a pet?) beyond the door. Standing across the threshold, Francine thought she saw a pair of eyes in the darkness.

"Mother?" she whispered, her heart pounding.

"Mother!" Another woman's voice, more girlish, repeated, following the word with laughter. Someone else giggled.

"Margaret?" Francine asked in a last, desperate hope. "Constance? It's me. It's your sister—"

There was a low, hurried exchange, and she strained to catch it.

"But he said she was with *them*—"

"I told you!"

"He'll be mad if you let her in. He'll get you—"

"But she's not a stranger—"

"She's not one of us."

"No..."

Francine Hazeltine Le Faye cleared her throat. "Perhaps... perhaps I've come at an inconvenient time," she offered, anxious to be in or out and have it done with. Suddenly the door was opened wide, and two figures stood before her.

The two birdlike women stood close together, as if they weren't separate individuals at all, but rather parts of a single whole. Their hair was equally brown and long, and they both wore it in the braids Francine remembered. *Yes,* she thought. Those were Constance's eyes, blue like Father's. And Margaret's mouth, the lips duplicating the curve of Olivia's and her own.

"Please," she begged them, not certain at all of what it was she wanted. She was no longer the actress, the worldly woman so sure of herself, but a sister again, a girl left out of a game.

"He said you were with them," the woman on the right stated.

"Constance?" Francine asked. Awkwardly, she reached for the thin figure. It was limp in her arms, unresponsive to her embrace. Her other sister reacted the same way.

"He said you went away."

"I—I did. But I came back to see you. Won't you let me in, just for a little while?"

The two sisters exchanged a look, then stepped back.

Francine crossed into the house as if stepping into a dream. "Is he . . . is *our* brother here?" she asked. Her sisters glanced at one another, then back to her, shaking their heads. The door was shut, and the world beyond it locked out. She felt a mixture of relief that Paul wasn't home, and the strangeness of having gone so far and come back.

"The town is so different," she said, trying to make conversation.

"We're different," Margaret answered.

"We always were," Constance added.

Francine heard the words, and with them the dimly remembered echo of her father's voice, and her brother's. "Of course," she agreed.

"We don't mix with *them*," Margaret said. Her inflection was that of a child, parroting an adult disdain she didn't understand.

"No, I suppose not," Francine said.

Her sisters had made no move to invite her in, to direct her to a particular chair or room. When she took a step, their bodies moved with her in unison. She pressed forward, staring into the dining room at her left. The china cabinet, the buffet, the table—even the Belgian lace cloth! It was stained and tattered, and the rich wood no longer gleamed but was nicked and scratched, dulled by years of neglect. She wanted to cry.

"I—I didn't know if you'd be living here still," she told them.

"But where would we be?" one of them asked as Francine's eyes drank in the familiar pattern of the carpet, worn and faded though it was.

"Then you're here? All of you? Mother?"

"Oh, she's gone," Constance said lightly.

"Gone?"

"Away. To be with Father."

Both her sisters, Francine realized, were dressed in white. The dresses were plain, a heavy muslin, but the simple cloth was cut and sewn into the full-sleeved, long-skirted style her mother had always worn.

"Could we...could I sit down, please?" she asked. Blindly, she made her way into the front parlor where she'd last seen her mother so many years before.

She fell into a chair rather than taking one; her sisters arranged themselves side by side, so close that their bodies touched as they centered themselves on a sofa. Clutching the arm of her chair, Francine felt the threadbare armrest. The cut velvet was so faded it was no longer possible to tell what color it had been. *Green,* she thought. Padding that had once been white poked out of it.

The room was familiar, but different, too. The furnishings hadn't been moved or changed, but neither had they been tended or protected. The once-prominent pattern of the flocked wallpaper could no longer be distinguished. In her mind's eye, Francine could see it as it had been—the room flooded with light that fell on the ivory keys of the piano. Now, it was hard to be sure where the window, overgrown on the outside and not cleaned from within, was. The piano keys were yellowed, like old teeth or fingernails, she thought. Of course it all couldn't have stayed the same, but still...

"When did Mother—go away?" she asked.

The sisters seemed puzzled.

"Was it a long time ago?" Francine prodded.

"A while back," Constance began.

"After you left," Margaret concluded.

"Were you angry with me for leaving?" She avoided their eyes as she softly asked the question, but their laughter called her gaze back to them.

"Why would we be?" Margaret asked.

"We have him, after all," her sister added.

Francine's fingers nervously knotted and unknotted in her lap. "I thought you might have been angry with me for not taking you when I left," she explained.

"But why would *we* leave?" Constance asked in dismay.

"This is our home!" Margaret answered.

Nothing has changed, Francine thought. Nothing, and everything. "But you do leave sometimes, don't you? You must go into town—"

"We don't mix with *them*," Constance reiterated. "We have everything here that we need."

"What would we want to go there for?"

"Well... for friends," Francine suggested to Margaret. "To visit companions."

"We have each other—"

"—and that's all we need. The two of us, and him."

"How—how is our brother?" Francine asked.

"The same," Constance answered.

"But he's not at home now, you say? Is he away on business?"

Again her sisters laughed, as if she'd told them a hilarious joke.

"What sort of business would he have—"

"—to take him away from here?"

"From us?"

Francine tried to explain herself. "I only thought that perhaps... well, that Paul had a business of some kind. After all, you need money to buy things—"

"We don't need to buy very much," Constance told her.

"Things grow. We put them by for winter..."

"And there's him, for the meat and the fish," Margaret added.

"But surely you must need to buy *some* things now and then?"

"There's the picture books," Constance told her.

"Books?"

Sighing, the younger woman stood and pulled a Sears Roebuck catalogue from under the sofa.

"But there are stores in Eastfield," Francine suggested. "New ones. So many of them!"

"They don't like us in Eastfield," Constance began, but a look from Margaret silenced her.

"It's us who don't like *them,*" she corrected her sister.

At that moment, Francine was touched by a deep, profound sorrow. *"I want to go with you!"* Constance had whined that afternoon, so long ago yet so suddenly fresh in her memory, when they'd been together for the last time. But Constance and Margaret, too, had been left behind. In taking her only chance, Francine thought, her heart heavy, she'd robbed them of theirs, condemning them to the life she'd feared for herself.

She'd hoped that somehow they might have been able to break away, to make lives of their own with at least a semblance of normalcy about them. But seeing that her sisters weren't really women at all but the girls they'd been when she left, Francine was filled with guilt. There was no way to change it; no will to change it. They had absorbed or inherited their father's exaggerated sense of superiority, and with it the underlying fear.

*Their father,* Francine thought. In seeking to distinguish himself and his, he'd marked them all in his way.

In wanting to give his family everything, he'd taken away the simple pleasures of human contact.

"Why do you dislike the town?" she asked gently.

"Father says!" Constance answered.

"You can't remember Father. You were too young!"

*"He* says," she insisted.

"Paul," Margaret amplified.

"But he's our *brother,* not our father—"

"He's the man," Margaret said simply, as though that ended it all. "The man is head of the house." She spoke without emotion, as if the words were an accepted statement of fact.

"No," Francine insisted, her emotions rising. "It doesn't have to be that way. Women...men—it doesn't matter. You can live your own lives—"

"But we do—"

"You could be happy," she said, her voice quivering as she tried to explain it all to them, to make up for the gulf of years and experience in a few short minutes. "There are friends. All kinds of people—"

"They laugh," Constance insisted.

Francine leaned forward, grabbing a sister's hand in each of hers.

"Not all people. There's the whole world, beyond East-field. It's different, Constance, and not at all like you think, Margaret. People—other people—have their secrets, too. They let you have yours and accept you in spite of them. For them, even—"

"But we are Hazeltines!" Margaret insisted, regally.

Francine remembered the walk from the train station to the house, the same walk she'd taken so often so many years earlier. The steps hadn't changed, but her bearing had.

"It's only a name," she tried to explain. "Once—when I was a very little girl and Father had the Buggy Works and his dreams of automobiles, it was a blessing, I suppose. We were the first family of Eastfield then, to be sure. And Father didn't let anyone forget it, either. Oh no! Paul Hazeltine was their savior and their future, and he wasn't about to mix with them or let them near his wife and children!

"He—he meant well, I suppose. Certainly he didn't mean us any harm," her words fell into a long sigh. "You

don't remember it, do you? Of course, you were too young!
But *I* can remember. I can see him on the platform that
Fourth of July, making his speech, making his promises.
They were afraid of him then. Afraid not to give him the
respect he demanded. But then...then the automobiles
didn't work out. Something happened.

"I don't know what it was, but everything changed.
Mother was pregnant, then she was sick. And Father, so
remote in that study of his, locked away from us all. Paul—
our *brother*, Paul—took on Father's ways. Mother let him.
She encouraged it, really, though I don't think she realized
it. The Works were lost...sold, I believe, and still we
stayed away. The people in town—well, Father had never
had friends, or let Mother make any of her own. And we
were told to keep to each other, all to ourselves!"

She was animated now, out of her chair, pacing in front
of the two seated women as she spoke.

The agony of the jeering stares she'd endured began to
seep through scars Francine had thought long since healed.
"They'd more than stare at us after that! They'd point and
whisper, and without Father's money, without the position
we once had...we weren't special any more. Or better.
Just—just different, do you see?"

She turned to them, entreating them to understand her,
or at least to try.

"*That's* why I left," Francine confessed, tears of her guilt
and for the lives she'd left them with filling her eyes and
choking her words. "I had to! I wasn't leaving the two of
you, or Mother, or Paul, even. You must understand that!
I didn't do it to you. I did it for me.

"It was—I was scared. I'd been afraid to stay here, and
once I left, I didn't know what to do. How to make my
life."

She paused, breathless, her body compressed with the

passion of the words that had waited so long to be spoken aloud.

"I was afraid for you, too. I used to wonder what was happening to you. I—I thought about coming back several times, but I didn't because I thought that I might not be able to leave again. I wrote to you. Cards, letters. I told you that I was on the stage, I'm an actress you know—in plays. You never answered. Did you . . . did you get my letters?"

They looked at her blankly.

"I—made a life for myself," she said, trying to reach them. It was like being on stage, like trying to capture an audience. Francine opened her bag and brought out a post-card-sized photograph of herself and Harry Johnson.

"That's me and Harry. My gentleman friend. He wants me to marry him. We're in Springfield now, at the Court Square Theater . . . well, the Bridgeway Hotel, of course.

"I made a life, do you see? A life of my own. I even changed my name—"

"Why?" Margaret asked her.

"We have a fine name!" Constance added.

"Yes—yes, of course," Francine agreed, eager to make and keep the fragile peace. "But I was young. A girl, still. And there were things I didn't know. It was a way to change myself and my life. You can do that in the world, you know.

"Oh, I wish you could see me on the stage!" she said. "I don't have the biggest parts, but I've had some lovely roles in my time. The costumes, the makeup . . . the lights and the applause. It's fun, really. Sometimes it doesn't even seem fair to get paid for it, I enjoy it so much. Of course there's the traveling, all the different cities and the trains and the hotels and that, but still . . .

"It's like when we were children together, do you remember? When we'd play? And people—the men who write the reviews—they say I'm quite good. They think

I'm pretty. One review—I have it in my bag—even said I was beautiful. Of course it was some years back. 'Her loveliest feature is her hair,' it said. It's hard to tell now, with it pinned up this way—" She touched her hair, then laughed, as much out of nervousness as anything else. On a whim, she pulled the pins out.

Like burnished copper, her long hair fell, cascading past her shoulders. "See?" she asked Constance and Margaret. "It's like Mother's hair, don't you think?"

She looked to them for some response, and for an instant their smiles were reassuring. Then Francine noticed something about those smiles that made her wonder, a quality she remembered from her own childhood as being indicative of sharing a private, unspoken joke. Her sisters eyes, she saw, weren't really watching her at all, but were fixed on a corner of the room behind her.

"What is it?" she asked them.

She waited for an answer, but none came.

It was then that Francine slowly turned, her eyes widening at the sight of the towering man who had silently come in without her knowing it, and who had been listening to her for how long she did not know. His cold blue eyes and the set of his features were so much like her father's that Francine felt she was looking at a ghost.

But the smile, so cruel and so evil, was one she remembered well.

And as her brother began to laugh, his sisters joining him, Francine began to tremble.

*Calm, calm, CALM,* she forced herself to think. Still, the word, like the laughter of her brother and sisters, rose to a deafening crescendo in her mind.

"You—you surprised me," Francine said at last, the words catching in her throat.

As suddenly as it had began, Paul's laughter stopped, and his sisters' ceased along with his.

"Did you think I'd be gone away, too?" he asked, accusing her. "Same as you?"

There was no reason to blush, Francine thought, no reason for her to feel ashamed. But the color rose in her cheeks as if she were a guilty child, and his undisguised contempt a punishment she had no choice but to accept.

"No," she answered softly. "I knew you'd stay. I never would have left if I hadn't known that you'd be here—" It was all she wanted to say, but he was waiting for more. "To look out for things," she added.

"It's us who should be surprised," Paul said.

"Yes, I suppose so," she agreed. The room and her heightened emotions had made her feel warm, but with Paul's appearance, that had changed. Francine felt cold, almost frozen. "How—how have you been?" she asked to fill the silence.

"Same."

The silence was back, heavier than before.

"Mother...she passed away?" Francine asked. "When was it, Paul? How?"

"She's not gone," he said.

For an instant, Francine felt her heart leap. She looked up, aware of the second story of the house. But it wasn't possible, she knew. Her mother had been sick when she left, well into her decline.

"She's with Father," Margaret said.

"Not gone. Just gone away with Father," Constance added.

"I see," Francine told them, though she didn't exactly. Then, without wanting to and without being able to stop herself, she was crying, sobbing. She wept for Olivia, for her sisters and the lives they had, and the lives they all might have had, even Paul. "I'm—sorry—"

"Get her some tea," Paul told his sisters. He took Francine's arm, easing her to the sofa. He made no move to comfort her as she cried, nor did he sit beside her. Instead, he took the chair where she'd been sitting before, watching her as if she were some strange creature, a specimen.

"If I could have something of Mother's," Francine asked through her tears. "Some little thing, for remembrance sake before I leave—"

"You will," Paul promised her. Constance and Margaret returned, carrying a cup of tea, setting it before their sister.

"Thank you," she told them, her hand shaking as she reached for it. The tiny pattern of the floral china, the old breakfast set, brought a new wave of emotion. She swallowed the hot liquid in big gulps to keep from another outburst. "What time is it?" she asked at last.

Paul looked at her blankly. "Don't keep a clock."

"There's no need," Margaret explained.

"We have no place to go," Constance added.

Francine finished the tea and set the cup down. "I have to be getting back soon," she said. "I can't miss my train."

She rose, but was overcome by dizziness. Her head felt ever so light, and at the same time, so heavy. The room began to turn, slowly and then faster.

"You wanted something of Mother's," Paul said. His words sounded as if they were coming from a great distance. His face, his malevolent smile, were larger than life. "So now you have her favorite. Her medicine."

*The tea! The same tea Olivia had taken with her drops!*

"No!" Francine wailed.

If they heard her cry, it had no effect. The sound was lost in the laughter as they danced around her, their hands joined in a circle. Then, as the sound grew and the movement around her sped faster and faster, as she felt her jacket being torn away, Francine tried to scream again.

When a sharp blow to the side of her head knocked her into unconsciousness, it was an act of mercy . . . of a kind.

Tossing, turning, she tried to wake herself, but she couldn't. The dream, the nightmare, held her like a tormenting captor, allowing her to realize that it wasn't really happening, but keeping her just the other side of wakefulness that could have released her from sleep. It wasn't happening, not really. Francine knew. In another minute, in just a moment or two, she'd wake to the sound of her own breathing, in a hotel room that was as familiar as any and all of them. Harry Johnson would be sleeping beside her, or perhaps even awake already, lifting her, holding her, rescuing her from the nightmare.

That would come later, but for now she was in another room, a room that was both strange and familiar. The darkness played tricks on her, giving her an uncertain sense of her bearings. There was an old-fashioned oil lamp turned down low, and it threw distorted, eerie shadows on the walls.

There were objects—a chair, a dresser—that she vaguely recognized, but everything was upside down. It was her mother's bedroom, she realized, far more vivid in detail than she remembered it when she was awake. Perhaps, Francine considered, she'd dreamed of it before, but had forgotten it when she woke. This time, she'd make it a point to remember.

Not that the details, as real as they seemed, were accurate: dolls and toys—her mother would never have let her sisters and her brother bring them into her room, much less strew them all about. Olivia Hazeltine had, above all, set great store in the importance of appearances. She'd have scolded Brigid for the heavy balls of dust beneath the bed, for the nicks and scratches on the heavy furniture that looked, even in the semidarkness of the room, as if it hadn't seen oil or polish for ages.

The angle from which she was looking at the room made no sense, it occurred to Francine. She could see the rug, stained and worn now; the sagging of the mattress and the broken springs poking out beneath it.

She was on the floor! How strange! How *very* strange, though she was aware enough to know that dreams often made little sense.

*"There's no use in fighting—"*

Who had said that? Someone in another dream, perhaps Francine thought as she tried to stand up. The simple movement brought a wave of sharp and searing pain. Her head hurt, and her breasts, and her back as well.

"...No use..."

It was part of an earlier, uglier dream, and the jarring hurt brought it racing back. She could feel the constricting pain around her neck as a hand, big and dirty and calloused, grabbed the collar of her blouse and clutched at it. The air was drawn from her lungs, and she struck out in blind panic.

Then her blouse was being ripped, torn away from her. Something—that hand, that *same* hand—was striking her. Someone was hurting her. There were other people nearby. She tried to make them notice, make them help her, but they only laughed. They were women, two women, but they were no different from the man. They were with him, against her.

He grabbed for her again, pulling at her skirt this time, and their eyes danced in the dim and sickly light. *It's a dream, a dream,* she knew, even then, but the pain felt so real, and the shadows the lamp threw on the walls were terrifying.

Again he tried to clutch at her, but this time she was more awake, able to pull her body back and away from him, to the opposite side and end of the bed. Even before she had time to think about being safe, even for a moment, the two women had come from behind the man, one positioning herself at the foot of the bed and the other coming around to the side near the window. Their movements were sudden and instinctive: wordlessly they'd gone from being observers of what the man did to being partners of his, knowing what to do as animals might, hunting in a pack.

With a strength her size said she shouldn't, *couldn't* possess, one of the women—the smaller of the two, though they were nearly the same size—thrust her arms forward, pitching Francine back to the man.

The three laughed again, the sound mounting as she cowered and begged them to stop.

Then, at some unspoken signal, they were reaching and pushing her from one to the other as she twisted on the bed. One woman grabbing at her stockings, twisting and pulling them till they tore away . . . the man tearing off her underclothes.

Her nakedness shamed her and amused them. She could no longer speak, not that she believed speech could help her. Desperately, pathetically she tried to cover herself, to close her body and her eyes. When some time had passed, a deceptive moment of time just long enough to let her breathing slow ever so slightly, to let Francine believe that perhaps she could open her eyes now and find the dream finished, they'd been there, the three of them, smiling at her and one another with satisfaction.

They began reaching for her, the man first, grabbing her

breast. She cried out as his fingers, with the nails jagged and broken, pinched her nipple. Her fist flew out at the same moment her body turned. She heard rather than saw it connect with him—his chest? his face?—then she felt him strike back, harder than she could have ever hoped to hit. Like rain the blows fell on her back and shoulders.

*"No use in fighting . . ."*

Whether he said it or she'd simply known it, it hadn't made any difference; whether she had realized that or not wouldn't have changed it. There were three of them, but they moved as if they shared a single will, as if they followed a common plan they had laid out well ahead of time.

They'd turned her over again, none of them speaking or needing to, and she had decided out of instinct for her own survival rather than reasoning that she would not fight them and see what that brought her. The man, though, wanted to see her resist, no matter how futile the effort. His hands wrapped around her breasts, his fingers squeezing harder and harder until she could no longer endure it.

The cry that had surged from her, filling the room, had been deafening, but none of them reacted as if it had been heard at all. The man's fingers dug into her soft flesh, bruising and hurting her. Each of the women grabbed one of her arms, holding them out to either side of the bed.

There was a sensation of relief when at last he let her breasts go, but it was fleeting. His eyes, she saw, were set lower on her body. She wrapped one leg around the other, and for some reason she found herself thinking of a small crucifix she'd seen somewhere—*somewhere in a room near this one! in another dream!*—years before.

Only a moment to remember it, and no time to think about the memory at all. His hands were on her chest, his nails raking her skin. They moved slowly, very slowly, toward her belly, leaving white furrows in her flesh. As the color returned to them, fine lines erupted with drops of her own blood. She struggled to free one arm, then the other, then both together, but it was useless. The two women only tightened their grip, cutting off her circulation.

"...*No!*"

Whatever happened, whatever he tried to do to her, she would keep her legs locked. Struggling against him, against all of them, she swore it to herself. She tried to center her full strength between her waist and her knees, willing her muscles to obey her.

But her thigh, though tensed, trembled when he touched it: she knew then that it was hopeless, as useless as the choked sobs that racked her.

He grabbed her legs, lifting and parting them as if they were twigs, matchsticks. Then, tired of toying with her, his hand rushed up, the shock of the defiling blow followed at once by the shock of his fingers inside her. They dug and scratched at her. When she tried to contract her muscles, to force him out, it only hurt her more.

The women's laughter and her own shame rang in her head. Francine closed her eyes. *It's only a dream*, she reminded herself. If she closed her eyes, tried to imagine something else, perhaps the dream would change.

*Harry* . . . maybe she could change it around, dream that it was Harry inside of her.

For a few seconds she tried, but the pain was too sharp and intense, the nightmare too commanding.

Her arms were numb. Her shoulders ached as the women twisted the limbs they held.

The man was still clawing at her relentlessly. When she could finally stand no more, just when a wave of blackness pitched toward her, Francine felt him stop. She wanted it all to be over, but was afraid to let herself believe that it might be. Eyelids clenched, she tested her legs ever so slightly. They seemed to be free.

There was a heavy step, then another. A sinking on one edge of the bed and movement, then several heavy thuds. For a brief instant, she indulged in the luxury of letting herself think it might be over. *Yes, yes! They were letting her arms go...in another few moments, she'd be able to open her eyes and the dream would be over, gone...*

She tried to calm herself, to catch her breath, to lay perfectly, unmovingly still and silent—

There was no warning before she felt something being forced down, over her face. They were going to smother her, Francine thought, gasping for air. It was dank and acrid. She tried to push the thing away and opened her eyes. She couldn't see the man's face, but could see his arm and hear him laughing as he held a worn, mudcaked boot, pressing so that the top of it cut into her flesh. The other women were undressing. They laughed as she struggled, helplessly and hopelessly, against the man.

Finally, he took the boot away, grabbing at her, pulling her until she was no longer in the center of the bed, but at its edge. With her heart pounding—it would leap out of her chest, through her ribs in another moment, she was certain—Francine trembled as the two naked women climbed beside her.

They began to caress themselves and each other, then they touched her, as if trying to determine whether she was of their kind. The man looked on, approving, an animal enjoying the sport of his young. The women were pinching her, stroking her. She'd wanted to die, to spoil their demented pleasure. But she hadn't considered that part of her body that was separate from her mind, independent of her will and wish.

Her eyes, open wide, looked up into the face of the man, her tormentor. The set of his features was a mixture of cruelty and pleasure, but beyond that, there was something she recognized. *The eyes* . . . they were her father's eyes! She couldn't stop the scream, or the frantic gasp for air.

The man only stared down at her with contempt. "Stupid," he said, spitting the word and his saliva at her. "You always were stupid, you know."

It was then that the dream had left her, or that she'd fallen out of it into darkness.

Another dream had followed. A hairbrush, of all things! Next to her, level with her head. What it could be doing there, she had no idea, but it held her attention.

It wasn't just any brush, a part of her mind told Francine. It was something special, familiar to her. Her eyes burrowed into the dark brown bristles, into the long strands of hair matted and coiled within them, then moved down to the ornate handle, the thick and heavy silver. She was surprised to discover that she knew the design. There was no need to trace the flowers that wound their way around the handle or to follow the fold of the leaves.

*My mother's brush,* she realized suddenly. It was part of the vanity set that Olivia Hazeltine had cherished, the brush and comb and hand mirror she'd used each night and morning, carefully setting them back in their precise positions on the marble top of her vanity table. She hadn't thought of it in years, all the years since she'd left the house, but there it was, so vivid she could almost reach out and touch it. Odd, and odder still to be so aware of her dreams, to know that she was only dreaming.

A hand reached for the brush, a woman's hand. Someone was brushing her hair, gently and tenderly, Francine tried to make her eyes work, but it took so much effort. She felt as if life was moving in slow motion.

Without the strength to speak, she tried to smile her thanks at the woman who was brushing her hair for her. The woman was naked, but somehow that came as no surprise. There was something about her features that was comfortingly familiar.

"Mother?" Francine asked in a hoarse whisper. Her throat was sore, and her mouth. Her body ached, but the pain was far away, or she from it.

The woman smiled. It wasn't her mother, as she'd thought at first, though the woman had the same high cheekbones and the same pale, alabaster skin. *My sister,* Francine thought.

"I've been thinking of you. Of the two of you, and Mother," she said. But the woman didn't respond, only continued brushing.

Because it was a dream, Francine decided that she hadn't spoken aloud. She closed her eyes, better to surrender to the pleasant sensation. It could lead her, lull her, back into sleep.

For several minutes, the brushing continued. Abruptly, it stopped. There was a metallic noise, a grating that disturbed her, and a quick tugging on her scalp. She opened her eyes and they were back, the man and the women from the earlier dream. One of the women, the same one she'd thought was her sister, brushing her hair, held a pair of shears above her.

"*No!*" The ache in her body became more real as she tried to move. Her strength, if she'd had it, would have made no difference. The man was on her in an instant, holding her down, with the other woman helping him. The other woman brought the scissors down, pulling Francine's hair and cutting it, pulling and cutting. Francine tried to scream and the man's hand came down on her face, hard, then sleep came again.

*A terrible night of terrible dreams,* Francine thought, waking on the floor. And now she was caught in another one. She felt less groggy than she had before. Images, vile and ugly, rushed through her senses, obscured only by the pain she felt as she tried to stand.

Just the effort to kneel was almost too much; she had to stop to let the pain subside. Slowly, a few inches at a time, she crawled to the dresser, wanting the dream to end, the enduring night to be over. Her muscles rebelled as Francine tried to clutch at the wood, to hold it and pull her body upward. As she forced herself to rise, her head throbbed. She tried, with all her being, to hold on to consciousness. Her body shook and quivered; the room spun around.

But as she faced the dresser, she understood that she wasn't looking at the room, but into a painting, lit by the light of an old-fashioned oil lamp that had been placed next to it. The picture was that of three figures in a bed, sleeping, their arms and legs intertwined so that it was impossible to determine where one body left off and another began. The angle of the painting changed as she moved her head, a strange dream-picture that had a silvery cast.

There was something about the bed, about the people in it, that she had seen or dreamed before. In spite of her pain, she inched her way closer to the frame to get a better look.

For a time, it was impossible for her to recognize the distorted head that replaced the peaceful painted sleepers. Even when she began to understand that it was not a painting but a mirror, that the thing with the bruised and swollen mouth, the eye half closed, was herself, she could not believe it. Only when she raised an aching arm to her head, when she felt the short, erratic patches that had once been her hair, as long and beautiful as her mother's, did Francine scream.

The agony of her own suffering, and of the truth, rushed

from her lungs, drowning out the sound of the footsteps hurrying toward her. The pain of her body obscured the crash as she fell to the dresser, and the burning as she knocked the lamp to its side, the oil igniting and pouring over her face and body.

They were kicking her, beating her and the dresser and the fire with blankets, but by then there was nothing more that they—or anyone—could do to her, or so she thought.

## - 5 -

"I WILL..." she began to say, but it was cold and the small window was so dark with dirt that the sunlight hid behind it. Francine sank into unconsciousness again.

"I will not die," she tried to say hours later, waking. The words would not come out. Her lips were cracked and caked with dried blood.

But she'd thought them, tried to say them, and there was a strength to be taken from them all the same. It was not enough strength to make her feel at all certain of herself or her whereabouts, no help in trying to sort out the hell she'd been in and was still in, for all she knew. She closed her eyes, and her mind.

"I am alive. I will live." Even the slightest movement of her mouth brought pain, but it reassured her that she was right.

Trembling from the cold and her terror, she waited, but they were gone. They'd left her alone! When she was as sure as she could be that it was no trick, that they weren't waiting to jump out at her, to ridicule her helplessness and her hurt, Francine allowed herself to feel other things, opening herself to the wounds of thought.

How long had they kept her their prisoner, she wondered? Hours or days? She'd lost all track of time.

There were limits, perimeters, bounds of agony that could not be crossed. The blows, the humiliation, the suffering...there had to be some reason, some kind of justification for the shame and agony.

*Later, later,* she told herself.

Her heart pounded, and frigid coldness stabbed at her. Achingly, she touched her skull, her eyes filling at the stubble of hair they'd left her. There were bumps on her head, and she vaguely remembered them carrying her, half conscious, out of the room, dragging her down the stairs so that her head hit the steps.

Light and darkness, she thought. Waking to suffer some more, then sinking away from it, and what now? Where had they brought her now, and for what insane purpose?

She was cold, freezing. She felt something rough and wet beneath her, a soaked cloth. It was a blanket, she realized. Filthy, but a blanket. If she could pull it over her bruised flesh, there might be some hope of warmth.

The cold was beneath the blanket. She felt it as her fingers tugged at the coarse, wet wool. She reached again, touching ice—

Ice! The icehouse! She remembered the night that she'd watched at her window, staring as her mother dragged her father's body from the house to this very place. He was dead, buried beneath the very spot where the cakes of ice they'd set her on rested.

She had to get up, to move away. The agony of her body didn't matter any longer. Francine managed to turn, pulling the blanket over herself. She was dragging herself to the end of the huge cakes of ice, one set next to each other so that their edges froze together and they made a solid monument of ice, when something made her stop.

*Another trick,* she longed to believe, but her breath hung in the air and her eyes were wide, as if frozen themselves.

*A dream,* she tried to tell herself in the instant when dreams and reality fused together.

Yet it was no deception, no figment of her conscious or unconscious imagination. There, beneath the ice, frozen into the ice itself, was a body.

Francine shook her head slowly as if to cast it out, but the sight would not leave her. The white dress, the coiled hair, the features of the face could not be denied.

She opened her mouth in a silent scream of anguish as the vestiges of reason left her. And beyond reason, beyond pain, she let the blanket slip from her hands as she backed toward the door, then through it, bolting, running, a raging wild-eyed woman, out of her mind, surely, fleeing from her mother's dead, frozen body, rushing through the yard, down the Way, into the traffic of the shocked motorists on River Road.

## - 6 -

PETER PUTNEY SAT up in his chair, then reached for the dial of the Emerson radio as the visitor entered his office.

"Wouldn't want you to put a story out that I was listening to 'The Make Believe Ballroom' or some such thing on the taxpayers' time," he said, shaking hands with his guest.

"Should be good for a headline. Maybe even a two parter," Vic Casey replied, smiling, taking the seat across from the other man without waiting for an invitation.

There was an easy camaraderie between them, fortunate, each of them felt, since the nature of their occupations brought them into frequent, necessary contact. It wasn't a friendship, exactly; the newspaperman was a recent arrival, having come to Eastfield and the paper only four years before, when the *Crier* had been sold to a publisher who owned papers in Greenfield and Northampton. The publisher had changed the weekly's name to the *Record*, then hired Casey as editor.

In the beginning, Casey hadn't understood the way the town worked, the way people felt about the distinction between news and their personal business. True enough, everyone enjoyed a juicy story in the *Sun*, or the *Mirror*, about Park Avenue debutantes who were found SLAIN IN

LOVE-NEST or NABBED IN WILD PARTY RAID, but a large measure of their pleasure was based on distance.

Those were New York papers, those tabloids, and the people who bought them at the newsstand by the railroad station or at the drugstore read them as novelties rather than news. The stories were true, or were supposed to be, but it really didn't matter. The people and events in them were so remote from the lives and experiences of Eastfield's citizens that they may as well have been fiction—stories of the same world seen in *Flaming Youth, Wild Wives, Jazz Babies,* and the shows that played down at the picture house.

There were no debutantes in Eastfield, and no real society at all. The few people with any kind of money at all hob-nobbed with the wealthy set in Springfield, and attended the parties given by the owners of the paper mills over in Holyoke.

There was a difference between a wild New York party where guests danced naked on tables, sniffed cocaine, and shot each other, and an Eastfield get-together where a farmer with a few too many drinks in him caused a ruckus, or a worker from the casket company flew off the handle and slapped his wife, and it was this difference that Peter Putney had tried to explain to the new arrival.

Putting it into words hadn't been easy. Putney had been handicapped by the immediacy of the editor's arrival. His eye was fresh, his mind unfamiliar with the history of marriages and friendships, the who-knew-whom and who-owed-whom of loyalties that went back longer than anyone could remember, in some cases, and made up the workings of the town.

Vic Casey, for his part, hadn't made an effort to take it in at first. He'd had big ideas when he came from New Haven, thirty-five years old and itching to do the kind of stories his managing editor there had always cut. Determined to make a good impression on his new employer, he'd ignored the proffered advice and suggestions.

Chief Putney had thought it was a matter of giving the new man enough rope, and it had been precisely that. The letters from readers—some of whom were the subjects of the stories—about the impropriety of running articles about domestic squabbles and divorces so prominently hadn't had any effect. But when Vic Casey went to town on the Tremont boy's breaking the window of the French church, the Tremonts had been outraged. The very next week, Casey had made the further mistake of questioning certain discrepancies between the official expenditures of the town council and certain records he found in Town Hall.

The mayor had gone up to Greenfield to meet with the *Record*'s publisher, and Vic Casey had been sent for in turn.

From then on, he'd better understood what was expected of him and what his obligations were. Certainly, it was his job to convey the news, but the good people of Eastfield were staunch New Englanders, ready to gossip over the fence or share a confidence over a cup of coffee, but not at all pleased about seeing "personal business" in print.

The paper, Casey was told, had another purpose. Trade of all kinds was coming into the area, and the *Record* had the job of showing Eastfield in the most favorable possible light. What town, after all, was without its drunks and wife-beaters and troublemakers? What purpose was served by giving them space that might be better utilized to emphasize the new sidewalks on Market Street, or the new junior high school, or any of the other things the town had every right to feel proud of?

Aware that his job was on the line, aware that he could play by the rules that had been made long before he came on the scene, Vic Casey had opted for comfort rather than crusading. He was already keeping company with an Eastfield girl whom he thought he might eventually marry. The salary was good, and like everyone else with a few dollars to spare, he'd gone into the market, using margin and tips from Andy Kallen, manager of the First Eastfield Bank, to accumulate several thousand dollars on paper.

Once he'd reached an "understanding" with Eastfield and the powers that be who ran the town, who "wanted only the best for it," Vic Casey had found the chief of police far more cooperative. In time, he'd come to realize that they were pretty much in the same position. Like himself, Peter Putney had people to answer to, wishes to accommodate. They never spoke of this common bond, though Vic occasionally alluded to it in a manner that passed over the chief's head, or seemed to, but they'd clearly arrived at a truce.

For several months, Chief Putney had been given prominent space in the *Record*'s campaign for more money from the Hampden County commissioners for the improvement of River Road. It was a major thoroughfare, after all, used not only by Eastfield and those who had business in town, but by all manner of passers-through. That was well and good, but the chief had cited the increasing number of traffic accidents, and pointed to the dangers faced by the young people of Eastfield, many of whom had to walk along the edge of River Road to get to school. The county, clearly, had the obligation of at least sharing the cost of sidewalks and perhaps a stoplight or two, as the town council had agreed.

"Did you get anything on her?" the editor asked that day in Chief Putney's office.

Peter Putney nodded, knowing exactly whom the editor meant.

"Yes and no," he answered, sifting through the papers in the wire basket on the corner of the desk. "Rape and beating, but we already suspected as much," he said, scanning the notes he'd taken after the call from Dr. Parrish at Eastfield Hospital. "She'll pull through it, though. Or her body will."

"She still hasn't talked?"

"Not a word. Doc says that she doesn't even know what's happening to her now, much less what happened to get her there."

"But she's conscious?"

"She was conscious when we picked her up, wasn't she?" the chief asked. He scratched his head and reached into his pocket for a Camel. He was accustomed to dealing with reports of physical wounds, but psychological jargon was a different territory—mostly a lot of mumbo-jumbo, if you asked him.

"She's what they call 'in a catatonic state,'" he read, "'probably as the result of shock and trauma'—whatever that means."

"Any inquiries?" the editor asked.

"Just one call from Springfield, but it doesn't really count. Some fellow with a traveling show lost his girl, and he's looking for her." He saw the editor's eyebrows go up. "Now, Vic, don't get excited. She's not our girl. The fellow is upset, but he got a postcard from the woman saying she was off. Recognized the handwriting as hers, but he still wanted to find her. You know those show people, how crazy they are.

"No, nobody's looking for our Jane Doe." He chuckled to himself. "And she didn't have a purse with her when we picked her up, you remember." The editor didn't smile, but Chief Putney thought it was pretty funny all the same. His pals at the Stop 'n Sip, where he had coffee and a sweet roll every morning, had made all manner of jokes about the naked woman who'd nearly caused a massive accident as she wandered down the center of River Road, oblivious to the traffic. *No sense of humor,* the chief thought, looking at the expressionless face of the editor.

"Any theories, Pete?"

The chief's demeanor changed. He'd thought about the case at length, of course, using the knowledge and insight he'd acquired from his police manuals and from a lifetime of devotedly reading *The Police Gazette* and *Crime,* and other popular magazines of the same ilk. He was pleased to have a chance to express his thoughts in an official capacity.

"The doctor says it's possible she was drugged," he began. "We know she's not from hereabouts. Nobody's filed a missing person, for one thing, and nobody's ever seen her before.

"We checked with the colleges—Smith, Mount Holyoke—and didn't get a thing. Of course she's older than that, so I didn't expect much, but I believe in doing my job."

The editor nodded.

"What I think," the chief continued, "is that she's probably a whore. Could have come from either direction, New York or Boston even. Looks to me as if she went on a party with a whole bunch of men and maybe they went from one tourist cabin to another with her on hand, and Christ knows how much hooch. Drugs, too. Things got out of hand at some point, and they beat her up and decided to dump her out of the car. Just our luck they had to pick Eastfield. Another few miles down the road, and they'd have done it out of our jurisdiction, in the county."

Vic considered the idea. "And you think they just dropped her off—'dumped her,' as you put it—and went on their way."

"That's my guess. Of course there's no way to check,

is there? Oh, she stopped traffic all right, but not for long. If anybody saw her being pushed from a car, they sure didn't stick around to tell me about it."

"You don't think there's a possibility that it could have happened here?"

"In Eastfield?" the chief asked. "Come on, Vic. You know the town by this time, and you know how these things are. We never have anything like this—"

"We have rapes, Pete—"

"Overexcited young people," the chief replied. "Not that you can expect much more these days, with that jazz and the rest of it. Girls hike up their skirts and roll down their stockings and wonder why they get poked."

The editor smiled in spite of himself. "Still, it's rape."

"And they pay for it. There's a lot of damaged goods taking the vows in Trinity Church, my mother always said." He winked. "Plenty of them with a bun in the oven, too, if you ask me. We've got our hotheads and our young bucks, Vic, but they're healthy men who get carried away. We've got our good-time girls, too. But nothing like this. The Jane Doe isn't even from around here. Doc Parrish says she has some fancy dental work, must've been down in some big city."

The editor cleared his throat. "None of the people who live out on the road saw her?"

"Nary a one. Now, she was going toward town, which suggests to me that she was probably dropped off a ways down the road—in the county, I believe. Could've passed out in the woods for a day or even two. Smelled to high hell, so filthy she was, and scratched, too, like she'd been lying in the twigs and leaves.

"There aren't really any people living out that way."

"There's . . . what's their name? The crazy people on the edge of town?"

Chief Putney leaned back in his chair and smiled. "The Hazeltines? *That* bunch? She could have knocked on their door to beat the band, and they wouldn't have let her in if she'd begged them." He shook his head and laughed softly. "They're hardly the folks to receive company, the Hazeltines. Now *there's* a story for the telling!"

"Really?"

"Come on, Vic. You know about *them—*"

"Not that much. Just little bits I picked up here and there."

"They're quite a lot. Used to be the first family of the town, my mother says, and not too proud to let everyone know it."

"They owned the casket company, didn't they?"

Putney nodded. "The Buggy Works, it was back then. The Hazeltine Buggy Works. My old man, rest his soul, worked for old man Hazeltine. So did everybody else hereabouts. You know, I can remember one Fourth of July a good thirty years ago or so. Big to-do at the Common, with old man Hazeltine making a speech, telling how Eastfield was going to do so well and the Works was gonna make cars instead of carriages. Spirits were high, I'll tell you."

"But he did it, didn't he?"

"Not for long," the chief explained, lighting another Camel, pleased to pass the time telling a story that had a natural element of law and order, pride and punishment, about it.

As the editor listened, Peter Putney recounted the litany of the Hazeltines' downfall. The old man losing the Works just about put everyone out of a job. It was only the casket company's coming in that saved the day at the last minute. Then him, going off and leaving Olivia—that's what his mother had always called her—and Olivia's children.

"Were they your age, Pete?" Vic Casey asked.

"Could be. I guess it's so. But they always kept to themselves—a crazy bunch."

His mother, now seventy-three and crippled with the rheumatism, had spoken often of the haughty ways of the Hazeltines, of how they'd paraded through the streets of Eastfield on those occasions when they deigned to come to town with their noses high in the air as if they were better than everyone else. School wasn't good enough for the likes of Olivia's children, his mother had explained. They had to be tutored at home, if you please.

While the Works prospered, the town had endured the Hazeltines, according them the respect and deference their position and power commanded. But that had changed with the advent of the casket company. Putney could remember his mother discussing the Hazeltines with Mrs. Tremont and her other friends, some of whom viewed "poor Olivia" as a tragic figure who'd been deserted by a husband who couldn't face his own failure.

His mother had insisted that, rather than being unfortunate, Olivia was proof of the old adage that "money goes to money." The plan for the automobiles had failed, but everyone knew that there was still a fortune in the Hazeltines' accounts at the local bank—not to mention the bank in Boston, where Olivia's people came from.

To Mrs. Putney, Olivia hadn't at all gotten what she deserved, but had settled into a life of luxury in her mansion, surrounded by servants and devoted children with no other purpose than to cater to her every whim.

Putney himself remembered seeing them on an occasional trip to town when he was a boy. There was a girl, not a bad-looking girl as he remembered her, but shy. And a brother—snotty little son of a bitch he'd been, even then. A couple of little girls. He didn't remember it exactly, and didn't mention it to the editor, but he could still recall a

day when he and some friends had teased Olivia's children
and the boy had given him some lip about getting his old
man fired from the Works.

"What happened to their mother?" Vic asked. "Olivia."

The chief shrugged. "Took sick, I hear. Always was a
bit touched up here." He tapped his head. "Her people in
Boston came to fetch her, oh, years ago. Put her in some
hospital, I believe."

"And the rest of them?"

"You've seen them, haven't you? Crazy as hoot owls,
the whole lot of them! Those that are left. The oldest girl
went off. I think I heard she went to her mother's people
in Boston and got married. The three of them that are left
are a sight!"

The editor's sense of a good story had been kindled, and
he pressed for details.

The chief supplied as many as he could, though when
you came right down to it, there was little that was actually
known about the lives of Olivia's children, and a lot of
speculation that was passed around town as fact.

He'd only been out to the Hazeltine place once himself,
when Paul Hazeltine had nearly shot a trespassing hunter
who happened to be a brother-in-law of the chief's wife's
closest friend, and who had, as a result, wasted little time
in reporting the incident.

"I drove out, and it's a shame, Vic," he said, sighing.
"That house was a fine place in its day. It's all run down
now—they don't keep up their property, not that they've
got much else to do with themselves."

"What happened when you went there?"

The chief shrugged. "Took them fifteen minutes to come
to the door—and then he had a shotgun in his hands. Told
me the man had been trespassing, and he'd fired above his
head as a warning. The way Tom Devlin tells it, he'd have

been dead if the shot had been a few inches to the right, but it's his word against Hazeltine's, and Hazeltine was in the right, when you come down to it. Told me so, and slammed the door in my face. That's the last time I've seen him, except for every now and then when they come to town. And that's only when they have to."

"But how do they live?"

"As well as they please. I took a look around, that time out there. They've got a few chickens in the dooryard. Fletcher totes a side or so of beef out to them from his butcher shop every year. They've got a garden. He fishes the river, I hear. And Dunleavy tells me they're always getting packages from Sears and the like." He sighed. "Crazy as they can afford to be, I guess."

"I guess so," Casey agreed. "You don't think it would be worth checking with them, Pete? To see if maybe they know anything about the woman?"

The man across the desk shook his head. "They keep to themselves, Olivia's children. I've lived here long enough to know a few things, and that's one of them."

The editor had been writing in his notebook. He closed it, slipping it into the inside pocket of his jacket.

"By the way, Vic, you weren't planning to write a story about the Jane Doe, were you?"

"It's news, Pete. Big news, really," he answered. His mind danced with the potential prestige of wire service pickup.

Chief Putney frowned. "Still, it's not the sort of thing we'd want to spread around, is it? Not a pleasant story, and no real story at all, since we don't know who she is. It would only get people stirred up, start them thinking that this kind of thing could happen here and all—"

"But people know already, don't they?"

"Those who need to, Vic. Some of the men. Fact is,"

he paused for effect, "a few of the boys asked me to have a word with you. They hoped you weren't going to spread the story in the paper. Didn't want their wives and daughters to get scared. You know how women take these things."

The editor nodded slowly. "I understand."

"Good," Chief Putney said, standing, coming around the desk and patting his visitor on the back. "I told them I thought you would. 'Vic Casey is one of us now,' I said. 'He wants the best for the town.'"

The chief's private line rang, and he excused himself as he lifted the receiver. "Chief Putney speaking.... He did, huh? No fooling. How'd it happen?" Vic Casey stood to leave, but the chief stopped him before his hand touched the door. "Here's a *real* story for you, Vic!" he said, covering the mouthpiece. "It seems that some congressman went up in an airplane, and the damn thing crashed right outside of town. Killed him, of all things!"

Vic Casey sat down again, waiting while the chief got the rest of the details. The *Record* went to press the next day. There were many people in town who didn't bother with the Springfield papers, and the fatal flight would be a real grabber.

With any luck at all, he'd be able to get Gary Parker, who ran the Eastfield Portrait Studio and doubled as the *Record*'s official photographer, out to the scene of the crash to get a good picture. The chief, he knew, would pull the necessary strings, and was already writing up the report his caller had given him.

All things considered, Vic Casey decided as he waited for the chief to finish, it would be just the kind of story his readers wanted to find in their paper.

## - *7* -

THE CHICKENS IN the dooryard clucked and cackled, rushing toward Constance Hazeltine as she held her apron and tossed them the kernels of corn that she'd brought from the barn. There had been a lot of corn this year, and the crows hadn't been bad: there was enough to can, enough for relish and meal for bread, as well as plenty left for the chickens.

She smiled as they clustered around her, and, leaving them to peck, she went to the back of the icehouse, where the hens roosted, to collect the eggs. She placed them in the wicker basket she used for the purpose. There were eleven of them—maybe Margaret would bake a cake!

Walking back toward the house, the chickens took no notice of her, not even trying to move out of her way. She set the basket down and, in a single move, scooped up one of the fattest of the hens, holding it at her side, pinning it with her body and her elbow so that the bird could neither escape nor flutter. Its throat pulsated and it turned its small, wide-eyed head frantically from side to side.

"Nice chicken," Constance cooed, stroking it. "Nice . . ." She picked up her basket in her right hand, then walked toward the house. "Nice chicken," she said again, setting the basket beside the door. Tenderly, as if she were playing with one of her dolls, she stroked and soothed the bird until the pulsations of its swollen throat were more regular. It didn't try to resist as she caressed its head.

Then her fingers were on its neck, twisting, strangling. Feathers flew around her, caught by the wind as the bird frantically tried to free itself. Kicking, clawing, it pulled its body from the crook of her arm. Constance grabbed it, trapping its wings, lifting the bird and crashing its head down on the solid slab outside the door.

Her brother, coming up from the Way with the mail in his hand, smiled at her. Wordlessly, he picked up the stunned bird and carried it to the stump of the oak tree between the house and barn. Constance held it then, beaming at her brother as he lifted the ax with its heavy handle, bringing it down with the full force of his body. Blood gushed from the bird, throbbing out with the rhythm of its still-beating heart. Ignoring the head for the moment, Paul kicked the chicken along before him, its blood making a wavy trail. Grabbing a hammer and nail from the tools in the barn, he nailed the dying bird's foot to the outside wall. The blood fell like paint on the faded, weather-bleached wood.

He wiped his hands on his pants, stopped at the chopping block to scoop up the warm head of the bird, then slipped the hand that held it around his sister's shoulders as they entered the kitchen together.

Margaret giggled as he tossed the chicken's head into the sink. She'd boil it later, with the feet and the remains of the chicken she'd roast for dinner that night, in her stockpot.

"Anything come?" she asked.

Constance took the pot of coffee from the stove, pouring a cup for Paul, stirring in the three teaspoons of sugar he took before pouring herself a cup and sitting at the table.

"Bank," he said, reaching into his plaid shirt, taking out a letter.

Margaret turned away from the apples she'd been coring as he tore open the envelope. It was odd for the bank to send anything this time of month: the statements came every three months, and there'd been one only a month before.

"It's not about..." she started to ask.

"Of course not!" he told her, annoyed.

"You musn't talk about *her,* Margaret. You musn't even think about her!" Constance insisted. She turned to Paul for approval. "Isn't that right?"

"Just right," he replied. Constance looked frightened, as if she still thought she might have spoken too quickly or said the wrong thing. He forced himself to smile at her, his long, thick arm extending across the table and his hand brushing her soft cheek. Her eyes beamed at him. Tenderly, her hands caught his and kissed it before letting it go.

Paul unfolded the letter, taking in the embossed address of the Eastfield Bank & Trust Company, established 1838. It was dated two days before, October 29, 1929.

Dear Mr. Hazeltine

The events of the past week, as you are aware having heard the news, indicate the severity of these troubled times in our nation's economy. No doubt you have been giving serious consideration to your current financial situation and your plans for your financial future as well.

Please allow me to take this opportunity to assure you, as a highly valued customer of many years' standing, that the Eastfield Bank & Trust Company is a sound and stable institution, and that your holdings are secure.

No doubt you've heard or read the addresses made by both our President and the Governor of the Commonwealth of Massachusetts regarding the gravity of the situation, which can not be denied. Panic, particularly on the part of large depositors such as yourself, will only further complicate the current condition.

As I'm sure you know, those ill-advised individuals who choose to withdraw their funds in an effort to protect their money face the dangers of robbery and other loss. It is my heartfelt hope that as a responsible American and member of the community, you will see fit to continue to allow our bank to serve you, and that you will accept my personal assurance to keep you informed at all times.

I look forward to the opportunity to answer any questions that you may have, and to be of service to you at your convenience

Most sincerely yours . . .

It was signed by the president of the bank.

"What does it mean?" Margaret asked.

Her brother studied the paper carefully.

"What events?" Constance inquired. "President Coolidge?"

"Hoover," Paul told her. "It's been Hoover since last year, remember?"

She shook her head. Presidents, governors, even the local politicians of Eastfield all worked far away. They had nothing to do with her, or Paul, or Margaret; why should she bother to remember other names? And besides, unlike Paul (who was the better of the two) and Margaret, she didn't know how to read. They read, and read to her, so there'd never been any need, no more than Paul needed to worry about the chickens, which she cared for. She heard only the names they read to her, and she much preferred stories, fairy tales in particular, to the news. There were names sometimes on the radio they'd sent away for, but she didn't hear them. Her head was filled with snatches of the songs the stations played, which she liked much better.

"It doesn't matter," Paul said. Furrows of worry and doubt had formed, etching themselves into Constance's forehead. At his reassurance, they disappeared. She smiled at him adoringly; he was her brother and oh, so much more.

He was her strength, and Margaret's, too, Constance thought, watching her sister set the apples to boiling on the stove for applesauce. The times she liked best were times like this one, when the three of them were close together. It was silly—she knew because Margaret and Paul had both told her so—but when he went into the woods to hunt, or even down to the bank of the river to fish, there were times when she was overcome by a great sadness. When she was doing something upstairs and Margaret was in another part of the house and Paul away, it was even worse. What if they left her? What if something happened and Paul didn't come back? If he went away as Father had, then Mother?

She'd asked Margaret these questions, tagging after her, getting in her way in the kitchen, which was Margaret's domain, but her older sister's promises that Paul would soon be back, that everything was fine, and that the three of them would always, forever, be together didn't always calm her.

Staring from the door or through one of the windows, she'd watch for the sight of him.

Over the years, the small animals that had come to think of the land around the house as their home had come to accept her as one of their kind. Rabbits, squirrels, jays, and robbins took no notice of her, or viewed her as more an object of curiosity than a threat. They seemed to sense that in standing her watch, in scanning the distance for her brother, Constance was much like them, looking for the way of her own survival.

"I'm heating up our lunch," Margaret told them, though it really wasn't necessary, for they ate at the same hours day after day, year after year. Still, Constance heard the signal and reacted to it, going to the cabinet and taking out dishes and silver. Once, in a time that she could barely remember, the dishes had been separated by style and color—this set for lunch, that for dinner, another for holidays and special meals.

Over the years, plates had chipped and broken, and the varied patterns had come together in an odd mixture of the three sets of bone china, one with gold trim, one with exotic Oriental blossoms, their color only somewhat faded by the years of being scrubbed in the sink, and one with a delicate design of tiny rosebuds, her personal favorite.

Constance set the dishes down, Paul's place first, then Margaret's, beside him, then her own at the far end of the table. She'd once said it wasn't fair that Margaret got to sit in the middle time after time, year after year, even if she was the next to oldest of them. But her sister hadn't yielded, and Constance had found contentment in being able to take her meals and look directly at her brother at the same time.

"Here we are," Margaret said as she took a dish from the oven. She carried it to Paul, who served himself from the pie she'd made of rabbit and carrots, onions and potatoes.

They ate in near silence, as was their custom. There was no need to compliment Margaret on her cooking: after so many lunches and dinners, so many breakfasts, she knew their tastes and prepared the meals accordingly. In the morning, they had bread and jams, marmalade for Paul and herself from one of the case of jars they sent for each year, the same Dundee Marmalade their mother had ordered from

S. S. Pierce in Boston. Constance preferred the apple butter
Margaret made.

The mornings were filled with work—straightening, re-
pairs, washing and hanging clothes to dry. In what they
called the Green Time, that time when things grew, there
was the garden, the picking and pruning that their mother
had taught them. Constance loved the garden and was to
a large extent in charge of it, though Paul helped with the
planting and heavy work. Margaret took the tomatoes and
beans, the cucumbers and radishes and the rest of it (the
squash, later on) and what they didn't eat fresh, she cooked
and stored in the pantry in the jars she boiled and sealed
with wax.

The Green Time, too, was the season of fruits. Blue-
berries and raspberries that grew wild in the woods around
them. Sometimes all three of them would go together, picking them, or they'd walk, led by Paul, deep into the woods
behind the house, all the way to the point where their property ended and an old farm with an abandoned orchard stood
in ruins. The birds and the bugs knew about the orchard
too, but there were pears and apples that escaped them and
they had all they could carry.

There was always lunch of some kind—a baked fish that
Paul had caught in the river. Beef cut from the side hung
in the icehouse, or from a deer he'd shot. Besides the chickens, there were the wild birds, the ducks and pheasant and
quail and turkey.

Dinner was similar, though they ate more—and more
leisurely, too. It was at this meal that Margaret served the
desserts that Constance loved—the rich cakes thick with
frosting; the puddings and compotes of fruit, simmered in
sugar, put by in jars to enjoy all year round.

After that meal, while Paul relaxed and the dishes were
cleared and washed, the three of them were together. Some-

times, they sat in the parlor, but that was more for the Green Time. Once the leaves began to turn and the air took on the first chill, they moved into their father's study, with its huge fireplace.

Each spring, the chopping of wood began, first with the trees that had fallen from disease, or as a result of having been struck by the lightning that terrified Constance in the spring storms. All summer, on and off, Paul went into the woods, cutting the wood, drying it in the sun, storing it in the bin in the pantry for the stove, and the box beside the fireplace in the study, with the rest of it left in the barn to be taken in as needed.

The fire lit, her sister would read to Constance as Paul looked through one of his own books. Margaret sometimes chose long stories, stories that lasted a whole book and which Constance found hard to concentrate on. Far better were the stories in the books she'd had as long as she could remember. Though she could not read the titles, she knew them by color. The pretty dust jackets had long-since crumbled and been lost, but the red book was *Grimm's Fairy Tales*, the green *Hans Christian Andersen*, and the yellow book, *Beloved Stories for Children*.

It didn't occur to Constance that there were other people in the world who read the same stories, and read them in fact from the same books. For they seemed to have been written just for her, for the three of them. Any kingdom became the house and the land around it. She and Margaret were the beautiful princesses; Paul every handsome prince and king.

Beyond the familiar domain was the wicked wood, the land of Eastfield with trolls and witches and all manner of dangerous people who, no matter how innocent they looked, wanted to hurt the three in the castle.

That was one reason why they had to stick together for

always, why Constance felt safest when the three of them were in bed, playing there or sleeping in one another's arms. No harm could come to them as long as they were all three together and no more, no intruders or strangers who envied them their happiness and planned their downfall and suffering.

Constance did not know what it was to have a secret, for everything—the food they ate, the work to be done, the pleasures of companionship and their own bodies—was meant to be shared. There were, however, thoughts that she didn't put into words, afraid that Paul might be angry with her. The idea of displeasing him was enough to bring tears to her eyes, and so she sometimes carried questions like eggs in a basket, chicken feed in her apron.

In the stories she loved, there were many kingdoms with princesses who seemed much like herself. How, she wondered, would they know if one of the strangers who came to the door was one of them come to visit? During the winter, the White Time, she'd think of this over and over again, particularly when the snow was high and driving, making going out—even to get to the barn—all but impossible.

Each spring proved her wrong.

While anyone who called on them once never called again, there was still the occasional salesman or minister newly arrived in town; the schoolboy selling magazines or a hunter who, rifle in hand, walked on their land as if it were his own. Paul stared them down, sent them away with the door slamming, or with the sound of his own gun firing above them as they raced back to the Way.

Eastfield was wicked: They were the Chosen Ones, the royal children.

The trips to town were even more proof, though they made them only when they had to. When the White Time

was gone, they had no choice. There were always a few
things to be bought, and Paul's visit to the bank, and arrangements to be made for one thing or the other. That they
were hated was a fact that Constance had always accepted.
Didn't people stare at them when they walked through the
streets, their steps the same, their bodies closely pressed
together?

Silence was their weapon; unity, a magic that would
protect them.

And as Paul had said so many times, those people, those
*others*, were stupid. Hadn't the man at the bank believed
that the letter they handed him had been written by their
mother's hand? That she had taken sick and was going, with
her eldest daughter who was to be married, to her family
in Boston. Her son, with the same name as his father, would
take care of things now.

And so it was.

Her mother had spoken, from time to time, of her relatives, particularly when she had begun to spend more and
more time in her bed, taking her medicine more frequently.
She'd asked that her family be informed if "anything happened," but Paul and Margaret had assured Constance that
there was nothing to tell them. Her mother had gone into
a deep sleep, was all. A sleep from which she'd wake, like
the beautiful princess in the story books, when Father came
back from his long journey and kissed her cheek.

It had been the White Time when their mother sank into
her deep sleep, and Constance had helped Margaret and
Paul to carry her out into the blinding snow. Her body had
cracked the snow's frozen surface, and she'd waited, more
snow covering her like a great white blanket. At the very
start of the Green Time, they'd gone to the yard and there
she had been, unchanged and beautiful.

They had made the unwelcome trip to town and had the

iceman bring a truckload, telling him to leave it just outside the icehouse door. When the sound of his horse and wagon disappeared down the Way, they'd begun to fix their mother's bed. Paul had taken a pick to the frozen ground in the dark, cold place. They'd set cakes of ice in that, then they'd lain their mother, carrying her carefully so as not to wake her, on top of them. Her flesh was ice itself, cold and hard and glistening. More blocks of ice had covered her, and she was sleeping, sleeping still, waiting for Father, who would one day return and reunite them all.

Except, of course, Francine, Constance remembered as the dishes were cleared and Paul went off to clean out the chimney. They'd only used it a few times, the Brown Time on them now and the White to come, but the fireplace had smoked, and the study had been thick with it. She stood at the sink, washing the lunch dishes as Margaret put the remains of the meal away.

Francine . . . her mother had spoken of their sister, as if, like Father, she might return and be welcome. But while their mother slept, Paul had told them the truth. Francine was bad, an outsider. She'd gone to the other side, the world of the others, against them. If she ever came back, it would be to hurt them, to try to take away what they had and what Father had wanted for them. This, of course, they must never let her do.

There'd been letters from her, cards, but they'd gone unread into the stove or fireplace.

Then, only recently, it had happened. The woman they'd seen from the upstairs window, the stranger who had knocked on the door. Francine, she said she was, their sister come back for a visit! They'd done as Paul said they should if she ever were to come and he wasn't in the house, and as he promised, he'd come back to save them.

She'd wanted them to believe that she cared for them.

She'd tried to fool her sisters. But Paul had shown them. First, the tea with some of the drops from their mother's medicine bottle, the bottle they'd always kept. Then, upstairs, where she hadn't wanted to play as they did, and had been punished instead. Knocking over the lamp—she had tried to burn the house down!

But they'd fixed her, putting out the fire, carrying her to the icehouse, and letting Mother decide. She hadn't chosen to welcome her daughter, but had slept and was sleeping still. Francine was gone, and Paul had promised they would not see her again, ever, as long as they lived. They were safe.

The two sisters went into the yard, taking the hen from the barn wall and plucking its feathers. Constance hummed as she plunged her hand (her hands were smaller than Margaret's, and better suited for the work) into it, pulling the innards out.

Inside again, they washed the bird, dried it with a towel and held it over the flame of a burner to singe the pinfeathers off the skin. Constance mixed an egg with stale bread and an onion from the basket in the cellar.

"Soon we'll have to take the apples in," Margaret told Constance. "The frost can get them in the barn." She stuffed the bird and put it to roast with potatoes in the oven, then, smiling at her sister, she began to mix the batter for an applesauce cake. Paul came through the kitchen with a barrel of ashes. They laughed at the sight of him, his hands and face black, so that his eyes stood out, all the bigger and bluer.

"Nearly dark already," Paul observed later, coming into the kitchen with an armful of stove wood.

He washed, and they ate the meal Margaret had prepared, with Constance having two pieces of cake. When the dishes were done, they joined their brother in the study.

Constance asked for a story, or a game of Chinese checkers, but Margaret wanted the radio first. It was a story about ghosts, and that was almost as good. The voices lulled Constance as she sat on the floor, close to her brother's chair, staring into the flames and picturing the ghosts in the fireplace.

The knocking, at first, seemed to be part of the story. But the radio characters talked on as if they hadn't heard it, and, at Paul's silent signal, Margaret turned the radio off. The two sisters followed him as he went toward the front door, walking carefully and quietly so that their steps couldn't be heard.

"Chicken!"

"Go on, 'fraidy cat!"

"You said you weren't scared of the haunted house!"

It was *them,* the outsiders, and more than one. Their voices sounded young, but young or old, they were all enemies.

"It ain't haunted. They're not home, see?" one voice said, closer than the others. He had to be just outside the door.

"Yeah? Well, if you want to join the gang, you got to get inside. If they ain't home, it should be easier. You got to get something from inside the house and bring it to us."

"Why don't you wait?" the closer voice asked in a whine.

"For what? So they can get us, too?" someone answered, and there was a chorus of laughter. "We'll see you later, Mickey—*if* you get something from inside."

"Come on," he entreated, but there was the sound of more laughter and of feet running away.

"It ain't haunted," the person on the other side of the door said to himself as Constance clung to Margaret, huddling behind Paul in the doorway.

After a few moments, Mickey knocked again, less forcefully this time, as if not wanting to disturb them if, in fact, they were inside. But as soon as the knock came, Paul swung the door open.

"Trick or treat," a frightened boy said weakly, but the words were barely out of his mouth before the strong hand was at his neck, pulling him inside.

"What did you say?" Paul asked him as Margaret shut the door.

"It's—it's Halloween, mister. Trick or treat. You know." The black of the ashes he'd cleared still held in the lines of Paul Hazeltine's face, and the pressure of his grasp on the boy's neck didn't lessen.

"It was just a joke," the youth said nervously. "We were kidding around, on a dare. That's all. The kids thought I'd be scared to knock on the door—"

"Why?" the man asked.

"On account of you're . . . well, you know. What they say in town. Hey! Let go! Lemme go!" He pulled and struggled, but Paul was dragging him through the foyer, into the study, then thrusting him into the chair where he'd been sitting himself, minutes before.

"What do they say in town?" he demanded.

"Nothing. Honest, nothing. Just talk. Kidding around, like. Please, lemme go, okay?"

A hard slap answered his question. For an instant, the boy seemed stunned. Then he tried to bolt from the chair and out of the room, back to the door. He wasn't quick enough, or rather Paul was too quick for him. He grabbed the youth by the collar and slammed him into the chair again.

"You answer me," he said calmly. "Who talks about us in town?"

"Nobody!" the boy insisted, but the threat of another

blow made him reconsider. "People. I don't know. Different ones."

"What do they say?"

"They—they say that the house is haunted. That there's ghosts, and—" It was clear he regretted not having stopped a word sooner. But the cold stare of his captor's eyes commanded him to continue.

"—and that you're crazy."

Rather than anger, Paul seemed to take pleasure in the confirmation of what he already knew. His head turned, and he looked to his sisters, his expression reminding them to remember what had been said.

"Why did you come here, if that's what you think?" he asked the boy.

The intruder was shaking now, his bravado completely gone. "I told you. It's Halloween. There's a gang of kids, a club, kind of. And I had to come here to get in. Lemme go, okay? I'm sorry, honest. I didn't mean to start no trouble—"

Again a slap silenced him.

"That's just what you meant to do, and it's done now!" Paul told him sharply.

The boy's eyes met his, flashing with anger and fear.

"You'll be sorry! I'm gonna tell. I'm gonna tell my folks how you dragged me in here and hit me!"

In that moment, with those words, the boy's future was decided.

When he spoke again, Paul's voice was light, almost pleasant. "How would your friends know that you were in the house?" he asked.

"I—I was supposed to bring them something. Over at Doug's house. He's having a party for the gang, and they're over there."

Paul looked at his sisters, then at the boy. "Something that came from here, right?"

The boy nodded. "It doesn't matter, though. Honest—"

Paul walked to the desk and picked up the brass Tiffany inkwell, part of the desk set that had been his father's.

"Something like this?" he asked, his voice as soft as if he were gentling a frightened animal. He held the object out to the boy.

"Gee, mister! That would be swell!" he said.

"You'll have it, then," Paul Hazeltine promised, just before he raised the hand that held the inkwell and brought it crashing down on the boy's head. The boy in the chair slumped without a sound, the look of surprise frozen on the young face.

"Oh, dear," Margaret said softly.

"We—we might have kept him, don't you think?" Constance asked.

"They'd come looking. They might look anyway. He's one of *them*."

"Yes, *them*," the sisters agreed.

"Now?" Margaret asked.

"I'll take care of it," Paul assured her.

Lifting the boy's body in his arms, he made his way through the house, the women following him to the kitchen door. He opened it in practiced silence, setting the boy down on the floor until he'd made sure that no more outsiders were about. Lifting the boy again, he began to walk through the yard, not taking the Way, but disappearing into the woods, the corpse a bundle in his arms.

The dry brush cracked beneath his boots. Owls hooted at his passage. There was a half moon and the sky was cloudy, but his eyes had long been in the habit of guiding him through nights like this one. The sounds of the wind and the trees and the low growth were all he heard for a time, then another sound joined them.

Softly, then louder as he came closer, the woody sounds were overcome by the noise of traffic rushing past on River Road. At its edge, Paul Hazeltine knelt and waited, checking the flow of traffic, his head turning right and left, right and left.

Thirty-seven minutes later, the moment he'd waited for came. A Ford sped by in the direction of Springfield. A station wagon made its way toward Amherst in the left lane, followed by a Chrysler.

Then there were no cars on River Road, and no headlights to be seen in either direction.

Crouching low, in case a car should come along suddenly, he made his way through the brush, then laid the boy's body down in the road. Hurrying back to the protective branches, deeper than before so that he could not be spotted, he hunkered down.

It was only a few minutes till the Packard came racing down the road. He listened and watched, a certain fear within him subsiding at the screeching brakes and the words that floated to him on the cold night wind.

"I didn't even see the kid! Jesus, I didn't see him—"

"Damn you, Johnny. I told you not to go so fast—"

Another car. Another explanation. "Oh my God!" and "I swear I didn't see him," and "Get an ambulance! Get the police!"

Soon, there were sirens, but Paul Hazeltine didn't wait for them. By the time they came he'd already run back to the house. His sisters had been waiting, grateful and adoring, eager to follow him upstairs to the bedroom, to satisfy him and themselves at the end of a day that was—with a single exception—no different from so many others that had gone before and would come after.

# - 8 -

"THIS WAY, Chief Putney," the nurse said. "Doctor is expecting you."

"Thank you," he answered, not certain if he was expected to take off his hat or not. Hospitals made him nervous, and he wanted to keep the visit as short as possible.

"Terrible about little Mickey Gaines, isn't it."

"Yes," the chief agreed. "A terrible loss."

"Of course, I tell my kids that if I catch them going near River Road I'll wallop the daylights out of them. Not that I'm sure the Gaines boy's parents didn't say the same thing. It's so dark, I hate when my husband drives it at night, I swear!"

Peter Putney nodded. "The mayor and the council are making sure the county hears about it," he told her. "Maybe this will make them give us some money to light the damn thing."

"It's a shame, though. Only twelve years old, the poor thing—"

"Thank you, nurse," the doctor said, joining them. She left without another word as the two men shook hands. "Sorry if she bent your ear, Pete—"

The chief sighed. "No, she was talking about the little Gaines boy. Whole town is riled, and rightly so. A terrible thing."

"Yes, yes it is," the doctor agreed, leading him down the pale green hall of Eastfield General Hospital.

"I wonder sometimes how you can stand it, Doc. All the sickness and death. The sadness of it all."

"So do I," the physician allowed. "She's in the last room on the right, Pete."

"Still hasn't talked?"

"Not a word. She doesn't acknowledge me, or the nurses, or anything else, for that matter."

"That bad, huh?"

"See for yourself," the doctor invited, opening the door of Room 310. He addressed the patient, a woman with bizzarely shorn hair and an angry red scar on the right side of her face. "You have company," he told her, but she continued to stare straight ahead.

"Does she know we're here?" Chief Putney asked.

"That's hard to say," the doctor replied. "We don't know too much about catatonia."

"What's that mean, Doc?"

"To put it simply, when something happens that's too much for the mind to accept, a kind of door swings shut. In this case, the traumatic shock was the attack. She's healed up pretty well, in the physical sense of it, but treating the injury to her mind is something else again."

Peter Putney stared at the unmoving, unblinking woman. "You mean she'll stay like that for the rest of her life?" he asked, bewildered.

"It could be," the doctor replied, sighing. "Then again, it might be a matter of weeks, months, years—there's no telling. Sometimes they snap out of it on their own. When the wounds have had time to heal, you might say. There've been some promising results with electric shock and other kinds of therapy. I expect they'll do all they can for her in Northampton."

"The nuthouse, huh?"

The physician winced at the vernacular term for the mental hospital. "We're transferring her tomorrow, as I told you on the phone. Physically, she's coming along nicely. They'll be able to continue her care."

There was something about the copper color of the short hair and the paleness of the woman's complexion that reminded the chief of someone, though he couldn't for the life of him think who it was.

"Can she hear me?" he asked.

"Only she knows that," the doctor answered.

The chief walked hesitantly to the side of the bed, leaning low so that he stared into the patient's expressionless eyes, as if to fathom her untold secrets. "Who *are* you?" he asked her. But there was no answer. No sign that she'd even heard the question.

"If it were as easy as that," the doctor said softly, "we wouldn't have a problem. There weren't any inquiries, I take it."

The chief straightened up and shook his head. "Nothing that crossed my desk. You know, Doc, in the case of adults, we don't make missing-persons reports the top order of business. A wife gets mad at her husband and goes to her mother's house. A girl has a fight with the boyfriend and decides to leave town for a week or so to make him sorry. It's a free country, after all."

The nurse appeared with a small tray. "I'm sorry. I can come back—"

"No, I think we're finished," the doctor told her. He turned to the man in uniform. "Unless there's anything else?"

"No, you folks go right ahead." Chief Putney was eager to leave, to get away from the hospital and the woman who had no more life about her than the body of the little Gaines boy, victim of a traffic accident on River Road, lying in a casket at the Breedlove Funeral Home. "I'll need the medical report for the record, Doc."

"I'll get it in the next day or so. Shall I have someone bring it over?"

The chief shook his head, and the physician's hand. "Mail will do. No rush on this one."

The two men left the room together, and the nurse drew the sheet back. Opening the patient's hospital gown, she began to swab the wounds with alcohol and cotton.

"Does it still smart, dearie?" she asked softly. "I know it must, but it's for your own good. And you're coming along so nicely. All that nasty infection gone."

That done, she gently spread ointment on the healing cuts and lacerations she'd cleansed. The poor creature was in a world of her own, the nurse thought, a real case right out of the textbook. Still and all, who was to say what she heard or didn't? Who could know except the poor thing herself? A little kindness couldn't hurt.

"Well," she said as she closed the gown and pulled the sheet back up, "I won't be seeing you again. I'm through for the day, and tomorrow they're moving you to the mental hospital. But they'll be able to help you there—and you try to help yourself, won't you? I'll remember you in my prayers, dear."

She patted the patient's arm and left the room.

*I fooled them all,* the actress thought.

*Harry didn't come and look for me. He didn't even try,* the woman mourned.

*They're moving me somewhere else, someplace where nobody will ever be able to hurt me again.*

A tiny smile stopped short of forming at her mouth, and a tear held itself back.

And Francine Hazeltine retreated to the formless, floating void that she had, at last, come home to.

part four
*1942*

## - 1 -

EXACTLY WHEN IT had started, she wasn't sure. She remembered what it had been like before, when she'd felt like her old self, but she could not define the point when it had started to change. The curse had stopped a year before, the flow inside her drying up, was how she thought of it, but the rest of it had begun long before.

There were the dreams, for one thing. Falling into sleep in her place on Constance's right, with Paul on her sister's left, Margaret Hazeltine's rest was disturbed by visions of her mother that made her wake with her heart pounding to find her body covered with sweat.

*What did the dreams mean?* she wondered.

Why did the image of her mother, her arms stretched out as if reaching for her, frighten her so? She thought of mentioning it, to get it out of her mind, but decided against it. There were times when she wanted to wake the sister and brother beside her, but she did not. Instead, she lay still, sometimes drifting into sleep again and sometimes fighting it off, concentrating on the steady sound of Paul's snoring and Constance's light breath against her skin until the morning.

Talking about her dreams of Mother would serve no

purpose. Constance would only get upset. It had been bad enough in thirty-eight, that March when the flood came, and the wind with it. They'd gone to sleep with the sound of the hurricane pelting the house, and the next morning, the barn had been blown down and the icehouse gone completely.

"Mother!" Constance had wailed. "Our Mother!" she'd sobbed and sobbed, and Margaret had looked deep into her brother's eyes for an answer, an explanation, a way of making it right.

"Father came for her in the storm," Paul had said.

"He came to take her away," Margaret heard herself add, as if it were a play on the radio that they'd practiced, or one of the stories she'd read to Constance so many times that she no longer had to look at the words to know them.

"Father came, and took Mother away, and the icehouse is gone as a sign," Paul told their younger sister as the hurricane raged outside.

A crash had punctuated his words as the wind hurled an elm branch into the roof, leaving a gaping hole over the rooms where the sisters had slept as girls. The three of them had worked busily to patch it as best they could, then the doors had been shut for good, since the rooms weren't needed any more. Constance, always easily diverted, had accepted the explanation. By unspoken agreement, Mother and Father had rarely been mentioned since.

There was no use speaking of her dreams, Margaret decided, for whatever Mother was trying to tell her would come to her in time, and besides, the dreams were only part of it.

Sweats and flushes came over her during the day as well as the night, striking with no warning. In the same way, there were times when she found herself feeling suddenly weak, moments at the sink when her arm felt almost weightless except for a tingling, as if she'd just gotten up from sleeping on it.

She'd thought it best to attribute an occasional broken dish or coffee cup to her own clumsiness, to laugh at it and make it into a joke the others could share. But there were more disturbing times when she was struck not by laughter, but sadness of a depth and intensity that she'd never known before.

The cold had worked its way into her bones, years of winters that left her fingers gnarled at the joints. Soaking them in hot water, which helped the pain, she'd find herself crying without knowing why. Catching a glimpse of her face in the mirror, she'd whisper, "I am old," as if seeing herself for the first time.

But when she stood with Constance in front of the same glass, they were so much alike that they could be twins, two thirds of the same whole. When she and Constance and Paul were together, she felt safest. Their unity, so ingrained, was a kind of protection and security.

Perhaps, she thought, that was part of it, too. She was rarely alone, but at those times when she was, when Paul was off in the woods hunting or fishing the river, when Constance went to gather the apples they kept in the pantry now that the barn was gone, Margaret was powerless against the panic that made her heart pound so hard she had to steady herself against the sink or the table or collapse into a chair, waiting and watching for their return.

What would happen if one of them shouldn't come back? What if there were an accident? What if some harm should come to one of the two people she loved, the two parts of her life that she adored. Their return would calm her nameless fears, but it could never fully exorcise them. They would wait, hiding in some dark corner of her mind, poised like a snake to strike at her again.

Things *could* change, she realized. She'd never considered it before, not really, but the signs were all around them, and perhaps Mother was trying, through her dreams, to warn her of something.

It wasn't the war, Margaret felt certain. For all the talk on the radio, the places called Japan and Germany, England and France were no more real than the kingdoms of Constance's beloved fairy tales. A man had called on them, knocking and knocking at the door and refusing to go away like the occasional unwelcome visitors who'd come to beg during the Hard Times. He was Civil Defense, he told them, as the three of them stood blocking the door. He'd craned his neck for a look inside the house, expecting to be asked in, but she and Constance had been silent, letting Paul say the little that had to be said.

When he'd finally left and disappeared down the Way, they'd all three looked at the brochures he'd left them, warnings about what to do if they spotted an enemy plane, pamphlets that said HOARDING IS JUST WHAT THEY WANT! and showed cartoons of men she recognized as Hitler and Tojo (she'd seen their pictures in magazines) laughing as Americans fought over rolls of toilet paper on a store shelf.

She wasn't afraid of the war, Margaret knew, but of something else, something closer but just beyond her ken. It was senseless, she told herself, wanting to believe it as she cleared the lunch dishes from the table. *Foolish*, she tried to think as she watched her brother brush the crumbs from his beard with the back of his hand. Constance carried the rest of the plates to the sink and caught her eye. Margaret forced a smile and reached to stroke her sister's hair.

"Might as well leave those for later," Paul said when she reached for the faucet.

"We can do them when we get back," Constance agreed.

For an instant, Margaret was totally bewildered. A mo-

ment later, she felt a sense of relief: *Eastfield*. Of course!
They had to go into Eastfield.... Relief gave way to a
sudden fear and sadness.

She'd never cared for the trips to town, but lately she'd
come to despise them more than ever. During the Hard
Times, it hadn't been so bad. They, the Hazeltines, hadn't
been touched by the Depression, and Eastfield had been
involved in its own troubles. Men had been laid off their
jobs, and farmers plagued by weather. Families had moved
away, and those that had stayed had been so involved in
themselves that she and Paul and Margaret had gone about
their business without much notice.

But the Hard Times were over.

All around, there were jobs to be had. The Springfield
Armory, Chapman Valve, Fiske Rubber...the new chem-
ical plant, and the paper mills down the river in Holyoke—
there was war work for everyone who wanted it, extra shifts
for more money.

Only a few years before, Margaret thought, they had
blended in with the town, though they clearly hadn't been
part of it. Now, she was conscious of the differences between herself and her sister and brother and *them*, the *others*.

The women of Eastfield no longer wore drab hand-me-
downs, but looked like they'd stepped out of magazines,
or out of the windows of the new stores that had opened
in town. Their lips were bright red, their pocketbooks swung
on their arms.

They saw the difference between the Hazeltines and
themselves, Margaret knew. She could see it in the smirks
the women exchanged when they passed them, in the nudges
and nods the men in their strange uniforms gave one another
as they looked at her, and at Constance and Paul, sometimes
not even bothering to hide their jokes and laughter.

She remembered what it had been like when she was a

girl. Whatever happened in town, however anxious she felt on the trips back then, she'd been able to breathe more easily once they began to head home.

That, too, had changed.

Eastfield no longer kept its distance. Instead, it spilled toward them, closer, ever closer.

There'd been a time when the building had stopped, then it had begun again. River Road had stores now, and though the man on the radio said there'd be no new housing for the duration, there was too much already, too many people living too close by.

"You can stay, if you like," Paul said, scraping his chair back. Margaret had long since stopped being surprised by the way he could know her thoughts, as if he could look into her mind and see them written there.

Constance pouted. "We go *together*, always—"

"We'll go together," Margaret said. "Of course."

"And I can get a new storybook!" her sister exclaimed with childlike pleasure.

"Yes, dear. Of course you can." Margaret assured her.

But when they'd closed the door behind them, when they stepped out into the early October afternoon and crossed the narrow path that led from the door, through the high grass to the Way, Margaret kept turning back to the house as if she might not see it again.

"I've got the books," Paul told her, patting the pocket of his red-and-black plaid shirt.

Margaret nodded, and with Constance between them, they began the unwelcome walk into town.

# - 2 -

"LOOK! THERE'S ANOTHER ONE!" Constance exclaimed with delight, pointing to the window of the house they were passing. Her tone quickly turned to petulance. "Can't *we* have one?"

Margaret glanced at the Gold Star decal, then, aware of a white-haired woman in black watching them from the porch, took her sister's arm. "I don't think so, dear—"

"But *why?*"

"We'll see. Maybe we can have one, after all," Margaret said softly. Perhaps she should have stayed at home; perhaps Paul knew best after all. They were hardly into Eastfield, and already she felt queer all over.

Their bodies were pressed closely together, their steps in unison as they continued down the sidewalk of Center Street.

*Nothing is wrong*, Margaret told herself. It was her imagination, her foolish imagination making her believe that hands were parting the curtains of the windows they passed, that people were stopping to stare at them as if they were freaks. As if they weren't Hazeltines, *the* Hazeltines, the first and foremost family of Eastfield!

"Look!" Constance announced, pointing to the window

of a shop. SET & STYLE SALON, its sign proclaimed. Three plastic heads stared back, their hair styled in the new pompadours.

"Come along," Margaret whispered, but Constance was pointing and laughing, bent over and giggling. "We don't want to attract attention," she cautioned, trying again, looking to Paul for help.

It was too late. Several women in the salon had seen Constance. They were standing up, looking out the window. Two, a stylist and her patron with rolled hair and a white smock around her shoulders, were already near the open door.

"A fine one to laugh, she is!" the beautician announced loudly.

"Crazy, the whole bunch of them, Trudy. I lived here twenty years, and I can tell you they're all crazy. My ma says they always were, Olivia's children..."

"You're hurting me!" Constance objected as Margaret took her arm and pulled her along. She turned to her brother. "Make her stop!"

But he was silent, taking her other arm and keeping the pace Margaret had set. *How old he looks*, Margaret thought. Where had the gray in his hair come from? Why hadn't she noticed it before? Was there something strange about the light here in town, or in the light at home? Paul was getting older, and so was she. Older...old. And Constance, too, in her fashion, though her mind was and forever would be that of a simple, trusting child.

They turned at Front Street, climbing the three steps to the Eastfield Bank & Trust Company. Holding Constance's hand, Margaret stood near the door as her brother paused with them before he went to the teller.

"...You ought to let Eddie fix you up with one of his

buddies," a blonde customer in a snood was telling a friend of hers with short brown hair.

"Are you kidding? My dad would fix my rear end if I went out with one of those guys from the base!"

The blonde laughed. "Well, the boys at Westover are our flying aces, right? It's your job to keep up morale, you could tell him. Hey, how about that guy over there? See him? Think your old man would go for him?"

The brunette was laughing, too. "Oh, Edna, you crack me up!"

Margaret felt a tingling erupt on her skin. It wasn't her imagination at all! They *were* laughing. They were looking at Paul, and laughing!

And they were making fun of her and Constance, the two women! Nudging one another as they passed, and giggling.

"Now there's a couple of blind dates for the fly boys—"

"Yeah, the *Jap* flyboys!"

Finally Paul approached the teller's counter, but his walk was different than Margaret remembered it. She saw the stoop of his shoulders, the slight hesitation in his gait. When had his straight, proud body begun to curve? she wondered. Why was it *now*—only now—that she noticed it?

She felt hot and flushed, and only out in the street could she catch her breath.

"...That new Bette Davis show is at the Poli, you know," someone was saying as they walked along.

"Me, I like the spook pictures best. Hey, look at them. The ones from the haunted house out there, you know, on River Road? Now *there's* something they could make a picture about..."

"Don't do that!" Margaret snapped as Constance turned

and stuck her tongue out at the man and woman who'd been talking about them. The couple's laughter followed them, and louder still, to Margaret, was the sound of her brother's silence.

Once, he would have stared them down, invoked their father's name, and that would have been enough. He no longer made the effort, or even acknowledged the insult. Was he tired, Margaret wondered, tired inside himself? Had the part of him that had burned so brightly with the blinding pride they'd inherited from their father dimmed? Or did he know—as she did, though they'd never spoken of it—that their name meant nothing any longer; their existence was a joke, a fact that Eastfield, at best, tolerated?

Mr. Fletcher, the butcher, had died some years before. Ralph, his son, had expanded the small shop into the Eastfield Consolidated Market. As they entered it, the shelves of food in their bright boxes and cans made Margaret all the more uneasy. So many choices! So many decisions! And it was changing, changing all the time.

"Can we get the cereal with the decoder?" Constance whined.

They regularly listened to the radio at home in the evenings, following the continuing stories of families and detectives. One program, sponsored by a breakfast cereal company, had frequent commercials that promised a secret decoder ring "in every box," and it was that brand that Constance wanted.

"They don't have it here," Margaret said quietly, aware of the women standing at the counter passing the time of day with the clerk; of the shoppers with their baskets in the nearby aisles. Even without making any undue noise, she and Constance and Paul attracted attention. Their clothes, their hair, the very infrequency of their visits made them conspicuous.

"How do you know?" Constance asked, pleading.

"Enough, now," Paul said, silencing her, and Margaret felt a grateful relief as her sister pouted.

"...too old, they told him down to the draft board," a woman was saying as they approached the cash register. "'Course, that's what *I* told him, the fool!"

Her companions and the clerk laughed. "Midge, you'd be singing a different tune if they took him," someone suggested.

"That's what *you* think!" the first woman insisted. "But Uncle Sam don't even want him!"

They were all laughing again, and Margaret waited.

The face of the young clerk was spotted with acne, and his mouth curled in a cruel smirk, older than his years, as he acknowledged the Hazeltines.

"Well, now!" he said, too brightly, too loud, his eyes sweeping the women he'd been talking with, bringing them into it. "And what can I do for you folks?"

Without a word, Paul reached into his shirt pocket and pulled out the ration books. Their standing order was delivered once a month, the first Monday always, and left beside the mailbox at the end of the Way.

"Anything special for you?" the clerk asked as he took the stamps for butter and eggs and milk out of their books. The chickens had been lost in 1938, and they'd never gotten around to replacing them. "Got some wild rice in—extra fancy—in case you're planning to do some entertaining," the boy said.

One of the women at the counter choked on her laughter.

"Stop," another told him, giggling all the same.

"You never can tell," the clerk went on. "Lots of people are opening their houses up for the boys in uniform. I just thought they might have a regular USO out their way—"

"Do you have any chuck steak?" Margaret asked, her

cheeks burning. "I'd like two pounds, chopped."

"—and hot dogs!" Constance added, her voice deafening. "Hot dogs, Margaret!"

The women erupted in laughter again, not even making the effort to hide it this time. Margaret moved toward the meat case, and the clerk followed, reluctantly leaving his audience.

*Another few minutes, just another few minutes*, Margaret reminded herself, choosing the meat. *It will be over in just a few minutes more* . . . as she took two cans of peas from the shelf. She was holding them but unable to feel them, as if they and her arm had become suddenly weightless.

Then they were back at the counter, Paul was paying the clerk and reaching for the shopping bag. The boy behind the counter gave him a mock salute as he turned to leave, and Margaret heard the laughter trail them as they left the store.

*A few more steps*, she told herself. *Another two steps and we'll be out the door, in the fresh air* . . .

But before she could take a breath, before the door had closed behind the three of them, a jangling noise and the sudden thrust of something being pushed before her face startled her.

"Red Cross—" the woman holding the canister said as Margaret's hand grabbed her brother's arm. Margaret's eyes were wide with wild, nameless terror.

"I'm sorry," the woman apologized. "I didn't mean to startle you. Are you all right?"

Margaret tried to speak, but her heart was pounding too hard. She managed to nod.

"You're sure?" the woman asked, looking at Paul and Constance as well.

Margaret gripped Paul more tightly, her fingers digging into the flesh of his forearm. He led them across the street, away from the woman whose eyes followed them until the door of the grocery store opened once again, and she approached someone else.

*I'm not well*, Margaret thought. *So jittery and jumpy! Imagining things! And hearing music, now, on top of everything else—*

"Music!" Constance announced, smiling with a child's delight.

*At least it's real*, Margaret thought. The sounds of cars and trucks and buses, the noises of the traffic and the day struck her as louder than usual, but she heard the music above them, the strains of a march being played by a band.

"Can we see?" Constance pleaded. *"Can* we?"

Before there was time for an answer, Constance had let go of Paul's arm and was away from them, running toward the source of the sound, her fear of the town overcome for the moment by the attraction of the martial beat. It was behavior that was out of character for her, but so much— Margaret realized in that instant as she watched her sister run and skip down the sidewalk, watched passers-by stop in their tracks to stare at the child-woman in the white dress and blue cape—was changing.

Paul was so quiet these days, and she herself was feeling old and sick, and Constance was acting as she had when she was a young girl, so willful and defiant.

"We'll have to go after her," Paul said, matter-of-factly.

"Yes. Yes, of course," Margaret heard herself agree, ignoring the pain in her mind and her body as they followed the figure that was disappearing in the distance.

They wouldn't run after her, they each knew, sharing some unspoken bond of communication. That would only make it worse, attract more attention. Instead, arms linked, they walked quickly down the street, turning the corner.

"There," Paul said, pointing to the edge of the Common.

The music was louder now, and there were more people. Margaret tried to focus her eyes on her sister, at the edge of the small crowd.

*The Common*...where they'd sat with Father and Mother on the grandstand at the Celebration, the tale told and retold so many times that the repetition more than the event was fixed in her mind and memory. Where they'd all sat, the Hazeltines, in the place of honor as Father made his speech introduced by the mayor...

The music—Was it the same march they'd played that day? she wondered—stopped. She could see Constance's face, set in disappointment.

"And now our new Mayor, Peter Putney," someone announced over a loud speaker. There was a burst of applause.

"Wait," Margaret told her brother, just before they were about to cross to the Common. She touched her chest, bewildered when she couldn't feel her body. "You—you get her, Paul. I'm short of breath."

His blue eyes studied her, deciding; then he nodded and crossed the street alone. Margaret tried to focus on the speaker's platform in the distance, and on a bright metal board that caught the sun and reflected it back. *My eyes!* she thought as the glow wavered. She tried to fix on Constance and Paul, but they shimmered, hovering in and out of focus.

A voice boomed in her ear, then faded, then boomed again.

"...And when the history of these difficult times is written, my friends, when the enemy is defeated and victory is at hand..." There was a roar of noise, a wall of sound, then the voice, loud and soft, louder and softer, as Margaret steadied herself against a lamp post. "Eastfield's place in that history will be one of sacrifice and honor. The names of our sons who gave their lives for their country will echo in our hearts, and our history—"

"'Scuse me, ma'am," someone said as a body collided with her own.

"I done tole you look where you goin'—"

Margaret fell against the post and turned her head. At the sight of the black man in uniform and the woman at his side, she fell to the sidewalk.

From far away, voices mingled and merged.

"...For this is not only a monument to memory, but to the spirit of sacrifice that is the foundation of freedom..."

"You done scared her half to death, the poor thing!" a woman's voice said, bending low but still far above her.

"Margaret?" It sounded like Paul.

"Oh, Margaret!" Constance gasped.

"I sure am sorry. Didn't have any 'tentions of upsetting the lady. Guess she never seen colored folks before..."

"What happened?"

"Who is it?"

"She needs a doctor!"

Voices and questions, apologies and suggestions, words and whispers.

"...The crazy ones from the edge of town there."

"You know, on River Road—"

"Olivia's children—"

"Why do they call them that?"

"I dunno."

"Move back, folks. Give the lady some air. Can I call a doctor for you, mister? Does she have spells like this often?"

"Yes," Paul was saying. "Often."

"Well, you'll want to get her home, no doubt. Do you have a car?"

"No car."

"Taxi! Someone get these people a taxi!"

Dimly, Margaret heard a car come to a stop and a door open. She tried to focus on her brother's face as he reached down for her, lifting her tenderly. He placed her right arm around his neck, but when she tried to make her left follow, it wouldn't respond.

She felt ashamed and frightened. She was causing such a problem, such a commotion! She tried to apologize, but her tongue was thick and the strength for speech gone.

"It's all right," Paul was telling her, his arms cradling her as the taxi pulled away from the onlookers. Constance was leaning close, brushing the hair back from her damp forehead.

"It will be all right," her brother said again, "as soon as we get home."

# - 3 -

THE FLOODS AND the traffic and the building had changed it all, he considered, watching the line float on the water. The deer had disappeared; the foxes were few. Even the rabbits were scarce, gone back into the far woods, avoiding the road and anything to do with it.

The river, too had changed. He couldn't remember exactly how long it had been, but it had been years since the salmon and the sturgeon ran. During the Hard Times, strangers had fished for trout and bass, but their numbers, too, were fewer.

A whistle sounded downriver. He looked up, and the gray sky was filled with a darker, grayer smoke from one of the factories. There were so many of them now, more all the time, in each direction and on both sides of the water. It wasn't just what he could see that told Paul Hazeltine this, but what the river itself showed him.

During the warm months, the Green Time, the river always smelled of the raw sewage that was dumped into it. Now, even in the cold of winter, there were other smells, something like paint at times, like lye at others. Besides smelling it, he could see it, floating among the branches and debris the current carried. Patches of foam, sometimes white as soap, sometimes a dark green or purple, floated by, or caught in bushes at the edge of the bank.

As if the memory of the things he'd seen and smelled triggered it, a racking cough seized him, and Paul Hazeltine had to set down his fishing pole. His chest rattled with the cough that felt as if it were trapped inside him, then it rose up, spilling from his mouth, thick and foul, brackish and bloody.

"Damn cough," he cursed, spitting again to clear the taste. He'd had it for months now, thinking it a cold in the beginning. He'd tried a tonic, and Margaret had made him a mustard plaster, before she took sick herself, but still it was with him. Deeper inside him, it felt, burrowed in for a long stay.

It sapped his strength and drained his energy, but he tried hard not to let his sisters know, to keep it down and back until he could go into the bathroom, or better yet, outside the door to let the poison out.

Maybe Constance was fooled. She was like a large child, easy to convince. But Margaret, for her sickness and the silence that was a part of it, knew. He was sure of it.

In the mornings, when he lifted her up from the bed and carried her downstairs to the rocker they'd moved into the kitchen—her favorite chair and her favorite room—he'd feel the muscles of her body tense. She wasn't resisting him, he sensed, but the effort it took from him, the carrying her down each morning and back up each night, he could look into her eyes and see that she thought herself a bother, a waste of time.

He could see that, and her future, and his own as well. At night, when he lay between the two of them, their heads against his shoulders and his arms around them, he could close his eyes and, in that hazy time before sleep, imagine that it was the way it had been.

They were safe and strong, special and chosen. It was as it had been, and always would be.

But then Margaret would wet the bed, not that she could help it, and he'd have to hold her while Constance changed the sheets. Or his own pain would stab him in the center of his chest, and he'd have to climb over one of them, then run the water in the bathroom sink as hard as he could to mask the sound of his lungs' contents spilling out of him.

"It's changing," Paul told the river, picking up his fishing pole. "It's all changing."

Something pulled at the line, and he expertly reeled it in. It was a perch, a small one. Once he'd have thrown it back, but now he'd come to take what he could get. He baited the line with one of the worms he'd dug and cast it out again into the churning current, watching and waiting.

Often when he came back to bed, his throat sore and his chest burning, he'd lie awake. The sleep that had once come so easily evaded him now. When it fell on him, it fell lightly. He'd see an image of the house as it had been, or his parents, and before he had time to dream the dream through (if it was a dream at all), he'd be wide awake, thinking.

His parents, at least, had been spared the passage of these years.

He could remember his father, his memory more vivid than the old faded photographs. He could recall the pride the man with eyes so like his own had taken in being above Eastfield, in his home and his land and his family.

"He shouldn't have left it all on me," he told the river, surprised by his own words. It wasn't a new thought, but for years, all the years of his own life as a man, he'd managed to hold it in check, to keep it inside.

There'd been times when it had threatened to fall from the tip of his tongue. He could remember the first of them, when he'd come down that morning and seen his mother, her battered hands and the madness in her eye. And the secret, the shame, under the newly turned dirt floor of the icehouse.

But his father's way had been the only way he knew, and he'd gone along with it, following his mother's lead, then—though exactly when, he wasn't quite sure—taking up the lead himself.

Protecting them all, keeping them safe... there'd been a challenge in it, and in his youth, he'd risen to it like a soldier. Then his mother, *"poor Olivia," they'd said in town*, turning to him as her son and her hope.

She'd been proud, too, in her way. Her flowers, and her house with its furniture and fine china. Then she'd been gone, too, and it had been on him, all of it on him to keep the secrets, to keep them safe.

Margaret and Constance had done their share, to be sure. And done it without question or complaint. He'd come to hate the other one (he could no longer think of her as his sister) for sticking him, so fully and finally, with it. He'd waited, that afternoon she'd gone off, a full two years at least before Mother, for her to come back. A doctor would be with her, he'd thought, or someone from town. But no, she'd gone with herself in mind and them out of it, and it had all been on him, all the weight of it.

His mother floating from one day to the next; Margaret and Constance turning to him to be told what to do. They'd managed it well, when you considered it, but why, he was no longer quite certain. The years had made the reasons for all of it, once as solid as the frozen blocks they'd kept in the icehouse, drip and melt away. Then the reason hadn't mattered, but the doing, the habit of it.

He'd done what he'd had to do, what he'd been taught to do, and if there was judgment for any of it, well...

A tug on the line pulled him from his thoughts. He concentrated on the reel. This one was bigger, a carp, he noted. He took it off the hook, and as he tossed it down to the ground, another spasm of pain overcame him. Coughing and choking, Paul Hazeltine sank to his knees, the bloody sputum rising within him as the carp, a few inches away, flapped and tried to soak the water up from the muddy ground. Its gills opened and closed faster and faster, then a few last, slow times, until like the perch, it was still.

He felt his sickness spill out of him, viscous and clotted.

Father and Mother gone, and the other one gone, and then—so many years later—with the nerve to come back! To stand there in her city suit and tease them, show them what they might have had and make it sound as if they still could! As if there weren't all the years when she'd been gone and they'd been home to mark them and set them off from the rest of the world!

He had hated her then and hated her still, wished her pain and suffering but not death, for death was too easy. Too peaceful, he thought, looking at the fish, thinking of the way the leaves turned so pretty when they died, and of the special colors flowers took when they dried, just before the wind bore their petals away.

Death was a rest from the world and its worry, he thought when he was able to stand, the pain in his chest dulled a bit. He took the fish and made his aching way up the steep bank, then waited beside a weeping willow for a break in the heavy traffic of River Road. Paul hurried across, his eye on the mailbox at the corner of the Way. The postal truck was parked alongside it, just starting up.

The driver leaned out. "Had a package," he announced. "Left it there in the same spot." He motioned to a thicket of leaves a few feet up beyond the rusted mailbox. "Long as you're here, you might as well sign the slip for me."

Wordlessly, Paul Hazeltine wrote his name on the form thrust at him.

"*Some* might say 'thank you,'" the postman observed.

Paul ignored him, carrying the mail and the package and the fish up the grade of the Way. His tread was slow and his muscles hurt. Finally, when he could hardly stand to move another step, the house was in sight.

He thought of his mother again, wondering what she would say if she could see it now. The woods had crept up beyond the hedge, or what was left of it. The stone paths and formal gardens were gone, the façade thick with vines.

He tried to remember when it had begun to change, or why he hadn't noticed it happening, getting away from them as it had.

"It's all changed," he said. Yet in the midst of it, at the very heart, there was no change at all.

# - 4 -

"DON'T YOU LIKE IT?" Constance asked petulantly. "Is there too much salt for you? Have just a bit more, then."

The pantry, where the rocker had been set, smelled of the apples that sat in bushel baskets, and the bunches of rosemary and thyme that had been hung on the walls to dry. The frail figure in the chair didn't answer or move; her lips neither resisted or eased the way for the spoon, lifted from the bowl of soup, that was guided between them.

"You have to eat if you want to feel better, you know," Constance said, "even if I'm not as good a cook as you. All the same, I think my cake turned out nicely, don't you, Margaret?" She blotted her sister's lips and dabbed her chin with the corner of her apron, then took the bowl of soup away, returning with a lopsided cake on a plate.

"I must have done something wrong," she observed, picking at it. "It *looks* funny, but it tastes good."

She laughed, delighted with herself. Margaret had always done the cooking, but after that day in town, Constance had been gratified to discover how much she'd learned without even being aware of it. Going through the familiar motions she'd watched her sister make for as long as she could remember, she'd turned out simple things first—broiled and fried meats; warmed-up vegetables that had been put up the season before, or the season before that—then she'd tried bread, and now, a cake!

"I wish you could have some," she told her sister unhappily. Looking into the sad eyes, made brighter and bigger by the flesh that had sunk into itself, she set the cake down. "Soon," Constance promised, kneeling, covering her sister's hand with her own. "Soon you'll be better, and we'll be just like we were."

The frail figure's breath rattled.

"Just let me change the water," Constance said, moving to the sink. The fish her brother had caught for dinner were soaking. Changing the water, Margaret had taught her, helped to take the taste of the river out of them and would keep them fresh for the later meal.

"I think I'll make a fish stock for you tonight. Won't that be nice?" Constance asked, wiping her hands on her apron as she turned. "Now I'll fix your hair for you, Margaret."

Gently, lightly, she took a brush from the pocket of the robe hooked on the back of the rocking chair and began to stroke her sister's hair. "I wish you could let me know if I pull too hard, dear. I'll try to be careful."

She giggled to herself, then added, "You're getting gray, Margaret! Like Paul. Want to see? I'll show you. Just wait right here!" she called over her shoulder as she hurried from the room.

*"Wait right here."* The words echoed in Margaret Hazeltine's head. As if there were any other place to go, or any way for her to get there. As if the sickness was a wrap she could shake off. As if she were one of the dolls that Constance liked to play with—

The twinge of bitterness had come quickly, and it left her as suddenly. It took too much of the little strength she had left. And who, after all, was to blame. Neither of them, Paul nor Constance, had done anything to her; nothing but kindness since that day in town.

The moments when she felt jealous of them, resentful

that their lives—that life itself—could go on without her, were like punctuation marks in days that turned into one another with a lethargy that she felt about the soup, and her hair, and all the rest of it.

Carried upstairs. Carried down. Unable to do the slightest thing for herself or by herself . . . she had come to take a strange pleasure in the sight of the skin hanging loose from her arms. The less there was of her, the less trouble she would be to them. The less weight to burden Paul each night and again each morning.

"I'm back!" Constance announced. Standing behind Margaret, she held a hand mirror to her sister's face. "Do you see?" she asked. "Gray hair, Margaret!"

It was all she could do to make herself look, not because she was concerned about her hair—it hardly mattered now—but because it was a struggle to lift her head. Still, she saw herself, and the image caught and held her.

How long *had* it been? Weeks? Months? How long did it take for a woman to become old, for an illness to etch itself into the lines of the face, for the skin to become translucent? She sighed inside herself; the sound came out as a wheeze.

"Maybe, when you're better, it will turn brown again," Constance was saying, chattering on. "Of course, I think it's quite pretty. Maybe I'll get gray hair soon, and then we'll *all* have it! Oh, Margaret, I *will* get it too, won't I? I'd feel so bad if it was just you and Paul."

She put the mirror down, then knelt to look into her older sister's eyes. "You do think I'll get it! I'm so glad!" Then she continued to brush Margaret's hair.

However long it had been, Margaret Hazeltine knew, it would not be that much longer. Each morning, when she opened her eyes, she was surprised. She wondered what it would be like on the day she didn't wake—if it would be like anything at all. Paul and Constance would go on. She could see them, picture them, going on in the house, Paul telling Constance a story about her going off to Mother and Father.

And maybe she would. Maybe it would be like the dreams she had of them, but longer—endlessly longer.

". . . Tonight we'll have the fish, and I'll make the cake a surprise for Paul. Don't you think he'll be pleased?"

Nothing could please her brother now, Margaret knew, for she understood that the same change that had transformed her life so swiftly was, more slowly but as certainly, transforming his. If there'd been more time they might have talked about it, shared their thoughts, prepared for it together.

"Oh, I forgot to tell you! The rubber sheet came in the mail. Paul brought it in. So you see, now if you—well, in the night, you don't have to worry, dear."

Margaret felt her eyes fill at Constance's sincere, obvious pleasure. She was a sweet child: exactly, a *sweet child*. Good-hearted, though highly strung at times. If they'd had time to talk, she and Paul, they might have had a chance to discuss what would happen to Constance; what would become of her. They were close, so much a part of one another's lives, that it had seemed impossible to imagine her—any of them—going on without the others. Yet in her sickness, Margaret had come to understand that it was to be their destiny after all, after so much . . .

"Shall I braid it for you?" Constance asked, still fussing with her sister's hair. "I promise not to hurt."

*She won't even know how to count the days after the curse, to know what time is safe with Paul,* Margaret thought, barely aware of her sister's hands at her neck. But maybe it didn't matter, really. Not any more. *Oh, Constance, I love you so,* she thought, wishing she could say it—just that—just once more.

"I love you," her younger sister said suddenly, bending and whispering the words, a kiss against the cool skin of Margaret's cheek. Margaret's head fell forward.

"There!" Constance announced after a time, pleased with her work. "You look so nice! And I suppose I should start supper, don't you think?"

The color was high as fire in her cheeks as she worked at the sink, humming to herself, talking to herself and her sister as she peeled potatoes and put them on the stove to boil, then began to clean the fish Paul had caught earlier.

"Do you remember the dinners we used to have?" she asked. "In the dining room? I do. It would be nice to do that sometime again, don't you think?"

But of course, the dining-room table was stacked with years and years of old magazines and newspapers, fragments of lives and days and decades.

"Oh, my—" Constance said suddenly, startled. She'd opened the belly of the carp, slicing the fish from the mouth to tail and unfolding it like a letter.

"What is it, then?" a voice asked.

She turned to her brother, holding the fish in her hands, a puzzled look on her face. In her cutting, Constance had nicked her finger with the tip of the knife, but it was not the sight of her own blood that bewildered her. "Look," she said, staring at the solid blue bubble her knife had exposed. It lay there, an unanticipated mystery in the gut of the fish, a thing of wonder, and terror.

Paul Hazeltine stared at it for a long time in his sister's open hands.

"What is it, Paul?" Constance asked. "Why is it there?"

He looked in silence, as if confronting the secret of life, or of death.

"Damned river," he said, finally, taking it from her, opening the kitchen door and flinging it out with all his strength. The movement brought on a fit of coughing and choking. Constance closed the door and slid a chair from the table toward her brother, He fell into it, his body racking and heaving, his elbows on his knees and his head resting in his hands.

As the spasm passed, Constance brightened, her worry transformed to glee.

"We don't need the fish," she said, smiling conspiratorially at the sister who, with her eyes open, had sunk into an endless sleep. She turned to Paul, lost in thoughts of his own, and brought a platter toward him, removing the yellowed doily that had been covering it. "See?" she asked, happy with her lopsided accomplishment. "I made you a cake!"

He didn't answer, so Constance said it again. His continued silence took away her joy. "Is—is something wrong, Paul?" she asked.

Paul Hazeltine looked at his own hands, then at Margaret, whose wide and lifeless eyes stared straight ahead of her. At last he turned to Constance.

"Nothing is wrong," he said, his voice soft and flat, his head turning slowly, as if with great effort, from side to side. "I—I'll be right back," he said, rising from his chair like an old man, stopping for a moment in front of Margaret. He left the room, his shoulders slumped, before Constance could see the tears in his eyes.

"See?" she asked the figure in the chair when Paul was gone. "I *told* you he'd like it!" Constance paused, her head cocked to listen to a voice that only she could hear. "Yes, yes you're quite right, Margaret," she agreed, displaying the cake, inspecting it herself with pleasure. "It isn't the way it looks that matters at all—it's how it is inside."

# - 5 -

RAIN CAME, hard and ceaseless, pounding against the roof, clouding the November sky until it was nearly impossible to tell day from night. Then, as the month ended, the rain turned to sleet. The pounding was louder, the beating against the bedroom windows a constant interruption of Paul Hazeltine's fevered dreams.

It had been two months since Margaret had lain in bed with him and Constance: "We'll leave her in the pantry. She'll be more comfortable," he'd told Constance, who'd accepted his word as always, agreeing that it would be best, even adding that perhaps it would be less tiring for her sister. But he and Constance took their usual places on the mattress, leaving the space that was, or had been, Margaret's, as if she might sometime rise from her rocker and climb the stairs to join them at night.

What was happening, Paul knew, was that they were to join her. He cursed his sickness, worse with the cold and damp, worse all the time now. It was eating away at him, draining him. He felt his strength, his manhood, leaving him, ebbing away in spite of the time he spent resting in bed, the soups Constance brought him—he could hardly swallow them, much less solid food—and the summoning of his will to make his body respond. It was failing him faster now, as if it had been holding out, holding on to Margaret. He could feel something—he remembered the blob of blue inside the fish, and pictured it as that—growing within his chest. Death was growing inside him.

Yet Constance, out of innocence or ignorance, acted as if nothing had changed or was changing. On those rare occasions when he dragged himself down the stairs, he found her in the kitchen, at the sink or the stove, carrying on a one-sided conversation with Margaret. Between her chores, she sat in the pantry, talking to the dead woman, chattering away merrily.

The cold and the dryness of the pantry, and perhaps the fumes from the stored apples, had had an odd effect on the thing that had been Margaret. She did not decay, but dried out, her skin becoming waxen, her limbs frozen in the position in which she sat.

Constance didn't know that her sister had died, or if she did, she refused to acknowledge it. Fatigue, in part, made Paul Hazeltine sleep, but sleep was also an escape from Constance and her sincere talk of what she and Margaret had spoken of, of what Margaret had "said."

Sometimes, he slept for minutes; at other times, he woke with no sense of feeling that more time had gone by, only to discover that entire days had passed.

It was no longer possible for him to hide the paroxysms of coughing, more intense, and frequent, and painful, from Constance: he hadn't the strength to get out of bed in the night. Sister and lover, she woke with him, held a cup for him to spit into, her fingers supporting his head when he was finally able to take a sip from the water glass she kept beside the bed and held to his parched lips. Her hand rested lightly on his shoulder or chest when the attacks were over,

her small fingers rising and falling with his irregular breathing.

And when the spasms passed, when he could sleep, he
was lost in dreams of his own youth; of his mother; of Father
himself. The house, in these visions, hadn't gotten away
from them. Instead, it was the showplace it had been when
Olivia had first been its mistress, instructing Brigid in the
details of its care.

He could see the high polish on the silver and brass, the
gleaming wood and glass. He could smell, in those dreams,
not the stench of his own sickness, but the scent of lemon
oil, and his mother's cherished flowers, and her perfume.

*"Keep us all together,"* voices told him, Father and
Mother. Waking, soaked with sweat and shivering in spite
of the extra quilts Constance had brought, he'd wonder what
the words meant.

The days passed, and the sleet stopped, replaced by snow
that coated the window, locking him further into himself.

As she had in the rain and the sleet and now the snow,
Constance went each day to the box at the end of the Way,
gathering the mail, carrying it up to the bedroom. Often,
he'd find her waiting when he woke, with letters and cir-
culars and magazines, and a cloth soaking in a bowl of cool
water.

*Did she watch him sleep, waiting for him to wake?* Paul
wondered. But Constance's expression offered no answer.
She'd smile, beam, wipe his brow and face and talk softly,
her touch light and loving, her eyes bright with the joy of
seeing him and having him look at her.

Each time, though, it was harder for him to see her, for
not only were his eyes watery and rheumy, but when he
looked at her, he could not see beyond the moment. There
had been a time when he had been able to look at his sisters,

at the house and land, and see years stretching ahead, un-interrupted. Now, there was only Constance, only days and maybe moments.

Beyond that was a blackness, a void that sickened him even more than the thing in his chest. Paul had to turn away at times, unable to look at Constance, into her heart and her love, without being overcome by a sense of shame at the realization that a time would come, and soon, when his eyes would not be there to meet her own.

*I've failed you,* he told her in the thoughts he could never put into words. Failure, when it was all over, as it so nearly was, was the Hazeltine legacy; the tradition of first father, and now son.

With Father, at least the rest of them had been together— Mother, and himself, Constance and Margaret, Francine— damn her!—for a time. But who would be left when he was gone? Who would there be but Constance, unaware of her own vulnerability, having been so completely protected, shielded to the point where she could not even recognize her innocence and dependence.

Unable to do more than wait, he waited for an answer, a sign of some kind.

But there were only the dreams, the voices telling him, *"Keep us together . . . keep the family together."*

There was only Constance, with the mail and the bowls of soup, the cups of tea he could barely swallow, the water that was never cold enough to soothe the burning inside him. Constance, lying next to him, watching, waiting to watch him . . .

And he would be unable to look back.

Once—whether it was day or night, or how long he'd been asleep, he did not know—Paul Hazeltine woke to find Constance again beside him.

She smiled as his eyes opened, the cloth already in her hand to sponge and soothe him.

"Soup," she said simply, tenderly, taking a bowl from the table beside the bed, bringing a spoon to his lips.

*I must not let it happen*, he knew, *I must not leave her alone . . .*

His back and shoulders ached as he propped himself up. His hands reached out as she brought the spoon closer and closer to his lips.

"It's good for you. It will make you feel better. You'll see," she told him with assurance.

*I will not leave her!* he decided then.

His hands, trembling, encircled her neck, but there was no strength in them, no strength left in him at all.

Without fear, with a blind and trusting love, Constance set the bowl down on the table, Paul's fingers a shimmering necklace around her throat.

"I know," she said softly, her own hands reaching out, caressing his matted hair and fevered skin. As she leaned toward him, he tried with all of the strength that was left to him, but the gesture only drew his sister closer.

"I know," Constance said again, her cheek against his, her lips lingering against his ear before she effortlessly eased back and again lifted the bowl of soup. "I love you, too, Paul."

Outside, a freezing storm raged.

And within the soul of Paul Hazeltine, a fire of a kind died.

# - 6 -

"SLEEPING, SLEEPING, SLEEPING!" Constance said, pouting.

She set the kettle to boil on the stove, then glanced into the pantry.

"He didn't even wake up this morning, Margaret—you know how Paul is *always* the first one up!" She sighed. "It's just as well, I suppose. He was up half the night with that terrible cough of his. I'll be glad when the Green Time comes again. Did you ever see so much snow?"

The water came to a boil, and she poured it into a cup, through the strainer with the pinch of tea she'd added. Before, she'd made a pot, but now there was no point. It would be better for Paul to have his fresh and hot when he woke.

With the chipped cup in her hand, she stood in the doorway of the pantry, sipping the steaming liquid. "Of course, winter colds are always the worst, aren't they? But Paul will feel like himself in no time. I'm sure of it. Don't you think so, dear?"

She waited, then smiled at the silence. "I do too. Yes, we'll all feel better once the Green Time comes again. Maybe we should be like the bears and just sleep the whole winter away. Wouldn't that be nice, dear? We'd all wake up when the snow was gone."

Cocking her head, listening to a silent voice, she giggled. "And maybe we'd find Goldilocks, you're right!" Her tone softened. "I miss the stories, Margaret—but oh, don't you feel bad." She giggled again. "I know most of them, anyway, without your even telling me. Briar Rose, and Rumpelstiltskin, and Rapunzel...I know tham all..."

She glanced out the frosted window and shook her head. "I *still* expect to see the barn and icehouse every time I look out there, don't you?" Constance turned and smiled at the still figure in the chair.

Somewhere a branch tapped against a window, and the old house creaked. "Those sounds are supposed to be scary," Constance said, as if imparting a great secret. "You know— the way they are on the radio, on "The Shadow," and "Suspense"? But I like them, don't you. They're...part of us, don't you think?"

She sensed, rather than knew, that Paul had awakened. "I'll be right back," Constance said, hurrying to the stairs, rushing up them.

The dim sound of a horn at the end of the Way made her stop for a moment. When she began to climb again, her step was brighter and her smile wider.

"Good morning, dear," she said at the doorway of the bedroom. As she'd known, Paul was awake, his body shifting slightly, his eyes watching her. "How are you feeling today?"

No words answered her, only a long spasm of coughing that bent and twisted him. She hurried to the bedside, holding the cup to his dry, caked lips. There was more phelgm now, thick and bloody. Wiping his lips, she put the cup aside.

"What you need, Paul, is something to drink. A nice fresh cup of tea, wouldn't that be just the thing? Oh—I heard the delivery truck from the store. I'll run down and put the water on. Maybe there'll be some eggs—I could fix you an eggnog, if they brought the milk. I'll be right back, dear. *Right* back."

Humming to herself, she went back to the kitchen, starting the kettle again.

"I'm only going down the Way to collect the groceries," she said to Margaret as she pulled her boots on and grabbed the worn blue cape to cover her shoulders. She opened the kitchen door to the cold wind.

The ground was frozen. Constance's steps made crackling noises as they broke the surface of the snow. Without breaking her stride, she reached down and cupped a handful of snow, not rolling it up, but tossing it high in the air, laughing as it fell back on her hair and face.

Across the lawn, she stopped for a moment, struck by the sight of the Way. Icicles hung from low branches; vines were covered with glistening frost.

*Like a picture in a storybook,* she thought, *a picture of wonderland.*

It was so beautiful that she wanted to stay, to stand still and admire it. But there were the groceries to be gotten, and the mail, perhaps, and Paul waiting, up in the bedroom.

But she could be Alice in her wonderland all the same; the Snow Queen as she walked down the Way; a princess in her private, wintry kingdom.

The postman hadn't come, she saw as she checked the box, but that was all the better. The mail was real, an intrusion on her imagination. The box of groceries, on the other hand, could be a thing of magic, a chest of treasures to be carried back to the castle.

"There *are* eggs and milk!" she told Margaret, delighted, not noticing that she'd forgotten to close the door, or that the kettle was boiling. "And butter, too!"

With her cape still wrapped around her, a magic cloak

now, she left the box and went through the parlor, up the familiar stairs.

"Tea or eggnog, Paul?" she called before she entered the room. "You can have your choice! Or both, if you like—"

She stopped abruptly. Another spell of coughing and spitting up, even worse this time. Clotted sputum stained his face and the pillow, spilling over to the sheet.

With a caress, she wiped his face. The movement was tender and light, but his head turned with it as she wiped his mouth, then it fell back again.

"Paul?" Constance whispered. She placed her hand against his forehead. It was cool: the fever had finally broken. "You sleep, dear," she said softly, pulling the covers aside, climbing into bed beside him. "You sleep, and I'll be right here when you wake up."

She would wait and watch him sleep, perhaps even nap herself, and then one of them would stir and kiss the other, like Sleeping Beauty and Prince Charming.

As she clung to her brother, surprised by the coldness of his body, Constance decided that it wouldn't matter which of them kissed the other, the way it did in the fairy tale. They would make their own story.

She held him as the morning sun rose higher, dozing and waking again a few hours later, when it had almost set in the late December afternoon. His body was cold and stiff.

"I'll wait," Constance promised. "I'll warm you." Outside, the sky darkened with the hour and with clouds.

She held to him that night, as the snow fell, heavy and silent.

She slept, imagining that he stirred and woke her, but when she opened her eyes, Paul's were still closed, and his body hadn't moved. "I won't leave you," she whispered, early the next morning, and again late the next day.

"Paul, oh Paul," she sighed, as she held him, as the snow fell, and as time within the strange and silent walls of the Hazeltine house ceased to be measured by clocks and calendars, but by the length of time it took for a heart to finally, fatally break.

# - 7 -

"FINE JOB VIC CASEY is doing, huh?" Officer Douglas Tremont asked as the police car drove along River Road. "Imagine, a war correspondent over in London. Just like Ed Murrow."

Lloyd Harris nodded. "It's a bit more exciting than the *Eastfield Record,* I'd venture."

The officer looked at the man beside him and smiled, wondering if the new man was jealous of his predecessor, who'd recently gotten the correspondent's job with the *Boston Globe.* "Give the town a chance, Lloyd," he said easily. "You may like it. Anyhow, it's better than being in the Army, being behind that desk of yours."

"I'd have gone if they'd have me. I'm Four-F." He tapped his thick glasses, and the officer, who'd gotten his job through the influence of his father-in-law, former police chief of Eastfield and now Mayor Putney, nodded, not mentioning his own deferrment. Instead, he changed the subject.

"Well, maybe you'll find a story out here. Of course, you have to consider that McCilligan is getting on a bit. And you know how mailmen are—nosy by nature, always reading postcards."

At first, he'd listened to the postman with a feigned interest. So what if some screwy old oddballs on the outskirts of town didn't take the mail in from their box? It was their business, after all, and besides the blizzard there'd been Christmas, with the usual traffic accidents, and more drunks to contend with—thanks to the soldiers in town.

"Bigger fish to fry," he'd said when the postman had stopped in again to tell him the mail was still piling up, overflowing the box, and to ask why no official inquiry had been made.

"Why don't you look yourself?" the policeman had suggested. "Go up and knock on the door if you're that concerned about them."

"I'm not 'concerned,'" the man had insisted. "They don't give me a word of thanks, much less a card at Christmas with something in it."

"Then what's the whole thing about?"

The postman had lapsed into a boring monologue about his duties as an employee of the federal government, and Officer Tremont had decided to check it out just to get McCilligan off his back. Something, though, had kept him from actually making the drive, a nameless thing at first that he hadn't been able to finger. It had gnawed at him, and finally he'd remembered it, the dare and the death and the funeral with Mickey Gaines's mother throwing herself on the child-sized coffin.

"Ever been out here before?" Lloyd Harris asked.

Officer Tremont bit his lip, not wanting to get into it, really, but grateful all the same for the company.

"Out this way a lot, of course. The house you mean?"

The other man nodded.

"Not in a long, long time. When I was a kid, we used to think the place was haunted. You know how kids are.

The Hazeltines never were the folks next door, so to speak. Some of the kids used to razz them once in a while, but my mom kept me away. Good thing, too, I expect.

"Not that they did any harm, but the road used to be pitch dark back then. A boy I used to run with got killed by a car one Halloween, right down the road a ways." He was no different from the criminals he questioned on petty charges, denying his presence before a question had even been asked, removing himself from the scene of the crime.

"People don't seem to know much about these Hazeltines."

The officer shrugged. "Olivia's children," he said. "That's what everybody called them. Don't know why. I guess Olivia was their mother's name. Now, they just keep to themselves. They like it that way and I guess the town does, too. Probably that's all there is to it this time—I feel a fool for butting in."

He pulled out of the center lane of River Road, parking on the shoulder, at the entrance of the Way.

"They don't have a driveway?" the newsman asked.

"Don't have a car," Officer Tremont answered, radioing his location back to headquarters. A check of the Eastfield directory, and a call to the information operator, had verified that the Hazeltines had no telephone, and who knew what emergency might come up.

He told himself that this whole thing was a waste of time that could better be used on real and pending police business, but as he glanced up the Way, his instincts and something more, something of memory and spirit, gave him a chill.

"They lived out here all these years, huh?" the newsman inquired.

"Long as anyone can remember," the cop answered, trying to keep his tone easy as they began to walk, fighting

against the urge, primal and fierce, that told him to go back
to the car, back to the station, to the relative safety and
normalcy of criminals.

The Way was so overgrown that it was impossible for
the two men to walk side by side. Out of a sense of duty,
Officer Tremont went first, holding back the icy twigs that
snapped forward from right and left and above, as if to deter
any intruder.

"Hell of a thing," the newsman commented. "They might
as well be miles out in the country, huh?"

The wind answered him, whistling through the Way like
a warning, drowning out the sound of his voice, amplifying
the crackling of the two men's footsteps. At the University
of Massachusetts, before he'd fixed on journalism, Lloyd
Harris had written poetry. But he was a newsman now, and
he told himself it was crazy to think that the frozen ground
was aching. He followed the officer in silence up the Way,
then, at its end, the two men stood, side by side and speechless.

"Jesus!" Officer Tremont finally said, staring at the
house.

"It's like something out of Hawthorne," Lloyd Harris
told him.

"Huh?" The other man's attention was still fixed, held
captive by the sight of the decayed house, with its crumbling
stone, its windows that were cracked in some places,
boarded over in others.

"Hawthorne. Nathaniel Hawthorne. The writer."

"Oh, yeah," the officer said without expression or
thought. He was thinking only of the sight before him, of
how he'd find the words to describe it to his wife, if such
words even existed.

"It looks as if nobody's lived in it for years," Harris said
as they began to walk toward the house. "And that roof—

it's practically caving in. Hell, it *is* caved in over on that side, do you see?" He pointed to a section that had collapsed and been crudely patched. "Aren't there inspectors or something that come around to check out places like this?"

The police officer cleared his throat. "As long as people pay their taxes..." he began. His voice trailed off as he knocked on the front door.

There was no answer, and he knocked again, louder and longer. "Police. Official business," he said as forcefully as he could. He waited, but there was no answer. The battered, rusted brass knob was frozen solid; the door locked.

"Might be a back door," he said at last.

The wind had heaped the recent snow high against the side of the house. It was difficult to navigate the sloped white wall that glistened blindingly. When at last they managed it, they turned to one another in stunned silence, shivering with a cold that had no relation to the temperature.

The back door was open, and drifts of snow had blown in. A jackrabbit huddled near the stove, staring at the two men in the doorway, its nose quivering. Rats darted from the kitchen table, and the box of groceries they'd been gnawing.

"Over there," Harris whispered, pointing beyond the snowy floor and the table, toward the open door of the pantry.

Officer Tremont tried to control his trembling as he made his way through the chilly room, to the figure seated in the rocking chair.

"Frozen?" the newsman asked.

The officer couldn't answer. Animals, birds and rats, had pecked out the open eyes and torn off bits and pieces of the dead, stiff flesh. He had to turn away.

As if suffering an agony of their own, the floorboards creaked beneath the steps of the two men as they made their way through the dining room, with its dust and debris, through the parlor, toward the stairs.

Even before they were halfway up the landing, the stench told the policeman what he would find.

"You might not want to see this," he said grimly, not wanting to see it himself. But the newsman followed him up the rest of the stairs, down the hall, past the rooms that had been shut and sealed, to the big bedroom, where the two decomposing corpses lay together in the bed, the shrunken arms of what had been the woman wrapped around what had been the man, the rotting flesh melding.

Yet there was something in the position of the corpses that, for a moment, made it seem that they weren't dead, that they had never intended to die, but had planned to hold to each other in an embrace for all eternity, an embrace of lovers.

# - 8 -

MORE THAN THE WEATHER, the time shaped the climate.

Eastfield was accustomed to rumors, and ever since the start of the war, they'd flourished with a new importance, gossip being given a new status. Everyone, or so it seemed, had a husband or cousin, or distant relative who had inside information. The news (suppressed by the government, of course, since it was bad for morale) that a Nazi U-boat had been spotted in New London; that Japanese bombers had been shot down over western Canada; that Hitler (someone had heard it on the official Berlin radio, on the short wave, it was claimed) had been shot—each story, no matter how outrageous or unconfirmed, was given the status of fact, or *possible* fact, for a time, however brief.

For in a world gone mad with such determined violence, a world that was coming to an end any day now—if you listened to the Jehovah's Witnesses who held forth in Common Park or went home to read your daily paper or listen to the radio—what wasn't possible?

Because of the climate of the times, then, and because of the place—which after all was home—and because it was a departure from the news of the war and worry and sadness about loved ones in uniform, stories about what had happened in the house out of town on River Road spread quickly and unchecked.

The official silence—the matter, Officer Tremont explained as patiently as possible in the face of repeated questioning, was still under official investigation—only added to the various conclusions and speculation.

They'd been murdered in their sleep, the Hazeltines, and the killer—a shellshocked soldier, escaped from the Veterans' Hospital—was still at large!

They'd killed themselves, the two sisters and brother, in a strange suicide pact; the note they'd left was in the police station, locked in Officer Tremont's desk.

Paul Hazeltine, the brother, had shot his two sisters, then himself. He'd been known to hunt—that was one of the few things that was known about him, when you came down to it—and there'd certainly been a crazed look in his eye on those few times when he'd come into town.

A strange new disease had killed them (which explained why the Hampden Country Coroner had taken an interest). The bodies were being studied, and the Connecticut River had been poisoned, perhaps by the Germans!

The older citizens of the town spoke of a "curse" on the Hazeltines, but nobody seemed to have the story quite straight, and everyone knew how old folks were.

Still, that story along with the others was dished up with supper and shared over lunch. Children who overheard and pressed their parents for details were told to "never mind," and to be sure not to play near old houses.

The Hazeltine house itself had been officially sealed, but at night gangs of teenagers rode out all the same, defying the ropes that blocked off the property and the notices on the door, rummaging through the bric-a-brac on dares and telling each other that they weren't the least bit afraid, that it was the cold that made them shake.

The official report, when it was finally released, was no real source of information. "Natural causes" were cited in the deaths of Paul Hazeltine, Jr., and his sisters Constance and Margaret. It was, however, noted that one of the sister's had predeceased her siblings, and that the second sister had "in all likelihood" died after her brother.

What, people asked each other, was so natural about that? And what had ever been natural about "Olivia's children," as nearly everyone now referred to them, though there were many who had no idea who Olivia was or had been.

Things were being hushed up, many agreed—dark things at that. Someone said that the autopsy had showed that the two sisters weren't virgins, and heaven knew they'd never had romances of any kind, so that meant only one thing. And wasn't it a matter of fact—right in the official report— that the body of one sister had been found in bed with her brother?

It was unnatural, people said. Sick and disgusting!

The gossip flared and spread as reporters descended on the town, intrigued by a story that would be good for feature space and a welcome diversion from the grim news of the war.

The Eastfield Public Library was besieged with requests for information, many of which were referred to the town clerk's office. The *Record* had played the whole thing down, but the *Springfield Union* ran a scathing editorial asking how the town could let such a thing happen—as if it was the town's fault that Olivia's children had decided to lock themselves away from the world, as if the town and not they themselves had decided to close themselves off from everyone and everything around them!

Then there was the reporter from the *Boston Globe,* stirring up more of it, asking questions, taking his pictures...

And what, really, could be said of Olivia's children? Nobody, after all, knew them. Even at the bank and the stores where they traded, they never exchanged so much as a passing word. So Paul Hazeltine, their father, had once owned a buggy works where the casket company now was— what did that mean, after all these years? Who knew exactly what had happened to him, or his wife, or the one "missing" sister, who'd done the sensible thing and left ages before, and probably wouldn't want to come back for the cremation of her brother and sisters even if she were alive and knew about it?

If some psychiatrist with a lot of fancy letters after his name was quoted, in the series in the Boston paper, as saying that, "It is not uncommon for siblings who are unusually close, particularly if they live a reclusive existence, to have shorter than normal life spans. It has been observed, too, that in these relationships, the death of one sibling may trigger, in rapid succession, the deaths of the survivor or survivors..." Well, what did that mean, anyway? Were people in their right minds supposed to believe for a minute that Constance Hazeltine walked into her house, set a box of groceries down on the table (leaving the kitchen door open in the middle of winter, mind you—it was all there in the official report) then went upstairs, found her brother dead in bed, and laid herself down beside him to die of a broken heart?

It was crazy, as crazy as Olivia's children themselves had been, and the only real tragedy was that they hadn't managed to kill themselves or each other or whatever it was without such a scandal, bringing shame to the town's good name.

Why the Boston stories had to be picked up and run all around the country was something that nobody in town understood, but something one and all resented. Who wanted to get a copy of the clipping from Aunt Grace and Uncle George in South Carolina, with a note that asked "What kind of place do you live in, anyway?" Or a page torn out by a son stationed at Camp Pendleton or Fort Dix with "Glad to see the old home town is still the same!" scrawled on it.

It was no laughing matter, that was for sure, and no business of outsiders, either.

When the old house burned down less than a month after the bodies were discovered, there were many who expressed the belief that if it was some kids who set the blaze by accident, it might have been the hand of Providence lighting the match: at least with the house gone, the busybodies with nothing better to do than poke their noses where they didn't belong could go elsewhere on their Sunday drives, as if gas weren't precious enough.

Like the fire, the furor died down.

There was the war, after all, and poor Vic Casey, who'd been the editor of the *Record* before going off to London as a correspondent, being killed in an air raid. Many who'd known him and many who didn't showed up for the memorial service in Trinity Church, and the ceremony in Common Park where Mayor Putney gave a moving speech.

With the exception of a few old men who liked to tell tales, largely of their own invention, on a winter's night, Olivia's children, and their passing, were forgotten.

And the town of Eastfield, along with the rest of the world, went about the more pressing business of its own slow death.